Reunion

Reunion

A Jack Marston Mystery

Carl Brookins

Brookins Books

Reunion

ISBN: 978-0-9853906-9-3
First Echelon Press publication December 2010
Brookins Books November, 2016

As always, I must, perforce, acknowledge my fine critique group of alert readers who save me from myself more often than I care to mention: Anne, Susan, Julie, Judy, Jean, Mary Monica, Kent, Michael, and Tim. Also a nod of thanks to my first editor and publisher, Kat and Karen Syed.

DEDICATION

The novel is dedicated to everyone, man or woman, who has had to endure attendance at a spouse's high school reunion.

1

Thick fluid slid down the long curved tines of the hay rake and congealed in the night air. I could see a small puddle that had formed on the thirsty ground. It was black in the moonlight, but I detected the hard-edged metallic smell of fresh blood as I went closer. The smell picked at the back of my throat and I snorted to clear the odor. A finger of breeze swayed the long grass growing around the rake and brought the fresh soft smell of new-mown hay from a nearby field. The harsh blood-smell remained.

The body hung suspended inches above the stubble, impaled on several upturned tines of the old rusty piece of farming equipment. The man was face down and not long dead. The harsh white beam from the flashlight in the sheriff's hand played over the still form. I only got glimpses, impressions of the man.

On the other side of the hay rake, a uniformed deputy sheriff squatted down and peered at the face of the corpse. "God, one of the tines got him in the eye. Why is the damn rake upside down like this, anyway?"

Behind them a door to the restaurant party room swung open and banged shut again. It brought a quick blast of noise and light. The Riverview Class of '89 was well into the first evening of its twentieth high school reunion.

I hoped Lori didn't notice my absence and come looking for me.

"It's Elroy Guteman," the deputy said softly. I heard a quaver in his voice. Cobb County deputies saw their share of bloody highway accidents in this rural county, but this was different, a lot different. Unless the man had jumped high enough to flip over and land face down on the tines of the old rake, he'd received some decidedly unfriendly help. Of course, he could have jumped off a building. Except there wasn't one, nor a tree, within twenty yards. I sighed. Cobb County and the town of Riverview were about to have a new scandal to chew over.

A little scandal and a lot of gossip had both been served up for the last two days, in the same healthy helpings as the meat and potatoes and gravy of nearly every lunch and dinner Lori Jacobs and I had encountered thus far during the weekend. Hadn't these people heard about high blood pressure and cholesterol? Each meal was a hungry farmhand's dream. I figured I must have gained five pounds in the two days we'd been in Riverview. The helpings were huge. Then there were the desserts.

"A piece of pie? Why surely you can eat more than that, Mr. Marston. Lori, you must do better by this young man. Now, we have apple, banana cream, blueberry, peach cobble, and of course, here's this marvelous lemon pie. I made it my very own self! Can't I interest you in just one more piece?" The solicitous voices mingled and blended in my memory.

Right now, even the thought of all that food weighed me down as I stared at the corpse. I hadn't known Elroy Guteman in this life, but I had an uneasy feeling I was going to know him better in death. One's history and experience sometimes works that way.

Old scandal and gossip out in smallsville were one thing, a new and brutal murder was quite another. I cleared my throat, sucked air into suddenly constricted lungs. "Sheriff Arnason?"

"Yeah...Marston?"

Not ten minutes ago we were Brad and Jack, having a sociable drink, watching Brad's classmates surge about the roadhouse banquet room, chattering and laughing, laying hands on each other in friendly fashion. Then a deputy appeared and whispered in the sheriff's ear. I got the message in the sheriff's voice. He was only using my last name now.

"I think I'd better go back inside, Sheriff."

"You feelin' sick?"

"A little," I admitted. "Besides, Lori might come looking for me and I'm pretty sure you don't want that crowd out here."

"Good thinking. Don't say anything to anybody just yet. Okay?"

"Sure." I wasn't exactly feeling ill, but the combination of this very recent, grisly death, the booze I'd ingested, and the dusty heat of the night were all contributing to a certain queasiness. I also knew this was about to cease being a fun weekend for Lori and her classmates. What I couldn't know then was how involved in the *sturm und drang* we were about to become.

I stumbled my way in my slick, leather-soled loafers over the uneven stubble toward the restaurant.

On my right just down the highway, the glow from the edge of town struggled to hold back the night. I felt the night sky pushing down on me. Odd how that same sky had seemed so soft and soothing when Lori and I stood outside this same restaurant the night before, after a pleasant dinner. Now I started to wonder what other secrets the night concealed.

Hell of a way to run a reunion, I thought. A quote from Shakespeare's Timon of Athens, one of the bard's lesser performed plays, came to mind. It is one of the weakest plays as well. *Th' ear, taste, touch, and smell, pleas'd from thy table rise; They only now come but to feast thine eyes* .... Some people considered it one of my less-endearing traits, quoting Shakespeare at odd and sometimes inappropriate moments. Lori puts up with it. God, I thought, this murder will devastate her.

Inside, the noise of multiple conversations in the stuffy room drowned out the music from the jukebox in the bar. That was okay. Somebody had stuffed the jukebox with a lot of songs from their senior high school year. It was not a memorable one in the music industry. It didn't matter; members of the Riverview Class of 1989 were having a high old time. I went to the bar and got a weak scotch from the pretty little barmaid. She was working hard, barely keeping up with the drink orders. Tiny beads of sweat had formed at her hairline and her small nose had gotten shiny. Everyone there, I thought, was still blissfully unaware of the macabre scene on the other side of the fire exit door. Or maybe not. Was somebody in that mob fully aware? Just waiting, smiling, drinking, wondering when it would come, the grisly announcement of discovery.

I rested one elbow on a sopping wet napkin at the edge of the bar. I was a stranger in a place that had suddenly grown a lot stranger. Then Lori Jacobs, whom I know quite intimately, appeared from the dark bar entrance, followed closely, too closely I thought, by Edgar Tomlinson. He had one hand on her waist. Tomlinson glanced quickly across the room. Tomlinson. I ticked through my mental rolodex of recent introductees. Yes. Big lawyer in town, prosperous, married to a classmate, Elaine? Right. A wheeler-dealer in this part of the state. He and Lori had dated in high school. Not exclusively, but almost, if I remembered correctly. Was he also a killer? He looked fit enough to be able to hoist the body of the dead man up onto the hay rake.

Lori looked a bit mussed, flustered even, I thought. Was it the heat? It was certainly hot and close. Lori saw me watching her, turned her head, and said something to Tomlinson. He leaned down, tall bugger that he was, then turned right and moved away without even a glance in my direction. Lori smiled at someone and came across the noisy room toward me, raising her hands to fix some errant strands of that gorgeous auburn hair. The action lifted her bosom. I inhaled. I saw a couple of glances directed at her. Envy? Recollection? She came up and leaned against me in that possessive manner she sometimes used, though not often in public.

"We making a little statement here?" I murmured under the din. I hoped my voice didn't quaver, didn't betray the turmoil raised by the scene I'd just witnessed outside.

"Well, sonny, you looked like you could use a statement. Or maybe a drink?"

"You see a tinge of the green jealousy? Or is it envy that's green? I can never remember."

"Never mind. Get me a drink, please, a weak scotch. Then come sit. I want to talk to you." She glided smoothly toward a momentarily empty table while I turned back to the bar for her drink. Weak was the only way they made them here. Like the coffee. Carrying the glasses, I slid into the chair beside her.

"I told you when we decided to come to this reunion it wouldn't be all fun and games. Small town stuff, petty jealousies, remembered passions, you know?"

"Hey," I said. "I'm eating too much and getting too little sleep, but if all this makes you happy, it makes me glad. Seriously, though, I have met some nice people, people I think I'd like to know better. I'm even having a nice time, at least some of the time." I detected a discordant note in my remark. I hoped Lori didn't notice and ask about it. Part of my mind still grappled with possible implications of Elroy Guteman's corpse impaled on the rusty tines of the old hay rake.

"Nice," echoed Lori. "I went out the front door for a quick breather when I found you'd gone missing. Eddie Tomlinson followed me. We had a little chat. It was pleasant, at least at first. His wife Elaine has become a drinker, apparently. Notice she's no longer here? After a few minutes, Eddie wanted to take up where we'd left off twenty years ago." She paused and looked at her drink.

"And?" I prompted. Did she want me to punch him out, I wondered?

"And, I know recollections are mostly edited. We remember the good and forget the bad. I certainly didn't recall him being quite so… aggressive."

"You want me to punch him out?"

"No!" She put her hand on my arm, alarm on her face before she realized I wasn't serious. "I suppose I let him think one little kiss wouldn't hurt."

"You did."

"Well, yes, I did think that, even if I didn't say it. But he went too fast, and too far."

I looked deep into her eyes, "And suppose he'd been gentler, less impatient, would it have made a difference?"

"Yes, of course, but not in the result. He wanted to kiss me, and I wanted him to kiss me. But even if he'd been a terrific kisser, that would have been it. One chaste kiss, pal. No baloney." She punched me lightly on the arm. She looked around. Then she looked back. "Hey."

"What?" Sensitive, my Lori.

"Are you all right? Is something else bothering you?"

I shook my head. "Tell me again about Elaine. Her maiden name is Flynn?"

"Right you are, soldier."

Lori and I were not married, but we live together in the Twin Cities. We have a good relationship, and keep it so by being straight and open with each other. At the moment I was concealing a horrible secret and even for the short while I knew it would be, it bothered me to keep it from her.

"Tell me," I tried on a smile, "about Elroy Guteman."

"Elroy? Well." Lori scanned the crowd. "First, I can't point him out 'cause I don't see him. He and his wife, whom I don't know at all, probably left early. They have this big farm out south beyond Wilson's Crick…Creek. They'd have early morning chores, I suppose." She sipped her weak scotch. "Elroy was the one who went right by us on the street yesterday when we first got here, remember?"

I nodded.

"He started with his family's farm and just got bigger. The farm, I mean. Any particular reason you want to know about him?"

"Nope," I lied. "Anything peculiar in his past?"

"You mean in high school?" She looked at me for a long moment. I knew that look. She was wondering why I'd asked. She knew I almost never asked idle questions or indulged in idle gossip. My job in student counseling made me super cautious about any sort of casual personal chatter.

The fire door at the side of the building opposite the entrance to the bar opened and the sheriff appeared, hatless, dark circles of sweat under each arm. He wasn't on duty so he wasn't wearing his uniform. He stopped just inside the door and I heard the faint sound of a siren as the door swung closed. Arnason caught Richard Borken's eye across the room. Borken, senior class president, had had a big hand in organizing the reunion and was nominally in charge tonight.

Borken rose and made his way over to Arnason. They conferred briefly, then Borken turned around and raised his voice, shouting over the tumult.

"Folks, folks! Quiet please. Brad here has to tell us something." The noise died, heads turned toward the two men by the door. I sucked in a deep breath and gently took Lori's hand.

2

It had started with an innocuous looking fat white envelope that arrived in the mail at Lori's apartment one sunny Saturday morning in early July.

Lori and I had spent a good part of the summer sandwiching weekends in remote, posh, northern Minnesota resorts, where nature rarely intrudes unless you go looking for it. We inserted these trips between her psychology client appointments and my duties at City College where I am happily ensconced as the director of the student services office.

Lori sauntered by that warm summer morning and I hugged her hips, stretching out one arm to stop her progress. She smiled and sank into my lap. For a moment we toyed with each other, savoring familiar pleasures of the flesh.

Lori sighed, "No more, sport. Duty calls. Actually, mail first." She slipped away downstairs to the apartment mailboxes. I went back to the story I was reading, a reprint of Fergus Hume's 'Mystery of a Hansom Cab'. It had been a best-seller at one time.

When she returned, she leaned hipshot against the edge of the small hall table, head down, shuffling through the usual wad of mail. We had similar distaste about certain kinds of mail and she discarded a goodly number of unopened pieces directly into the wastebasket at her bare feet.

A minute later I heard a soft, "*Hunh!*" Lori raised her head. In one hand she held a fat white envelope. She stuck one corner between her lips and there was thoughtful amusement in her glance.

"What?"

"I am now about to subject you to that greatest of all relationship challenges. This should seal our destiny as a couple forever. And just remember, you brought it on yourself."

Wait a minute, I thought. Forever? Where had that come from? What dire deed had I proposed to accomplish? "What if I don't rise to the challenge?"

"Oh, you always rise to a challenge," Lori smiled, moving now. She came around the table, lifted one slim leg, and swung it over me, plunking herself astraddle my hips. The chair creaked alarmingly. She leaned forward to rest her elbows on the chair back, one on each side of my head. The effect was to thrust my nose into the sweet-smelling valley between her breasts, territory I was always eager to explore. I tilted my head a little so I could breathe and dipped my tongue into the hollow at the base of her throat.

"Feeling a little randy, are we? I would have thought after last night…."

"And again this morning," I reminded her.

Lori chuckled. "Try not to sound so proud of yourself. Just listen." I heard the sound of paper tearing. "Here is your ultimate test." Reading then. "Dear 1989 graduate of Riverview High School. Our twentieth graduation anniversary will soon be here and plans are well under way. The response so far has been terrific and we have organized a great reunion. This note is an acknowledgment of your reservations and includes a current list of those planning to attend. I know you're looking forward to renewing old friendships."

"Ah," I murmured. "Reunion. Reservations. With an s. Plural. I do now remember."

"Exactly. Since you persuaded me against my original judgment to accept the invitation, you now have to face the challenge that *we* are going to Riverview for this reunion. Together. As a couple."

Considering the position I was in, in delightful danger of almost smothering, and considering my feelings for the woman in my lap, I wasn't about to have second thoughts. This was a challenge with which I could certainly cope. I actually welcomed the weekend sojourn into Lori's past. I was sure my companionship at Lori's high school reunion would be a good thing for both of us, out there in Cobb County, on the border between Minnesota and South Dakota.

The next two weeks were filled with preparations. Not mine. None of Lori's classmates had ever so much as laid a single eyeball on me. I would go as her escort; we would make a few minor ripples in her small home town, since we weren't married and would be staying in the same motel, in the same room. I didn't have to think much about my appearance or my attitude, so long as my fair friend was happy. I would play the benign consort and be as circumspect as need be. I recalled a small poem which had much meaning in our early times together.

If that the world and love were young,
And truth in every shepherd's tongue,
These pretty pleasures might me move
To live with thee and be thy love.

"So, my little dove, how much do you think the good folks of Riverview know about your life since you left town?"

"I have no idea. Haven't been in close touch with any of my classmates."

I wrestled a suitcase onto the end of the bed. "So it may come as a shock that you are now reasonably well off, have a PhD in Psychology and a successful practice, plus you're living with a fella in unmarried bliss. In my admittedly biased view of small town attitudes, I should think you'll have a lot to answer for."

Lori smiled. "It's that last that will cause the most talk." She stopped packing and looked at me. "Maybe this trip will give *us* time to talk more."

I divined what she meant. Until this invitation, I'd known she hailed from small-town western Minnesota, and she'd grown up on a farm and had no living relatives, but no other details.

She frowned. "Look." She twirled around holding up a long shimmery summer dress. "Does this make me look fat?"

I have been privy to intimate conversations between spouses. As a very young graduate student I'd been married, a union that lasted several years and resulted in a fabulous daughter and an amicable divorce. I recognized a no-win question right off. Lori was waltzing around in a favorite dress. One she'd worn to a couple of important occasions at the college, where she was also employed, part-time. I could attest to the fact that clothed or not, she never looked fat. She wasn't fat. She worked out, her job helped keep her trim. Hell, she was never going to look fat. Dowdy, frumpy, they were remote possibilities, but even they were really, really remote. Long years away remote.

"Of course not," I said, smiling. "No way," I assured her, thinking, "I may be just a minor college administrator, but I'm not dumb."

3

It was a pleasant enough drive on Highway 7, that August morning, almost straight west from Minneapolis to Lori's hometown of Riverview. The sun shone down from the cloudless blue sky, the temperature was reasonable, and the highway was in good repair. There wasn't much traffic and the worst parts of the highway had recently been repaved.

I thought about the upcoming festivities. I guess I was having serious third and fourth doubts when I looked at the weekend objectively. Here I was, a very urban, unattached fellow, venturing into the hinterlands. Small town, ruralocity. It was just not my kind of scene. What would I chat about with these folks? A discussion of Shakespeare's history plays probably wouldn't be of much interest to the local banker or farmer.

On the other hand, what I knew about crop yields and E85 or Ethanol, you could stuff in a thimble with room to spare.

Lori's senior class of 1989 was seventy-five strong. If they all showed up and all brought their spouses or partners, it would be quite a party in a town of only twenty-six hundred people. I'd looked up the population when Lori didn't know. Research.

"Can't happen," she remarked when I raised the question of anticipated attendance.

"Why not?"

She was immersed in papers sent to her by the organizers as we rolled west in the warm morning sun.

"Everybody never comes to these things. And Tessa Larson is a widow."

"Really?"

"Her husband Ron died several years ago, I think. It was some kind of terrible road accident. Maybe five years ago."

"What's that you're reading?" I asked, maneuvering around a slow-moving machine pulled by a big red Farmall tractor. We were on a standard rural two-lane highway. No freeway ran from Minneapolis to Riverview.

"This is an advance list of early registrants. I think Dick Borken sent it mainly to tweak the curiosity of the Reluctant Virgins, among others."

"The what?"

"Yep," she said with a small grin. "You like the name? They were a small clique of girls at school. Most of them in my class, girls who often hung around together. I heard later they let a few others in who really begged. They weren't great at supporting school social activities. Always off by themselves. They didn't date much either, but when they did, according to rumor, things went pretty quickly, even on a first date, but never all the way."

"Things?" I looked over at her.

"Things."

"Were you a member?"

Lori gave me a sharp glance. "Nope."

I nodded, sagely, I thought. It's something I occasionally practice to help me set the right tone with students. "Is there anyone in your class I should pay particular attention to?"

"Well, Brad Arnason is the Cobb County Sheriff. Played football. Then there's Dick Borken. He's wealthy and probably owns half the town by now. Al Steiger still lives in the area. He'll come, I guess. And Donna Andrew, but she lives in California. I think she's a writer, or reporter, or something like that." Lori went on reading the roster of still living classmates. There was a subtle change in her voice.

"I know Ed Tomlinson will be there, he and Elaine."

"Do I detect a certain something in that tone?" I glanced again at

Lori. She looked back, all wide-eyed and innocent.

"Possibly, but don't make too much of it. Okay?" There was a slight touch of defensiveness in her voice.

"Hey. Easy. I don't know these people, remember? Or your relationships to them. I don't want to put my foot in my mouth unnecessarily." I smiled.

"Sorry. Surprised myself there. Edgar T. and I had a little thing going for a while back then. I hear his wife Elaine has become something of a drunk. She and I were pretty close in high school. Worked on the yearbook and newspaper together. She was bright. A good writer, even then. We all thought she'd move away and be a professional writer, or a journalist of some kind. Instead, she settled in and married Edgar. Or married Edgar and then settled in." She sighed. "I don't know. Knowing me, and knowing you, I'm beginning to think my first reaction, to skip this reunion, was the right one."

We rode in comfortable silence for more miles. I reminded myself that we wouldn't be there if I hadn't noticed the invitation on her desk. Lori'd waved it off and when I pressed her, she'd been oddly resistant at first. At least it had seemed odd to me.

"Don't you have something going on at the college that weekend?"

"Nothing I'm aware of. Whatever is piling up on my desk can wait for a few days. We're only talking about a long weekend, right?"

"What is this, a test of our relationship? Okay. Okay. We'll go." And we'd dropped the subject. I wondered then if she just didn't want me there, a foreigner observing the place and the people who had shaped her outlook, her attitudes on life. Had I forced the issue? I didn't think so. On the other hand, she knew I was a true urbanite who rarely ventured beyond the city limits. I knew about farms and where milk came from. I knew life in small agricultural towns like Riverview was slower, less stressful, more peaceful, or so it was always said.

I did have an ulterior motive.

Lori and I have been together for almost two years. Although technically eligible since my divorce, I didn't date much. Lately, however, I'd been thinking more seriously about my relationship with

Lori and about what the future might bring us. It seemed to me that we had to get on with things, make some decisions about our long-term relationship. I was pretty sure Lori was falling in love with me and I knew for damn sure I was in love with her.

This reunion could be an opportunity to develop our relationship further, and maybe, finally settle some issues between us.

We stopped for lunch outside Hutchinson, then went on to Montevideo and soon, *The Corner.* As Lori explained it, *The Corner* was just an intersection. A state highway running north and south crossed another state highway running east and west. That was Highway 7, which we were on. Over the course of time, I learned, that particular highway intersection had become known to those who passed over it as *The Corner.* There was even a faded, banged up sign on the dusty lot that said, 'Welcome to The Corner'.

Two gas stations squatted there, with a small restaurant attached to one. On another corner was a closed service station desperately in need of repair or razing. On the southwest lot, was this big ramshackle roadhouse, surrounded by what appeared to be several acres of cracked bumpy asphalt. The place looked a little like several small buildings had been smashed together into a single structure. 'The Junction,' the big sign said. Appropriate name.

"There it is," remarked Lori, squinting through the windshield. "Looks just the same. In fact, if I half-close my eyes, it could be twenty years ago. Amazing."

I rolled the car to an almost-stop under the blinking amber traffic light and checked right and left. The brassy sun glared down on the drowsing countryside. There was no breeze. We'd been on asphalt; now the roadway changed to concrete. Old, cracked, seamed concrete. I looked at my watch. It was just after two p.m.

I made the left turn to the south and looked across my companion toward The Junction, to a scattering of cars in the big lot, including a dusty police vehicle. COBB COUNTY SHERIFF was neatly lettered on the door.

Heat waves shimmered and blurred the scenery in every direction. We rolled south, uncertain rhythms from the tires on concrete giving our vehicle a sort of rock-and-roll feeling. Now that we were closer to the Little Chippewa, tiny streams feeding it were more in evidence. Small groves of trees showed up on the horizon and in clumps closer to the highway. Big old cottonwoods, shelterbelts planted during the thirties, an occasional ash or elm.

"There's the Worckowski place," Lori said softly, looking off into the eastern distance. "They used to have barn dances and sleigh rides every winter."

"Worckowski, isn't he the one you told me about?"

She nodded. "Right. Terry was my buddy in high school. We were best buddies. Watched over each other in a casual sort of way. Like a brother and sister might, when we weren't squabbling. I helped him with book reports and history and he helped me with science projects, stuff like that. He was big, even in high school. So he never had to throw his weight around."

Conversation waned. Lori's family was gone, parents and one brother dead. She'd not been back home for a very long time. Not since her sophomore college year.

Now this approaching high school reunion, with a lover instead of a husband in tow. It was a chance for me to take a look through new eyes at the places where she grew up, at her friends and class-mates. Was this a good idea? Trepidation and second thoughts joined us as passengers.

"Jack?"

"*Ummm?*" Her fingers grasped my wrist.

"Be...patient, okay?"

"Relax, honey. I'll even try to stem my usual biting witticisms. And I'll even keep my more obscure Shakespearean *bon mots* in check"

Her dark head lolled to my shoulder and she placed her left hand on my thigh. High on my thigh. "Promise?"

"Promise. To try."

"Gee, I just knew this would be a fun time, you and me in Riverview, for a long weekend." Her tongue flicked my ear. She'd appar-ently decided to make the best of whatever discomfort might arise. I smiled. Maybe this would all work out for the best. Probably so.

"Uh, it's early" I said. "Isn't there some place we could pull off the road? Find a little shade under one of those trees?"

Lori sat up straight and flashed me a mischievous smirk. "As a matter of fact there is, but I'm not going to show it to you today."

The big blue sky seemed to widen out and the hills got flatter; the horizon seemed to go out west past forever. The grass was a little grayer and there were fewer fences. We rumbled over a bridge spanning the Chippewa River and a few minutes later rolled serenely into Riverview, Cobb County, Minnesota, right there at the edge of the plains.

4

Lori had booked us into one of the two local motels, this one on the west side of town. Since it was Lori's first school reunion and she hadn't been in touch with any of her classmates, it wasn't surprising we hadn't been welcomed to another grad's home. Turned out it was just as well.

"Besides, I assume it's common knowledge by now that I'm living in a state of sin." Lori's voice floated out of the bathroom where she was preparing to shower off the dust of the long road home, as she'd put it.

"Beg your pardon?"

"Sure. You can bet as soon as my reservation arrived for the weekend, the word went around. Lori's here, in a motel, with a man she's not married to. *Tsk.*" The bathroom door closed.

I raised my voice. "How would anyone know?"

"I didn't enter us on the reunion reservation form as Mr. and Mrs. So naturally the committee jumped to the correct conclusion."

"Naturally." I wondered if people really cared. The sound of the shower intruded. I briefly considered joining her in the steamy bathroom, then decided the timing wasn't right.

Lori emerged from her shower a few minutes later wrapped in a big white towel, her wet dark hair hanging on her bare shoulders.

"What now, my little poppet?"

"You shower, we dress, and I'll give you a quick tour of Riverview."

"So I shouldn't get lost, if we're ever separated, I imagine."

"Ah-ah-ah. Don't be condescending. You promised to leave the witty cracks at home, remember? And you could lose the W. C. Fields impersonation attempt permanently."

With a shrug and a raised eyebrow I took myself to the shower. We were soon cruising down Main Street at a sedate crawl. River-view's main street is also the state highway through town. It's wide, wider than the highway. Cars could park diagonally head-in at either curb. There was enough room to park cars nose to tail down the center of the street, a reminder, I supposed, of the days when teams of horses and wagons had to maneuver through town. "But they only did that on heavy nights, like Fridays and Saturdays," Lori assured me. "I sup-pose you know that farmers don't use horses and wagons any more. Except in parades."

"Good," I said, "so I won't have to watch this heavy bumper-to-bumper traffic for horse carts in addition to all the other vehicles." At the moment, we were the only car on the street that was moving. Four others in the next block were parked at the curb in front of Buddy's Tavern.

"I guess the rest of the time they use the space for U-turns." I stomped on the brakes to avoid a dirt-caked pickup that squealed across the entire width of the street to whisk by in front of our bum-per.

Lori chuckled.

Half a block ahead, the pickup swayed back and forth and then zipped into a parking spot at the right hand curb. It was not a tight squeeze, the pickup being the only vehicle besides ours in that block at the moment.

"There's the bank." Lori pointed. A tall man in a straw hat and dusty work clothes stepped out of the dirty pickup and hiked up on the sidewalk. "Oh, that's El Guteman. Gee, he hasn't changed much. A little heavier, maybe."

"Who is?" I said, glancing left and slowing for a passel of giggling pre-teen girls who suddenly swarmed across the street in front of us.

"El-Elroy Guteman. Farmer. Lives out southwest of town almost to the state line, if he's still on his dad's place. Inherited it and bought more property, I read. Got two kids. Married some nice girl from away."

"Away?"

"Yup, not from here. From away."

I nodded. Made perfect sense. Away. We proceeded to another intersection.

"Turn right here. The high school is just up the block." Lori gasped softly when the building came into view through the trees on the boulevard. "Goodness, it's huge! I expected to see the same dinky little brick box I remember."

The dinky box was there, all right, built of dark, reddish, weathered brick. A square two-story building that screamed school, even if you couldn't read the word chiseled into the granite lintel above the black-painted double doors. The box was attached to a much newer, rambling beige stone building that almost surrounded it. The new one had shiny aluminum window frames, frames that winked and glinted in the hard sunlight, as if sending secret messages or suggesting they knew interesting things. Maybe they did.

"Let's go back and park on Main," Lori said, gazing at the school. Her voice was wistful, remembering perhaps, a time in her life when things were simpler and more obvious, at least on the surface.

"Okay, babe, it's your party." I whipped the wheel over and turned into a gravel alley mid-block. I was about to reverse into the street when Lori straightened up from her slouch and peered through the dusty windshield.

"Oh look. I think that's Stacy Frommer. Boy she's changed. I don't remember her being so sexy looking." A tall female with a heavy head of flaming red hair extricated herself from a well-polished fire-engine red Mustang. She walked away from us, hair bouncing in rhythm to her steps down the trash can-cluttered alley. She moved carefully in high heels, and with some trouble on the uneven gravel ruts. I noted she wore a loose white shirt and tight shorts. I particularly noticed the shorts because of her long slender legs. Lori leaned out the window. Before she could hail her, the redhead turned and disappeared into the back of one of the buildings.

"Huh," I grunted.

"Back doors to some of the upstairs apartments are along there," Lori said. We proceeded to Main and went left this time, heading back the way we'd come.

"Park there," said Lori, pointing.

We got out into the heat of late afternoon. I watched Lori, who was gazing across the street at the upper level of the solid row of commercial buildings. Except they weren't all commercial spaces on the second floor. Curtains in some of the windows hinted at private rooms.

"Stacy lived in one of those apartments."

"Maybe she still does."

"Uh uh. She moved to Fargo. Owns a beauty shop up there. I bet she's looking at the place they used to live."

"They?"

"Yes." Lori stopped and frowned. "Stacy lived there with her dad. He hit her sometimes."

"Excuse me?" Lori looked back at me and then across the street again.

"That's right. Her dad sometimes beat up on her. With his fists. When she'd stayed out too late or something."

"She told you that?"

"Yes. After I saw her naked at the swimming beach by the river."

"Naked. In the river."

"Jack. It wasn't anything. Sometimes a few of us did that. When there were just girls, you understand, alone at the swimming beach. A couple of times we took off our suits for a few minutes." Lori smiled at the recollection. "Anyway, I came out of the water one day beside Stacy, and saw some yellowish spots on her side. They were old bruises. She didn't want to tell me about them, but I made her. Said her dad hit her sometimes. When he was drinking, or mad at her for something."

I swung my gaze away from the quiet street and looked up at the partly curtained open windows. Framed in one of them stood a dark figure. From the outline of the head, I thought it might be the same woman we'd seen in the alley. Stacy Frommer.

5

Lori and I strolled down the street, not speaking, just absorbing the town. Occasionally Lori would mutter something under her breath or exclaim softly. "That's where Mr. Jimson had his candy store. He was a nice old guy."

The space she indicated was now an empty, weed-grown gap between two painted pale-blue, cinder-block buildings. They had false fronts rising above the street.

"There's the hardware store. Steve Parsons was in my class. His sister was a year younger, a bright girl as I remember. She skipped a grade, so then she and Steve were both in my class. I didn't see their names on the list of people who have signed up. Maybe they're out of town."

We approached a two-story, solid-appearing brick building. It stood aggressively on the corner, crowding the sidewalk of tipped and cracked concrete slabs that reflected waves of shimmering heat into the air around them.

"Bank," I said.

"Yep. Houck's bank. He owns a lot of the town, I guess. There were stories about how he got his hands on some of the real estate. I heard a few things when I was in school. Wonder if old J. L.'s still alive."

"If this is your first trip back in however many years, how is it you are so up on things?"

Lori smiled and cut her eyes at me. "Something I learned in school, babe. Research, research, research."

I nodded.

"In my storeroom there's a big old bureau from my mom's room on the farm. I keep the weekly Cobb County Chronicle in one drawer. From many years ago, too. Once we definitely decided to come to this reunion, I started boning up on the life and times of the citizens of Riverview."

"You have a subscription?"

"Yep. Ever since I went away to college. First Mom gave me the subscription, then I just kept it up. I have old yearbooks and other stuff as well."

"Memorabilia," I said.

"Research documents." Lori went on a few paces and then must have realized I wasn't beside her. She stopped and looked back to where I was standing a little bit away, staring across the street. From the edge of my vision I saw her turn and come back toward me. I lifted my chin in the direction of the opposite sidewalk, across the broad main street. "Look at that," I said.

She looked where I indicated and her shoulders stiffened.

Five young men were standing in a loosely shifting group on the sidewalk outside a dry goods store. They appeared to be ordinary young guys, talking and laughing loudly among themselves. They were all heavily tanned, looked like your typical farm workers, in their late teens or early twenties.

"What's that about?"

"Puts my very thought into words," I said, shifting slightly on my baking feet. The young men dressed to show off their nicely muscled bodies, wore tight jeans and old work shirts. The sleeves were ripped off at the shoulders and all five had their shirts open to the waist to frame their laddered abs.

What had attracted my attention in the first place, besides their raucous laughter, was the way they moved about on the sidewalk. Most people in the light flow of foot traffic went by easily, but a few were crowded toward the curb, forced to change direction, and step around the group. The boys were fairly subtle about it, never really looking at their targets, shifting by degrees to block or open lanes for passersby. Unless one watched for several minutes, the disruption would have been seen as accidental.

A slight, elderly, Asian gentleman shuffled along toward them. Now the sidewalk was completely blocked. Lori and I watched the old gentleman hesitate and then step into the street between two cars. He bowed his head and walked around the boys, stepping back carefully onto the curb after he'd passed the blockade. The men laughed and punched each other on the upper arms. I smiled at Lori. There were small red spots on her cheekbones, and they weren't there from the heat of the afternoon.

"Looks like something that's happened before, several times probably. Wonder how many people know about it," I said.

"Not enough. Or they're ignoring it."

"Well, I can't ignore it." I stepped into the street.

Lori grabbed my arm. "Wait, Jack. We're guests here. Remember what you promised?"

I turned my head and looked at her. "I remember, but that was disgusting." I pulled my arm away and walked across the street.

"Hey!"

Five heads snapped around and stared at me as I walked directly toward them in the street. They turned and stood shoulder to shoulder, making a line along the store front just under the edge of the awning. I am slender and not over average height, not a dominating physical presence.

"What do you think you're doing, hassling people like that?" I demanded.

As I drew nearer, I could make out their shadowed faces a little better. The biggest youth, maybe twenty years old, stepped forward and flexed one arm in a habitual gesture. The right one. His tanned muscles rippled. "You lookin' for a party?" he said. His voice was surprisingly light, boyish almost.

"Brian? Brian Worckowski? Is that you? You look just like your father did at that age." Lori's testy sounding voice floated from over my shoulder.

One of the other young men confronting me flicked his gaze

briefly toward the sound of Lori's voice. When he turned back he said something to the others. Without another word, all five stepped back and turned, and disappeared around the corner into the side street.

I stopped and smiled inwardly, feeling how my heart was beating faster and then noticed the sweat dribbling down my sides. Lori came up beside me.

"One against five? Jack, they could have done you some serious damage."

"I don't think it would have gone that far."

Lori fished out a tissue and handed it to me. I wiped my palms. She tugged my arm. "C'mon. People are looking at us."

The incident put a damper on our spirits for a few minutes, but then we continued introducing me to Riverview. A block further along we saw a tall metal tube-like structure surrounded by a big dusty graveled lot. A flat-roofed two-story concrete-walled rectangle stood beside the tube. It had a large floor-to-ceiling plate glass window fronting the street. Above the window a freshly painted sign in large block white letters on black proclaimed, MARTIN'S IMPLEMENTS.

"Joshua Martin," said Lori. "Sort of competed with the bank at times. Owed money by a lot of farmers in the county."

"Yeah? Common situation, I suppose." Being city raised, I had little knowledge of the more intimate shadings of agricultural business deals.

"Mister Martin was a bit of a hard-nose when it came time to pay up. No more latitude, or so the stories went. The bank had regulations and an attitude of staying in for the long haul. Tried to work things out if the farmer was in trouble. Martin, on the other hand, apparently made deals that he knew would cost farmers money they couldn't afford. He advanced money and loaned equipment to people who couldn't get a bank loan. The result was he, Martin, acquired some choice property."

"Ah, sort of like the S&Ls in more recent times," I said.

"Except it looks as if he's still doing business in the same way."

A big stake truck came around the corner of the dealer's building and pulled into the street. Lori squinted at the driver, who appeared to do a double take at us and stomped on his brakes in the middle of the street.

"Lori? Lori Jacobs? That really you?" The man at the wheel had a big booming bellow.

Lori squinted in concentration and then recognition washed across her face. "Terry? Terry! Hi guy." Suddenly years younger, she dashed into the street and hopped up on the running board of the truck. From my vantage point I could see the two of them grinning at each other like young fools. The man hesitated, then leaned forward and pecked her cheek. She grabbed his head and kissed him soundly on the mouth. By then I had reached the truck and smiled up into his seamed and weathered face.

"This your guy?" He offered his hand through the open window. I grasped a strong, rough, workingman's hand. I felt the power behind the grip, but he made no effort to demonstrate it. We had a good firm and friendly handshake

"Terry Worckowski, meet my guy, Jack Marston." . I tried to see a resemblance to any of the five young men we'd encountered earlier, but it wasn't there. A horn beeped behind us as a car swung wide to get around the truck. Lori waved.

"Hi, Jack, very pleased to meet you. Your lady here an' me, we go back a few years. She's one of the good 'uns."

Lori's wide smile continued to cast light over us as she hung there on the running board, clutching the big bracket holding the outside rear view mirror. "You too, Terry." His smile at her compliment appeared a trifle embarrassed.

"Sure glad to see you. Hey listen, I gotta get going. Chores, you know. You going to dinner at Georgina's tonight?"

"Georgina's?"

"Sure, that's right. Guess you didn't know . The 40-Mile Club. It's called Georgina's now. She came in for a partnership and a few years later, bought the whole thing. So she changed the name. Owns half the motel too. Well, see you all later then."

Lori stepped down and Worckowski gunned the motor. He eased the clutch out and the big truck rumbled into motion. It surged down the street. Lori and I stood at the curb watching it go.

"There goes about the best friend I had all through high school."

Hot acrid dust swirled by in a tiny cyclone and unseen fingers dusted my eyelids with grit.

"We've never talked about my childhood out here, have we?" She took my arm and we started strolling. "I grew up earlier than most of the girls in my class." She gestured at her bosom. "A few of the guys started noticing me. They made cracks, figured out ways to jostle me. Kid stuff mostly."

I nodded.

"Some of the girls were jealous of the attention I got. A few of the boys occasionally drove by our farm real early in the morning while it was still dark. Later there were the gropes." Her mouth turned downward in distaste at the memory. "My folks were never sure I wasn't partly responsible."

On the trip to Riverview, Lori had told me that right after she graduated from high school, her mother died. Her dad sold the farm and moved to Illinois. He'd parlayed the money from the farm sale into a string of successful investments and when he died, left each of his children a tidy fortune. It had allowed Lori to continue her higher education.

"Terry," she said, pulling me along the sidewalk, "was the proverbial friend in need. Almost every time things got hairy, he'd show up. Just drift around a corner and lean against the lockers with his big hands in his pockets. Smiling. A truly nice individual. I'm sure that was his son in that group we saw earlier. He looked just like Terry did in high school."

We walked slowly back into the center of town, this time pausing beside the bank. I looked up at the gold lettering on the main doors.

"Huh, two lawyers. Didn't think the town would be big enough for two."

"Oh, it is if one of them is Ed Tomlinson. He's strictly business. Only deals with the big farmers and the big businesses in the whole area. Several counties. Half the state. The other one handles everything Ed doesn't."

"Isn't he the one…" Lori nodded at me.

"Right. We dated some in high school. He'll be easy to recognize at the banquet tonight. Tallest boy in our class." The sharp clack of hard heels crisply stamping along interrupted our conversation. Lori looked back over her shoulder.

"Goodness. Marge. Margie McMenny! How are you?"

"How should I be?" The woman's voice was hard, sharp, like the footsteps. I turned around. She was taller than either of us. I saw a slender woman, with dark, almost black, lustrous short hair carefully shaped around her head. A long brown filter-tipped cigarette hung from the fingers of one hand and a wisp of smoke trailed from her open lips which were colored a vibrant red. She wore a loose open-necked white blouse over a black skirt that cut across her legs about an inch above the knee. Her high spike-heeled shoes and her hose were black.

"Do I know you two?"

"Margie! It's me. Lori Jacobs. This is my friend, Jack Marston."

"I see. I'm pleased to meet you." The words were right, but there was no real feeling in them. Her dark carefully made up eyes flicked over me and returned to Lori's face. I got the message. I was dismissed. "So, Lori. In town for the big reunion, I guess."

"Um, yes. How've you been?"

"Tolerable. But I've got to run. Lots of errands. Dick gave me the rest of the day off. I guess he'll close the shop early, on account of the big doings."

"Dick?" queried Lori.

"Oh, right. You wouldn't know. Remember Dick Borken? He owns Martin's Implements now, too. That's where I work." She stalked off, the brittle image of a hard woman.

"Who was that?" We resumed our stroll.

"Marge McMenny. We're the same age, but she missed a lot in ninth grade so they held her back. It made her unhappy to fail a grade and when she finally graduated from high school, she was two years behind us. Never dated much, never seemed to be part of any group. I seem to remember she was not a very happy kid in school. I'm surprised she's still in town."

"Really?"

"Yep. Meeting her like this brings back some of the gossip about her."

"Gossip is usually nasty and only sometimes accurate."

"Exactly."

"You know everybody in Riverview?"

Lori smiled. "Just about. Remember I told you on the way out there were only 75 in my graduating class."

In the next block, after Lori had pointed out some more locations that had figured in her childhood and adolescence, we arrived back at the place where we'd parked the car, only across the street.

"Hey, babe, what about supper?"

"There are a couple of choices. We can eat at the motel, we can go to Ralph's, if it's open, or we can eat in the regular dining room at the 40-Mile–Georgina's," Lori said. "Do you want to choose?"

"Do I remember right that the banquet tomorrow night is at Georgina's?"

"You do," said Lori.

"Let's go there. We can eat like regular folks and I'll be able to decide if the food's okay for a repeat tomorrow." I winked at Lori before she had an opportunity to protest my crack.

A door beside us opened suddenly and a man hurried out. He brushed by and began to walk briskly up the street. Lori looked after him, mouth slightly agape.

"Elroy? Elroy Guteman. Is that you?" she called.

Guteman stopped and looked back, gave a hesitant half-wave. Then he hurried on again.

"Well, that's certainly odd. You'd think he didn't want to talk to us."

"Another classmate, right? Did he recognize you?"

"Yes he did, but I wonder why he didn't stop?"

I didn't reply. I was looking through the half-shut door Guteman had just exited. It opened on a long flight of stairs leading to the second floor. I noticed the black silhouette of a woman framed in a door at the top of the stairs. Her body seemed to radiate tension. I remembered the woman we'd seen in the alley and the woman I'd glimpsed earlier behind the window.

6

The dining room at Georgina's 40-Mile Club was big, low-ceil-inged, and about half-filled. The air conditioning worked well and was whisper quiet. The cool dimness was a welcome relief from the heat of the outside prairie. Lori and I sat at a table near the center of the room.

"On your left, two tables over, are Steve and Yolanda Parsons," she said in a quiet voice. I looked over at the man facing us. He noticed Lori and smiled, beaming in recognition. His sister barely glanced around at us. Even with just a quick view of the woman's face, I thought they looked related. Both had dark hair and dark complex-ions, although I couldn't tell whether it was natural coloring or tan from the sun. Both wore dark clothes. Her long hair was gathered at the back of her head and fell straight down, flowing over the back of her chair.

"Their dad had the hardware store. She was smart enough to skip a grade up to ours. Didn't I mention that?" I nodded. "Steve didn't like it, though. I think he thought it cramped his style."

"Did it?" I noticed an old man on the other side of the room, very erect, sitting at a table against one wall. Facing him in profile was a much younger woman I already knew to be Georgina Maxwell, owner of the place and a classmate of Lori's.

"Did it what?"

"Cramp his style."

Lori smiled. "I don't remember that he had much to begin with. Yolanda on the other hand is bright and she had a rep as a real party girl. How's your roast?"

"Tasty. Good gravy, too. But much too much."

"Well, eat up. They'll be offended if you don't. And there'll be dessert, too."

"Lori, this is a restaurant, after all."

"Doesn't matter. Great big meals are normal out here. Don't clean your plate and they'll remember. They won't say anything, but they'll remember."

"Lori? Lori Jacobs. It really *is* you. My, my, it certainly has been a long time." The short round man who'd materialized beside our table had a big, carefully articulated voice that belied his size. Lori looked up. Then she nodded.

"Reverend Ames. How nice to see you again. Yes, it has been a long time." I put down my napkin and fork and started to rise. "Reverend, let me introduce my good friend, Jack Marston."

I smiled and stuck out my hand. The Reverend Ames turned his head and surveyed me. "Oh, oh yes. I'm…pleased to make your acquaintance, Mr. Marston." There was just the slightest hesitation, then he took my hand and pressed it once between his warm soft fingers. It wasn't a handclasp, exactly, sort of the male equivalent of the air kiss you sometimes see among women who are trying to be polite but don't really care, or don't want to smudge their makeup. Lori watched us with that peculiar gaze she sometimes uses on me. I think of it as her specimen-examination-look.

"Will you join us, Reverend?" Lori indicated the empty chair. Reverend Ames dropped my fingers and leaned away a little. I noticed others in the room watching, both openly and covertly.

"Oh, no, no, my dear. Don't let me disturb your dinner with your friend. However, if you have a chance, I know an old man would appreciate a visit. At the rectory, of course, if you find an opportunity. We've had no Jacobs in our congregation since your brother, Stanley, left Riverview." He bowed slightly at the hips and walked away. I sat down and resumed eating.

With a sardonic twist to her lips, Lori said, "See? I told you people know about us and they have their opinions."

Loud voices, from an alcove at the end of the room where part of the bar intruded into the dining room, drew our attention. Three men in work clothes and boots stood at the end of the bar along one wall. They'd been there when we entered, over an hour ago. They looked like they'd be there when we left.

"Know those three?" I asked, waving away a second piece of chocolate pie offered by the waitress.

Lori peered over her shoulder. "One of them. The one at the very end of the bar is George Hermansonn. He drank in high school, too. Even when he played basketball." The object of Lori's comment turned slightly. His beer belly hung out over his wide belt and even at this distance in the low lighting I could see he had the look and mannerisms of a long time drinker. Running up and down a basketball court was only in his past.

We finished the meal and decided against an after-dinner drink. Georgina Maxwell and her table companion were still closely engaged in conversation, heads close together across the table. "Who's the old guy with Georgina?" I asked as we went out the door.

"Oh, that's J. L. Houck. The banker. His son runs the bank now, but I think old J. L. still owns it. At least most of it. He's a descendant of one of the original homesteaders in Riverview. So's Josh Martin."

The sun had gone during dinner and the street lights on the main street glowed as we drove sedately back to the motel through quiet, peaceful, Riverview. "How 'bout a short walk?" Lori's voice was calm in the thick darkness. "I'm not ready to go in yet."

"Sure." I parked and, hand-in-hand, we crossed the empty road. We strolled along the grassy verge back toward town. Dust in the air tickled my nose. I thought about the day. Lori seemed more relaxed now, but I still felt an undercurrent of tension in her. "About Reverend Ames."

Her fingers pressed my palm. "What about him? Didn't I tell you some people would object to our living arrangement?"

"I'm sorry if that was embarrassing. I guess we all carry an image of ourselves from our school time. My being here with you like this must be challenging that image," I said.

"I predicted it, remember? You're right, of course, but I left Riverview a long time ago. Coming back is…interesting, but not embarrassing."

I digested that in silence. At the edge of the town park, which smelled like it had recently been watered, Lori tugged my hand and we went down a gentle grassy slope. Ahead of us a small grove of trees marked the bank of the stream around which a small park had been built. Night creatures raised a growing cacophony of high-pitched sounds. There seemed to be a lot of them, all congregated along the banks of the meandering stream that fed into the river farther on. The growling croak of frogs along the water's edge lent a foundation to the chorus. The sounds of humankind, engines, talk, sounds like that, were non-existent. The air was heavy and still.

"Our old swimming hole was right over there," Lori murmured, pointing off to the left. "Now it's part of the city park. I saw a pool in the park. Twenty years ago there were just a few trees along here beside this wide spot in the river. In those days it was outside of town. It was a popular spot then, the only place deep enough to swim in for miles around. There are quite a few stories about this place." I could hear the smile in her voice.

We had gone forward a few more steps when I heard a splash and stopped again. Lori pulled my hand and we squatted beside a bush. Directly across the swimming hole, the moon was rising as if from the surface of the pond itself. Into the rippling slash of light, a dark figure appeared from the far side. A second figure appeared, both wading out until the black water was up to their waists. Even with just the moonlight, I could see they were both women. They drew closer and embraced.

7

Early the next morning, Friday, I was awakened by a thunderstorm that rumbled across town like the freight trains must have done, back in the day when trains ran through Riverview. Today only the rusting tracks remained. The depot was gone. Grain in the elevator at the edge of town now came and went by truck.

After breakfast we drove south over fast-drying streets into the countryside. Lori had decided she wanted to visit the farm where she'd been born and had lived until she went away to college. After her father sold the place, the homestead had remained empty. The land went to neighbors and nobody wanted the buildings, Lori explained. Ten miles south and east of Riverview we turned off a gravel road and parked in a forlorn weedy driveway.

"Sad looking, isn't it," Lori said, gazing wistfully at the small house. White paint was peeling from the lap siding and there were many missing shingles, but the ridge pole didn't sag. A soiled curtain hung limply askew over the single unbroken window facing the car. Lori got out and walked a little ahead, silently absorbing strange but familiar sights.

"My mother found that well," she said, turning around, pointing.

"Your mother?" There was no pump anymore, just a two-foot length of rusty pipe sticking out of the ground. It was barely visible above the weeds and crabgrass outside the kitchen window.

"Before she found it, we had to haul water from the well by the barn. She witched it."

"You mean with a willow wand? Your mother was a water witch? You never told me that."

Lori shrugged. "Well, she used a crowbar, not a willow stick. But yeah, she found water here, and over on Thompson's farm once. We kids were sort of embarrassed about it. I think she was too, sometimes." Close together but apart, we walked across the dusty yard, disturbing grasshoppers and other unseen critters, to the sagging barn, which stood open and partly filled with rotting straw. The odor was overpowering, but not entirely unpleasant. "We had horses, you know. Even after he got a tractor. Dad used them for all sorts of jobs on the farm. Tim and Diamond they were named. Big, gentle beasts. There are still farms around that keep work horses." She blew out her breath in a gusty sigh.

"That's the chicken house and there's what's left of the shed where my brother Stanley raised sheep for 4-H. I never did that."

"Did you all do chores and help in the fields?"

"Sure. I even learned to plow and disk with the tractor. I was good at it too, but my folks were getting close to retiring when I was in high school. Then mom died and dad sold everything and moved to Peoria." Lori's voice was pensive, quiet in the heated air of summer on the plains. She stood with her legs a little apart, firmly planted on the ground, shading her eyes and looking out across the dusty green fields.

"Who owns the place now?"

"I'm not sure. Dad had borrowed from Martin and the sale of the place paid off the loan, I guess. But I don't know who bought the house and buildings. Maybe nobody. There was some money from the stock and the machinery."

The house and what buildings remained were situated on a small rise, so you could see almost forever in every direction except on the north side. During the thirties a shelter belt had been planted to protect the home and buildings from the ravages of the north wind that blew harshly across the prairie. There were shrubs and cottonwoods and Russian Olives and other trees I didn't recognize. I looked west all the way to the horizon. All the way into South Dakota. In my mind arose visions of hunting parties of the Lakotah, riding their ponies in and out of the shallow valleys, through the tall, waving grass. Before the railroad and before the settlers. Before the fences and the plows came.

The wind blew in gentle puffs, bending the tall grass around us in the corners of the yard. Heat rose in shimmers and the sky was cloudless. The sounds of the vast silence were a soft murmur in my ears.

When we got back in the car, Lori leaned her head on the seat's headrest and closed her eyes. I backed the car out of the driveway and continued slowly along the gravel road. We passed a fence line with sagging barbed wire running at right angles to the road. She sighed and turned her face up to me and touched my arm.

"Thank you," she said. Her eyes were wet.

We turned east and re-entered the county highway. It was a wider road with a better grade of gravel.

"Where now?" Silence. I looked at her. Lori was staring through the windshield, biting her lip. "Lori?" We were rolling slowly south, the sound of the gravel crunching under the tires.

She sat up and muttered something I didn't catch. Then she said. "Let's just keep going for a couple of miles. As long as we've come this far, I'd better go by Wilson's Creek."

Wilson's Creek? It hadn't ever come up in conversation that I could remember. I didn't say anything, just increased our speed slightly. Ten minutes later we turned left onto yet another gravel road. This one dipped into a small valley with a meandering creek on its floor. The road was like an earthen dam across the little green valley, except there was a big silvery culvert in the middle that carried the stream under the road.

Part way across Lori abruptly said, "Stop here a minute."

I eased to a halt at the edge of the gravel and Lori got out. I started to join her, but she didn't wait, just walked away, gazing down toward the creek. Ever since we'd left her parent's farm, I'd felt a kind of agitation growing in her; there seemed to be a separation growing between us so I didn't go after her. Instead, I watched her receding back for a minute, then went around behind the car and stood looking out over the little valley. The ticking sound of the cooling engine intruded.

It was apparently pasture land running all the way to the horizon, dusty green land with dark trails I assumed cattle and other animals might have made as they went down through the small hillocks to the water. It was a huge open expanse. During spring runoff the stream must have been deeper and much wider. I could see strips of bare earth on either side of the water, pock-marked with the tracks of cattle and deer, perhaps. At the bottom of the slope, partially buried in the mud, was a broken plowshare, the arm sticking straight up in the air. It was one of the few things I recognized out in rural America, a plowshare. The steel plow that broke the plains. I stared at the thing. Tied to the rusting upthrust brownish arm was a small bundle of flowers. From where I was standing, it looked like other flowers, faded, crumbling, had been tied there before. I could see dry stems and leaves of dead plants scattered on the ground. The bundle tied to the plowshare had been there a while. The blossoms were colorless, loose, barely hanging on. I heard a loud squawk and looked back along the road the way we had come. A big bird with a colorful ring around its neck and a long tail ran along the road and disappeared into the ditch on the other side of the road. Behind me, gravel crunched as Lori returned to the car.

"Let's go back to town for lunch. You up for that?" she said in her normal voice.

"Sure thing."

We had a large dinner–no way could it be called lunch–served family style at a long table in a small place on the main street of Riverview named Ralph's Cafe. The menu listed espresso along with tea and the usual coffee. A big shiny commercial espresso machine squatted on a counter at the back of the place. Heat radiated off the machine, but it remained unused while we were there. The food was excellent. Several people stopped to chat with Lori and some even shook my hand.

The afternoon passed with brief visits to some of Lori's parents' friends who still lived in town. We didn't stop at the rectory to see the Reverend Ames.

Back at the motel as the afternoon wandered down toward evening, I scanned through the packet of material that had come to Lori when she registered for the reunion. The heat helped us decide that neat but casual dress would suffice. I wore light-weight dark olive slacks with a summer-weight, off-white button-down dress shirt and no tie. My shoes were well-shined dark brown loafers. Lori looked fetching in a short, dark blue, shirtwaist dress that buttoned down the front. She caught it at the waist with an intricately twisted, brightly colored scarf, held in a complicated, multiple-ring gold clasp.

"I think I'm going to be sorry I wore pantyhose," she remarked as we walked to the dusty Miata. We'd elected to drive out here to River-view in Lori's sporty red Miata instead of my older station wagon. As we crossed the asphalt parking lot, the smell of the hot fields pressing against the back of the motel was strong in my nostrils.

"I wonder if there's a carwash in town. This thing could use a rinse."

"Well, if there is, we're likely to find it on the way to 40-Mile," Lori said, sliding across the warm car seat. The drag of the seat fabric, when she slid over to unlock the driver's-side door, pulled her skirt up high on her thighs. I noticed and smiled. Lori glanced up and caught my gaze.

"Hey, you. Later." The smile on her face told me she liked my looking.

We drove sedately through town, turned right at the intersection and headed south on the main drag.

"Look over there," I said, pointing. "Carwash." I wheeled into the service station, filled the tank, and ran the Miata into the car wash. The big soft brushes inundated the car with soapy water, covering the windows. We were caught in a private cocoon of our own, blind and isolated for a brief time from the world. We were silent, each in our own private space. I was learning new dimensions of my companion, where her contemplative silences came from. I wondered how she felt about our growing intimacy and how it might affect our relationship. My instincts told me now wasn't the time to inquire. I touched Lori's fingers where they lay quiet on the cushion.

She didn't look around, but her fingers curled over mine in a lov-ing squeeze. The separation between us began to dissolve.

The washing process continued for so long I began to think the machine was stuck. Then there was a clunking sound, the car was jostled, and the rinse and dry cycles brought us back to the hot Minnesota prairie.

The sun flashed a million messages from the drops of water sliding across the hood, all indecipherable. We wheeled across the highway and into the restaurant's parking lot. There was a growing collection of cars, pickups, even a semi tractor, outside the entrance. The graduates had begun to gather.

When we went in, hand-lettered signs directed us to a large, cool banquet room at the rear of the place. There was a big computer-printed paper banner over the door at the end of the hall. **WELCOME GRADUATES OF 1989!!!!**, it proclaimed.

Inside, the room had been arranged with white-clothed tables in a series of rows. The chairs were light-weight padded plastic, black, with thin rose-colored cushions. Fluorescent fixtures hung upside down, sending harsh light to the ceiling of textured tile. The floor was some sort of dark tile. It was an altogether ordinary banquet room.

About half the chairs were occupied and several more graduates stood in small clusters or circulated around the room, talking. I made a quick estimate: there must have been fifty people in the room already. The noise level was on a sharply ascending curve, punctuated frequently by high-pitched squeals of recognition. I caught fragments of, "…you haven't changed a bit," and "…don't you look wonderful," and deeper bellows of "hello" and "son-of-a-gun," and once a "hey shit-head!" which caused the gabble to dip dangerously toward silence for just a moment. A brown wood-grained lectern with a shiny microphone attached stood on the empty table at one end of the room. In the corner opposite the entrance was a swinging door, presumably leading to the kitchen. Beside the door was an opening in the paneled wall with a ledge serving as a temporary bar. On the other wall of the room a large brown metal door with a panic bar bore a sign that warned FIRE EXIT ONLY.

The waitress, doubling as bartender, quickly slapped two drinks in my hands and I went back to where Lori had found seats in the middle of the room. Lori remained beside me for ten minutes, whispering in my ear, pointing out people she remembered, waving and smiling as more graduates and their spouses filtered into the room. Twice she stood to hug another classmate. The room filled and Lori was carried away. I waved her off, smiling. I'd anticipated being left to myself from time to time.

A large man eased himself into the chair across the table. He stuck out a paw. "Arnason, Brad Arnason. You must be Lori's friend, Jack?"

"Right. Jack Marston. We're colleagues at City College in Minneapolis." I shook the other man's hand.

Arnason had the look of a man who had seen and done some hard things. Football and wrestling and girls had been his high school interests, he said. Later law enforcement. Did a hitch in the service, then back to local law enforcement, and up through the ranks. Then came a chance to run for election and now he was the sheriff of Cobb County, had been for a bunch of years. We chatted amiably for several minutes. Occasionally Arnason would nod and smile, mentioning the name of someone who stopped by the table. Somehow we didn't seem to be as popular as most others in the room. I recalled my experiences a few years earlier standing alone with a detective in Minneapolis at a college function. It was more of the age-old reluctance to be too friendly with a cop, even a high school friend.

"Terry Worckowski. Good farmer. County commissioner for a while. Lives out north of town."

"You married, Sheriff?"

"Yep. Her fifteenth reunion is comin' up in two years. See the couple just came in? That's the Tomlinsons. He did law school back east somewhere, now handles big business deals. Elaine is his wife. Bright lady."

There was something in Arnason's tone that I picked up on, a wistfulness, perhaps. The handsome man he had indicated was slender and tall, easily the tallest person in the room. His wife was a good looking Scandinavian type with fine blonde hair combed back from her high smooth forehead. Both were impeccably and expensively groomed. She looked a little flushed and I noticed Tomlinson holding her firmly by her upper arm.

From the door leading to the front lobby of the motel, there came a burst of laughter. A man in a short-sleeved white shirt and tan slacks entered, shook hands and talked animatedly with several people close by. Others walked over to quickly embrace him or shake hands. I recognized him. It was the man Lori had identified on the street earlier as Elroy Guteman. He seemed popular among his classmates. I recalled Lori remarking he'd been starting quarterback of the football team during their junior and senior years. Seeing Guteman reminded me of the flame-haired woman–Stacy? I rose a little from my seat and swept the room. She didn't appear to be present.

"Brad, darling, how nice to see you."

The woman, who had drawn our attention in another direction, was also a blonde, this one a dark blonde. She was a petite woman dressed in a light-weight somber-hued dress. Arnason, who had risen to greet her with a friendly squeeze and a quick peck on the cheek, introduced us.

"Tessa Larson, this here is Jack Marston."

She smiled brightly and gave me her hand; her fingers exerted a tiny pressure that almost wasn't there. "Married to one of us?" Her voice was almost lost in the rising tumult of sound.

I shook my head. "I'm a guest of a classmate of yours, Lori Jacobs." I was a little uncertain what to tell Lori's classmates about our relationship. Lori's family had all moved away, but this was, after all, her hometown. I certainly wasn't going to mention the way we occasionally made love on the living room carpet, back in Brooklyn Park.

"Oh of course, the handsome Jack Marston. You have some sort of responsible position at that college in downtown Minneapolis. Am I right? Lori has told me about you. I thought you'd be taller."

"She has?"

"Oh yes she has. She suggested that the 'ol swimmin' hole' might be a pleasant venue later on for a little gossip and late night schmoozing."

"She did?" My glib tongue had deserted me, and that didn't sound at all like Lori.

"She did. You've apparently had a positive influence on our tight-assed little Lori." Her bitter laugh hung in the air over us as the woman turned and switched away without waiting for a response. There wouldn't have been one.

After a moment Arnason nudged me across the table. "Close your mouth, Jack, you're catchin' flies."

8

A loud explosive bang sounded at the end of the room. I looked over to see a fair-haired man in an open-necked short-sleeved white shirt banging his fingers on the microphone at the lectern.

"All right, folks, let's settle down. I'm calling this twentieth reunion of the Riverview High class of 1989 to order." Quickly the room quieted as people took seats and looked expectantly at the speaker.

There followed several comments about who was not expected and what the business of the evening and the next day was to be. Then Richard Borken, implement dealer, leading businessman, and president of the class of 1989, turned to his left and said, "Elaine, as class secretary, would you take over now?"

We all watched the plump, pleasant-looking woman I had noticed earlier rise and push back errant wisps of fine hair from her forehead. She bent her head and picked up a sheaf of papers, then walked slowly to the lectern to scattered, polite applause. When Elaine Tomlinson turned toward her audience I saw an expression on her face I would describe as trapped. She wasn't desperate, but she appeared resigned, as if she'd rather be somewhere else—anywhere else.

Mrs. Tomlinson smiled around the room and dipped her head again. She took a sip of water from a glass, and shuffled the papers she held. Then came a period of introductions of strangers in the room. She had been using the usual labels to describe the spouses of graduates in the room. When it came my turn to rise and smile, and wave one hand, there was just the tiniest pause and a slight emphasis on the word friend. Then she went on. Throughout, I had the feeling she was being extra careful, the way an experienced drinker who has had just a little too much wine might act.

"Al Steiger wanted me to tell you all his wife can't be here tonight but she'll be around tomorrow." Polite clapping. Lori was still busy across the room. Steiger, a short, squat man, waved and smiled briefly when his name was mentioned.

"Now, we have this nice gift certificate from Denny's Walgreen Drug for the person who came the farthest. And I guess that's Edie Kronk, all the way from the West Coast. Edith? Where are you?"

A woman rose from one corner of the room and walked carefully to the podium. She was dressed and made up in a smooth exotic style that was definitely not Rural Midwestern. The dress, with its spaghetti straps and deep cleavage, her golden tan and carefully tangled hairdo, spoke of sun and sand and ocean beaches. California or Florida, perhaps.

"She's still trying to make it in Hollywood, I hear." Lori's voice was pitched low in my ear. She'd slid into the next chair while I'd followed Edith Kronk's progress to the front of the room. Everybody in the banquet room was watching Kronk. Her gaze swept the room when she turned toward us after receiving the certificate. It was a cool laid-back gaze, almost predatory. She was checking out her audience, just as the audience was checking her out.

"Edie was one of *those* girls in our class."

"A Reluctant Virgin?" I shifted slightly in my chair, so I could look directly at Lori. She nodded with an amused tilt to her lips.

Elaine Tomlinson continued awarding more gift certificates in several categories. The program slid by with hardly a pause. Borken reclaimed the microphone and Elaine went slowly back to her seat. He reminded the graduates of the upcoming schedule and then asked everyone to briefly vacate the room so the staff could set up for dinner.

I lost track of Lori and found myself in brittle conversation with Mary Jensen, another former town girl. She took pains to assure me that her second husband, a Minneapolis attorney with a different last name, was not present, trailing her restless fingers down the front of my shirt.

A few minutes later we were called back into the room and found the tables set for dinner. I didn't see any redheads in the crowd. There were a few minor jostles as people tried to sit with those they most wanted to be with and others appeared to be trying to avoid those they didn't wish to be near. Lori and I chose the table with Brad Arnason and one empty chair.

"So, I hear there's a plan afoot to visit the ol' swimmin' hole later on," I said.

"I beg your pardon?" Lori looked bewildered.

"I've been given to understand that's the plan for later."

"Who told you that?" Lori looked more than a little puzzled.

"I think it was your friend Tessa Larson."

"How odd. I never said any such thing to anyone, least of all to Tess Larson." I decided to leave Tessa Larson's other comment for later when we'd have some privacy.

Black-haired Richard Borken was back at the lectern. I wondered if it was a dye job.

"Now, folks, I want to remind you all that this is no ordinary restaurant dinner. A lot of good folks in our class did the work and prepared this meal. We are in debt to Dolores Holbrook for arranging our menu and supervising the volunteer kitchen crew. Not that Georgina's regular cook isn't a good one. Don't mean nothin' by it. Georgina's been great, but her staff couldn't handle this banquet plus their regular Friday night customers." He gestured in the direction of the main dining room.

Somebody at the head table said something to get his attention and he leaned over to listen. "I've just been reminded that many of you won't know who Dolores Holbrook is. Well, she's the new owner of Ralph's Cafe here in Riverview. And there she is." He pointed toward the kitchen door. A tall solid-looking woman of about thirty-five, in apron and chef's hat, stood in the door. She nodded and briefly smiled in acknowledgement of the polite applause.

Arnason leaned toward me. "You catch that? *New* owner of

Ralph's? Miz Holbrook has been here four years. Some folks will call her the new owner for *another* ten years."

I nodded.

"Great cook. And a baker. She'll have fresh pastries 'most every morning. She even brought an espresso machine in."

Three waitresses, carrying heavily loaded trays, entered the room. The food wasn't fancy, but it was properly prepared, hot and plentiful. We feasted.

* * *

"C'MON, JACK, YOU can handle another helping of meatloaf and potatoes." Lori smiled across the plates. I politely declined, feeling a little stuffed already and knowing dessert was still to come.

The sounds of eating reduced the conversational roar to a general murmur and an occasional raised voice.

"Say, Bob," I heard from a nearby table, catching Brad Arnason's amused glance. I watched Brad shovel in another forkful of meatloaf. Chewing slowly, he reached for the gravy boat the waitress had put on the table, and sloshed more steaming brown gravy over a big mound of mashed potatoes, his second helping. Maybe it was his third.

Whoever was with Bob went on. "Say, Bob. Where's Elroy? He's s'posed to give us a ride. Said I should leave the truck here overnight, he said."

The female voice that answered was definitely not Bob. "Gee, Thad, I think he's gone. Said something about a sick cow."

I leaned toward Lori and said, "I notice you haven't introduced me to your best high school girl friend." Lori nodded agreement.

"How come? I thought everyone had a best buddy in high school."

"Did *you* have one?"

I admitted that I hadn't.

"See? Something else we have in common. No close girlfriend. Partly it was because I was a farm girl and we bused in and out." She shrugged dismissively. "Terry was the closest to a best buddy, and he was definitely a guy."

After the main course was polished off there was a short recuperative lull. Back the wait-staff came, this time loaded with large servings of pie. There was lemon and apple and blueberry and banana cream and cherry. One could have more than a single piece, with or without ice cream, thank you very much.

By the time coffee arrived, we'd been in the restaurant almost three hours and it was getting close to eleven. People drifted in and out, and the bar in the corner was doing a steady business. Few, if any, appeared ready to end the evening.

"Excuse us, Brad? I want to introduce Jack to several more people he won't remember tomorrow morning." I arched an eyebrow and Brad nodded. He wore that sleepy, well-fed smile some big men get. He leaned back in his chair, thoroughly relaxed.

Lori and I made our way through the tables toward the lectern at the front of the room. The classmates we greeted all seemed genuinely pleased to see Lori and to meet her guy. That's me, I thought, *her guy*. We stopped to chat with Terry Worckowski. He was sitting with a pleasant woman named Marybeth Wilson.

Marybeth and I hit it off immediately. We had read some of the same books and our political views meshed. Lori looked at me and slid out of her chair to the beckoning smile of another classmate. The noise level got louder and friendlier again. People surged back and forth among the tables.

From behind Terry a conversation between two women filtered into my consciousness.

"Who's the man Lori brought?"

"The one with brown hair?"

"Him. He looks right at you when he talks to you. Like he's really paying attention."

"He's got nice eyes."

Terry leaned across the table. "Don't turn around," he murmured.

"He's here with Lori Jacobs. I don't remember his name."

I looked a question at Terry. He winked.

"…married?" said the first woman.

"Don't think so, but they're registered in the same room at the motel."

Crowd noise rose and drowned out the rest of the conversation. I furrowed my brow at Worckowski and leaned back to take a sip of my drink. The crowd shifted and I never did see the two women who'd been gossiping about me.

At the head table, class Secretary Elaine Tomlinson seemed to be putting her drinks away pretty steadily. Or perhaps it was the same drink and she was just sipping on it. I wasn't spending a lot of time watching her. Marybeth rose to move on, and as we said goodbye, I looked over her shoulder to see Elaine being guided, or helped, toward the entrance by two women I hadn't met. Her husband seemed to be among the missing. There was a lot more traffic in and out of the place as people went out to smoke or into the bar, or just looked for a quiet place to rest for a moment.

I decided to take a break and find someplace cooler and more quiet. Scanning the milling crowd for Lori, who was not in immediate view, I made my way across the big banquet room to the fire exit, which someone had propped open a few inches. I went out into the prairie heat and discovered a field that had the smell of new-mown grass. Crickets sang. By the hundreds. Or maybe by the thousands. I had a sense there were people in the darkness, but no one close. As my eyes adjusted, I began to make out bushes and trees near the wall. I strolled away from the building, breathed deeply.

Off to my left, about thirty yards away, I heard rustlings in the grass and glimpsed the faint outlines of several figures in a tight group.

A bright flashlight flicked on and someone said, "Jesus!"

I picked up my pace and angled toward a piece of machinery that was the center of attention. The flashlight went out.

9

Arnason's announcement of the discovery of Guteman's body was met with stunned silence, then a few low murmurs. Nobody screamed, nobody fainted, although I could have sworn the temperature in the room went up a few degrees. The sheriff's almost laconic statement was brief and to the point. He avoided mentioning that the circumstances didn't appear accidental. Lori looked at me and her hand tightened in mine.

I'd been observing Lori's classmates. I always did that in new situations, part of my instinctual attitudes relating to my work with adult students at City College. In this case I hadn't expected to do much more than examine my collected observations relative to Lori. The circumstances had suddenly changed. Here we were in River-view, next to the Chippewa River, hard by the scene of what appeared to be a murder. I realized my outsider observations might be useful to the investigation, but I didn't want to be involved. I suspected Lori wouldn't want me to be, either.

"You already knew, Jack." I nodded at Lori's soft spoken comment, still watching the crowd. I whispered that I'd stumbled on the scene a few minutes earlier and the sheriff had asked me to keep it quiet until he was ready. A few women had tears in their eyes and I heard a muffled sobbing. I couldn't detect the source.

Sheriff Arnason and his deputies began methodically writing down the names and addresses of everyone in the place. That included not only reunion classmates but several strangers who had the misfortune to be in the main bar or who were staying at the attached motel. Preliminary statements were being taken from many of them, Brad commented when he walked through the room, but it appeared that local people were not being closely questioned. I wondered about that.

Dick Borken reappeared at the microphone, a somber expression on his face. "Well, folks," he said. "We've discussed this at the head table and we think we should end this evening's fest-activity of the reunion. I know it'll be hard, but I believe El would have wanted us to carry on with the rest of the plan during the remainder of the weekend." There were nods of assent from a few listeners. "So you all please be at the high school tomorrow morning according to the schedule we've distributed. The building will be open for the exhibits, there'll be a few announcements, and the buses will leave for Kronk's at ten sharp."

Borken paused and licked his lips. "Sheriff Arnason tells me he's got what he needs from everyone here in the banquet room for now, so we can leave. He also said for me to tell you he may be in touch with some of you again during the weekend."

People began to stream out, some hurrying as if glad to leave the scene of Guteman's murder. Others stood in tight knots jabbering at each other. Forming mutual alibis? Gossiping? Probably a little of both, I thought.

In the car, I sat beside Lori while we let the engine idle, the air conditioner slowly expelling the oppressive heat and moisture from the Miata. The parking area was crowded with cars and trucks jockeying into line to get out of the place. Dust and exhaust fumes billowed and swirled in the headlight beams.

"Jack. I have a feeling there's something you haven't told me about this."

"Right as usual." I looked at her profile. She was staring through the windshield, blinking slowly.

"It all seems so unreal. There he was, so vital, going down the street only this morning. What aren't you telling me?"

"His death wasn't an accident."

"Oh, my God! What happened?"

"He was found skewered on an old hay rake out in back of the restaurant."

"Jesus, Jack. That's awful!"

"Deputy found him still warm."

"God. Was he killed by the rake? Could he have fallen?"

"I doubt it. He'd had to have deliberately climbed up on the thing, way the body was positioned. Someone strong put him there."

"But why the hay rake?"

"That could be an important question."

"I can't believe it. Nobody ever talked about him. I mean, there are always stories, gossip about people. Some of it can be pretty nasty. But I don't remember hearing anything about Elroy. Riverview's mostly such a peaceful, straightforward little town. Nothing much ever happens here."

"Sure."

"Did I ever tell you about the county superintendent of schools?"

"No, I don't think so." I wondered at her abrupt change of subject.

"I never knew the man, hardly ever saw him except at graduations, or the Christmas concert. Olafson, I think his name was.

"Anyway, Dr. Olafson resigned the year after I graduated. Quite abruptly. Nothing was ever said about it, just a tiny announcement in *The Cobb County Chronicle*. It was right in the middle of the school year, just after Christmas. My mother sent me the paper at college.

"Anyway, it seemed odd he'd resign in the middle of the school year like that. Next summer back home I asked mother about it. She got this funny look on her face and brushed me off. She changed the subject. It turned out he'd been abusing children. Both boys and girls. Elementary school kids, on some of his visits around the county. I guess he never actually had sex with any of them. But he would hold them on his lap and fondle them. Touch them *inappropriately*, as we say today."

"Jesus!"

"Apparently it had been going on for a long time. Years. Some people knew about it. And for a long time they just kept silent, but finally, he was forced to resign."

"They should have arrested him."

"Yes, but remember, this was twenty-some years ago. He was a respected member of the community and nobody wanted a scandal. Et cetera, et cetera." Lori's voice had become harsh in the telling. She abruptly switched back to the present. "Guteman's death, odd circumstances aren't they. A hay rake."

"Yeah."

"Jack, does Brad have any ideas how it happened?"

"If he does, he's not sharing. I hope they get it sorted out so we out-of-towners don't have to stay beyond the weekend."

"Poor Elroy. I wonder what he was doing to end up dead behind the club. I wonder how his family will get along now."

"Do you know them?"

"Not very well. I may have mentioned on the way in yesterday that he married an out-of-town girl. I think they have two kids. Teenagers by now I guess. God, poor Elroy." Lori fixed me with one of her looks. "You aren't itching to get involved?"

I wanted to ask her whether she knew any of the children who had been molested. I wanted to ask Lori if she was a victim. I decided asking those questions right now wasn't a good idea.

"No thank you, ma'am. Just because I'm curious and always looking at behavior, this is not my territory and sure not my area of expertise. There's a difference between being aware of our surroundings, as I am even more so now than before Guteman's body was found, and actively participating in a murder investigation. My years as a Navy investigator are long behind me as you well know. I'm an outsider here, my only connection is you. I'll stick to wrestling with student issues at the college. Besides, your Brad Arnason strikes me as a pretty competent sort."

"I guess he is, but this just goes to show you never really know, even about people you've known all your life. Who understands all the dynamics in these small towns?"

"True," I said. "Everybody has secrets they don't talk about, even when the secrets aren't particularly important."

Lori's mouth curved in a small sad smile. "I guess that's so. Even between lovers." Her hand came to rest on my thigh.

"Me too," I responded.

"I'll confess I do sometimes process you or use you, but in a good way, I think."

"Meaning?"

"You're like a benchmark for me. Sometimes I think, 'how would Jack behave in this or that situation?'"

"Gee, I'm flattered, I think."

"*Ummm.* Why'd you want me to come out here this weekend? For that matter, why did you come along? Most men would run screaming from their wife's or lover's high school reunion."

"Couple of reasons. When you showed me the invitation, that was my first reaction, although I was pretty sure you wouldn't even ask me to go. I was a little surprised when you blew it off. The reunion.

"However when I thought about it some more, and about our relationship, I thought it could be interesting for me to meet people from your past, get a little more familiar with some of your old friends."

"Same reasons I wanted you here. I thought it would be good for you to have a look at my formative influences, so to say, once I was persuaded to come at all."

I shifted the Miata into drive. "Later, though, you seemed to change your mind…almost as if you regretted asking me along. And then today at Wilson's Creek, I…."

Lori put her fingers on my lips. Leaned closer "I know, babe. There are some things I still have to sort out. Things I kind of forgot about until we actually got here. I've been a little surprised at myself. I'll explain later. Promise."

"I'm a patient man, my love." I was thinking hard. We'd been on a plateau, relationship-wise for a while, and I hoped this reunion would move us forward. I still felt that way, but now murder and other secrets were intruding. Why had Lori suddenly brought up the pedophilic superintendent? *Well, we still have time to work it out. Plenty of time.*

10

Saturday morning we were up by six. It had become my custom to jog for half an hour or so several mornings each week. Just trying to keep the old bod in some kind of reasonable shape. So I threw on a t-shirt and my running shorts and shoes and slipped out while Lori was in the shower.

"Back before breakfast," I said, as I went out, shutting the door and walking to the rear stairs.

Outside, the air was already heating up. A momentary second thought inserted itself when the humidity smacked me hard in the face, but I went forward like a good soldier and jogged west out of Riverview, staying on the shoulder of the road to avoid traffic. There wasn't much to avoid. The few autos that rolled by ignored me. A stake truck headed the same direction came up behind and blew its horn as it swished by, pushing an invisible wave of dusty hot air across the lane at me. A mile or so out of town I crossed the highway and started back the other way. Farm fields stretched out on either side. On my left was what I recognized as a bright green field of corn. The motionless stalks reached toward the horizon. On my right an expanse of what might have been wheat or barley stood golden on the ground. I made a mental note to ask Lori what the grain was, if it was even a grain. Identifying growing crops was not one of my talents.

Back in our motel room, Lori was absent. A scribbled note said "Meet me in the coffee shop."

I showered and changed into comfortable slacks, a short-sleeved shirt, and a clean pair of white and blue cross-trainers. Downstairs in the coffee shop, I saw Brad Arnason. He was facing me, sitting at a table in the center of the room with a woman. It was Lori. Both had coffee in front of them.

"Good morning, Sheriff," I said, pulling out the third chair. He looked up. No smile.

"Sorry to bother you folks so early," Arnason said, "but Elroy's killing is going to put a serious strain on county resources if we're going to avoid holding you out-of-towners over beyond Sunday night."

"Is that a possibility?"

"Yep. Legally a little shaky, I guess, but unless someone lodges a protest, folks tend to cooperate. Besides, by the time anybody gets a lawyer to appear before a judge, we'd likely be through. I hope we can cut down any inconvenience by establishing the whereabouts of as many folks as possible. Right now I'm concentrating on visitors. Out-of-towners, like you folks. That way we can release people who couldn't have been involved. When I saw you running out on the highway, I assumed Lori was also awake, so I called your room."

"I was just getting out of the shower." Lori had an amused glint in her eyes. I looked at her and then back at the sheriff. What was amusing?

Brad pursed his lips and then scratched his forehead. He looked away. Odd. Something was bothering him as well. "So, Jack, you were at the reception the whole evening?"

"Right. I saw Guteman come into the room where we had dinner, not long after we got there," I said. "Must have been right around six."

"Was there anybody with him?"

"I don't think so." I shook my head.

Arnason nodded and wrote in the notebook he held. "I hope this isn't too difficult," he sighed, "but I have to ask you these questions."

"Go ahead, Sheriff."

"You two were together the whole time, is that right?"

I raised one eyebrow. This was interesting. "Are we suspects?" I held up a hand. "Yes. The answer is yes, we were…." I paused. "Well, that's not quite right. We were in the same room."

"Mostly," interjected Lori.

"Um," said the sheriff.

I looked at Lori. The glint was stronger.

"I take it you two are not married, is that right?"

Where, I wondered, was this going? "That's right, Sheriff," I answered, "although I don't see what business that is of yours."

Arnason stared at Lori who obviously knew what was up, but wasn't about to help the man out. Or me either. He sighed. "Well, a couple of people have told us they saw Miss Jacobs here and Ed Tomlinson in the parking lot at one point last night. And…"

"And he wants to know if I'll verify that," Lori interrupted. "I told him I couldn't verify who might have seen me–us–because I wasn't looking around at the time."

"Ah," I said, trying to look wise and urbane. Not something I practice. I was getting the point. My great and good friend Lori Jacobs was playing a game with us. "Well, Sheriff, I suppose your sources also told you Ms. Jacobs was, rather intimately, shall we say, *socializing* with Tomlinson out there in the parking lot."

"That's correct." He nodded. Was Arnason blushing?

"I can tell you that I observed Ms. Jacobs and Mr. Tomlinson in close proximity, when they appeared in the entrance to the banquet room at about nine-thirty last night. Coming in the door. She'd been out of my sight for about thirty minutes, I think. Understand, Sheriff, I didn't check my watch and I haven't any way of knowing how long she was dancing with Tomlinson in the parking lot, but it was within ten minutes of when I left you in the field behind the restaurant. She looked a bit flustered. A little mussed, you could say." I took Lori's hand. "She told me she was the recipient of some unwelcome advances in that parking lot. As she could very well have explained to you much earlier in this conversation."

Lori briefly dropped her gaze, mostly to cover a smile. "Sorry, Brad. I know this is serious business, I just couldn't resist a little dig when I realized what you were driving at and why you were a little antsy."

Arnason glanced at each of us and nodded. "Well, I guess I'm relieved. I didn't much like the idea of causing a fight between you two." He frowned at Lori. "You shoulda told me right from the get-go that Jack already knew."

"You're right and again I apologize, Brad. I guess this reunion is affecting my maturity. You're sure Elroy was murdered, I suppose."

"Jack told you how we found 'im?"

"Yes, basically, but…"

Arnason raised a hand. "No, I ain't tellin' you any more details. There's still too much down home in me. Now I know where you both were during the critical period, and that things are okay between you, I have other questions, and a request." He looked at me. "You mentioned last night you were an investigator in the Navy before you went into the education business, so you're an experienced observer. Think about last night. Think about where people were in the room and how they reacted to the news about Elroy. I'm going on the trip to Kronk's, but extra eyes will help. Let me know if you see anything out of place today. Right now my list of people with the opportunity and some who might have a motive is mighty long. I'm not asking you to become a deputy, but as I say, I can use the extra ears. And eyes." He rose to leave and I shook his offered hand.

"Sorry this is messing up your enjoyment of our reunion, Brad," said Lori as he turned away.

"Yeah, well, think how it's messed up Elroy's."

After he left and we both ordered breakfast I said, "I have a question about last night."

Lori nodded and sipped her coffee.

"I wondered if you knew any of the kids who were molested by that Super?"

"No, I didn't. Actually, I don't know that for sure. I wasn't one of them, and I think if any of the people I knew well, like Terry or Elaine or Ed Tomlinson, had been I'd have heard about it. You know, hints, sidelong looks, dropped comments."

I wasn't so sure, but I was relieved that Lori hadn't been subjected to the guy. Our breakfasts arrived and we tucked in. Tension always seems to give me an appetite.

"A change of subjects," I said, around a mouthful of eggs. "I wonder if Sheriff Arnason knows about Stacy Frommer and Guteman?"

"Excuse me? Stacy and Elroy? Knows what about them?"

"I can't be positive, but I strongly suspect it will turn out those two were having or starting or maybe ending an affair."

"Jack! How could you know that? Stacy lives in Fargo. Elroy is—was married and works his dad's farm out west of town. He has a family."

"Yes, but we saw a woman in that alley when we first got here, remember? You said you thought it was Stacy Frommer."

"Sure, but—"

"And then we saw Guteman come out of that door on Main and go down the street without even stopping to say hello. Remember that? You were looking at him, but when I glanced up the stairs I saw the figure of a woman, and it sure looked like it was the same woman we saw in the alley.

"I think if we check we'll discover that Guteman came from a stairway to the second floor just about where you told me Stacy used to live."

"I'll be damned. Pretty thin, though. They sure wouldn't be *my* candidates for lovers."

"You know as well as anybody that attraction between two people can take odd twists."

For a moment she stared silently over my head. "Why didn't you tell Brad?"

"What if I'm wrong? If what I think I saw isn't correct, it's just more pain for Stacy and Guteman's family and more gossip for the town. I can't see that waiting a few hours for proof will hurt anything."

"I understand." She fiddled for a moment, then stopped folding her napkin. "Meaning, I suppose that you plan to do a little detecting? More than just be a secret watcher for Brad?" She sighed when I nodded. "Do I get the idea that maybe you aren't entirely sure of the sheriff?" I nodded again. Lori dropped her napkin on the table and blew out her breath. "If you're ready, let's get over to the high school for the next event."

We drove to the high school where we found most of the class already assembled. The main topic of conversation for the first twenty minutes of milling around was, of course, the death of Elroy Guteman. More and more people, I noticed, referred to Guteman's death as a murder. I learned that Arnason and his deputies had been discreet so my presence at the actual scene was still unknown. For that I was grateful. It also raised my estimation of Arnason's competence and ability. Gradually the conversations around me shifted into more ordinary channels.

"Darlene, I have to tell you, you still look real good. Texas life must agree with you."

"Sure does, Marybeth. I just wish Benton could have come along for you-all to meet him."

"Hey, George, I heard down 't the elevator, Amundson is thinkin' 'bout sellin' that eighty-acre piece you were looking at last year."

"Yep. I'm gonna call him on Monday, see if we can get together on it."

Lori caught my attention and whispered, "See, even a murder doesn't stop the normal interests of people in Riverview."

11

"All right, everybody, all right! Let me have your attention now." Class president Dick Borken leaned over the podium mike on the low platform, trying to quiet the chatter. We were clustered in the old gymnasium where we'd already endured a brief welcome by the current school superintendent.

Some of Lori's classmates and their spouses were strolling around the perimeter of the hall, looking at the trophy cases filled with artifacts of bygone eras.

"There'll be time for talk and wandering about in a minute. I just want to go over the schedule once more." He looked up in what I took for an expression of mild desperation and smiled in my direction. I thought it more probable he was smiling at Lori. "You'll have an hour now to tour the building and wax nostalgic about your former classrooms...the old parts."

"Yeah, like how we feel about our old parts," someone behind me muttered.

"Then at ten-thirty, we've arranged for school buses to take us to the Kronk ranch for a big barbecue. And there'll be a few surprises as well. The buses will return here at five." As far as I was concerned, we'd already had one surprise too many. "Supper will be here in the gym starting at six-thirty, so you won't have much time to get ready. Then, after the meal we'll hold a brief ceremony outside here on the practice field." Borken pointed his finger at the south wall. After a couple of additional bits of business he released us.

Down the corridor we sauntered and passed through an open set of double doors. The smooth tile floor changed and we were now walking on a highly polished, slightly uneven wood floor that had supported generations of students. We had gone into the old brick high school building that once sheltered a mere four hundred young people in four grades during Lori's time in Riverview. The smell of the floor wax used by every school in creation was apparent, even though it looked to my eye like the floor now had a thick coat of shiny clear acrylic.

"Here," said Lori, "this way. My homeroom is down here." We walked slowly along the hall, past small knots of people, until we came to a big, square sunny space. There were no desks or chairs today, just a wide expanse of polished board flooring and long tables arranged around the perimeter. On the walls hung a series of large black-and-white photographs of students, many in a similar location, but wearing clothing of a bygone era.

Lori stopped just inside the door. "The room seems a lot smaller than I remember, even without the desks and chairs." We turned toward a display. "Oh," she said softly, "this is different." Then she went closer to the nearest panel of several mounted photographs. "Look. Here we are in tenth grade."

We spent the next several minutes going along the walls looking at more photographs, some of them so grainy from being enlarged, the people in them were almost unrecognizable. At least to me. Lori gave me a running commentary, sometimes happy, sometimes wistful, about the people and the events depicted. Most of the pictures were informal photos of events. The others were posed group pictures. Class photographs. The guys' haircuts were mostly short. The girls had ponytails. Their clothes didn't look much different from today. Jeans, some with cuffs, a few plaid shirts, a skinny tie or two. The girls seemed to have only a single hole in each ear lobe. No nose or eyebrow rings. There were no visible tattoos. I didn't see anyone wearing jeans with artfully placed rips, but there was one girl in what looked like leg warmers. The movie 'Flashdance' was big then, I recalled.

The participants seemed to be happy; smiling and laughing, having a fine old country time. I thought Lori looked cute as a button in some of them. I didn't tell her that.

She was a picture ahead of me when I heard her say, "Oh." Something in her voice made me look hard at her face. She was standing before yet another group shot. I saw her take a deep breath. She put one hand up to touch the picture as she turned toward me. "This is our ninth-grade class picture. See, here I am, in the short braids? And here's Mary and Elizabeth and Ed and Elaine. Brad. Here's Tony–Anton Litvek." There was something, an odd tone in her voice. "I guess I'd forgotten he would be in these earlier…."

"What is it?" I looked at the boy in the middle in the front row. He was small with dark hair and a prominent aquiline nose. He had large, very dark eyes, and he wasn't smiling. I got an impression he was darker skinned than the others, but it was hard to be sure from the grainy black and white photograph. Even for a ninth grader, he was handsome.

"Tony--Anton…died…the next spring. Actually…he was killed…in an accident."

"Lori?" Something was wrong.

I moved closer and touched her shoulder. Suddenly I had a flash of insight. "Does this have anything to do with Wilson's Creek?"

She nodded. "It was so sad. We were on a class outing, right after most of the snow melted. At Wilson's farm, out by their creek. We were on sort of a field trip to look at lichens and early plants. After a while, we just started horsing around, you know? Most of us were jumping back and forth across the creek. We were going downstream so the creek got wider and faster and pretty soon we were daring each other because it took longer and longer jumps to get across. Finally at one place, just a little way above the culvert where it goes under the road, Tony refused to do it."

"He was the smallest boy in the class, wasn't he?" I murmured, looking back at the picture.

"Yes," she said. "He was about the smallest in the whole school. Well, you know how kids are. We kept daring him and started calling him names. Tony on one side of the creek and all the rest of us on the other." She stopped. I saw tears in her eyes. She looked away from me and stared at the photograph. "There were really only four or five of us close by. I didn't really...." She stopped and bit her lip. "It was Edith Kronk and Elaine and Elroy. Terry was there too. The whole class. Oh, a few of the kids tried to stop the teasing. Some crossed back to his side to egg him into trying the jump."

She didn't say so, but I would have bet Lori was not one of those who led the teasing.

"He eventually tried to force himself to jump, running to the bank, then stopping. He must have been scared. The third time, Elroy pushed him off when Tony ran by. But he didn't make it."

"What happened?"

"He landed in the water right at the edge in front of us, with his arms on a little ledge and his legs and lower body in the water. Landing like that must have stunned him, because he just hung there for a few seconds. Then the current pulled him into the creek. It wasn't very deep, you know, but it was deeper than usual because of the snow melt. We could probably have walked across in it, except for the current. But it was icy cold. One of the boys waded in after him, but he couldn't grab Tony. Before most of us realized what was happening, Tony was pulled down the stream and right into the culvert that carried the creek under the road. We could see him, his hands reaching up, his mouth open." She stopped and sighed.

"His head hit the edge of the culvert and there was blood. It seemed like a lot of it." She stopped again, recalling the scene. I pulled her into my arms and she rested her chin on my shoulder. A couple of people walked slowly by and eyed us, questions on their faces.

Lori eased out of my arms and wiped her eyes with a tissue. "I ran up on the road to get around the culvert. The class was spread all over the pasture. When he came through he looked like he was unconscious. Some of the boys who were already across the road scrambled down and dragged him out. His face was really bloody from the cut. Nobody knew what to do, exactly. They tried to dry him off. After a while Miss Simms, our teacher came back, and then the sheriff arrived. They took him to the hospital in Montevideo. Two days later he died. Never regained consciousness, they said." Lori sniffed and dabbed at her eyes again with a tiny handkerchief. "They let all of us out of class to go to the funeral. I remember his sister sobbing, sobbing, through the whole service. They were close in age, I think, but she was two years behind Tony in school. I don't know why. The family moved away later that summer.

"God, Jack. I haven't thought about all that in a such long time."

I looked at her and squeezed her hand. *This was what had been bothering her about the reunion. This was why she hadn't been back to town since she left. There's guilt here. She still feels it.* Knowing what was bothering her didn't make me feel any better, especially since I'd kind of egged her into the weekend.

She showed me a tremulous little smile. "I still feel bad about it." She wiped her eyes. Took a big breath. "With all my expensive training, you'd think I'd have realized long ago why I've been reluctant to come back." She took in another big breath. "Enough. It was a long time ago and I know I don't need to beat myself up over it any more. C'mon, the buses will be leaving for Kronk's."

"We don't have to go. I get the feeling you're forcing yourself in this reunion. Christ, Lori. You don't have to do any of this." I could hear the irritation in my voice. Not at Lori, at my helplessness to shield her from the unhappiness. It didn't come out quite that way.

She gave me a sharp glance. "And miss the bus ride? You never rode a school bus, did you?"

"No. And I don't think it scarred me for life."

"Well, maybe not, but you ought to experience it at least once. Plus, if we don't go, how will you do any detective work?" A small smile appeared. "I'll get over this. Again." She gestured at the picture and we turned out of the room.

Lori was strong and not given to periods of depression. She would get through this, I thought, but I now realized our relationship might be affected by how this all played out. I knew then I wasn't going to let the sheriff's request for a little help divert me from attention to Lori the rest of this weekend.

12

Lori and I were almost the last ones to get on the third big, ugly, yellow school bus, a somewhat more modern version of the vehicle she and most of the others had ridden from isolated farms to the little school in Riverview. We were about the only ones who remained quiet in the gabble of conversation the entire ride out to Kronk's spread. I had a sense everyone was trying to put the murder away so they could all spin out their good school memories and have a grand reunion.

Spread was the right word for the Kronk place. As we bounced over the gravel road that went straight as an arrow shaft south off the highway, Lori pointed at a fence line.

"Now, except for the county road, we're on Kronk land."

"How far west does their land go?"

"Farther than you can see, babe." We hit a pothole and I felt an instant of air between me and the seat I was on. *Weren't there any springs in this thing?* I grabbed the handhold on the corner of the seat in front. Lori merely swayed to the awkward rhythm of the bus. After ten minutes on the gravel, the bus ground up a gentle hill and turned right, into a winding gravel driveway between two large rock-and-cement pillars. Powdery clouds of dust seeped under the door from the wheels of the buses that had preceded us.

When we alighted, I discovered we were in a wide sweeping driveway edged with tall poplar trees. On our right a paved walk led to the front door of a three-story split-level white house. It was a big house. We approached the east side where all the windows had drapes drawn against the morning sun. The wide overhang of the hip roof shaded the upper story windows already, even though it was not yet noon.

"Huh, they've added to the house," said Lori, shading her eyes against the glare. She slipped on a large pair of dark glasses I'd never seen before.

In front of us, to the left of the row of nose-to-tail buses, sat a large building that looked like an overgrown two-story garage. Farther to the left was the end of another white building that stretched a long way west.

"That's the stable," said Lori tugging at my arm. "C'mon, we go this way." A brick walk carried the seventy or seventy-five celebrants and spouses between the garage and the north end of the house to the west side. Along the way I discovered that the house was built in the shape of an L, with the longer leg oriented east and west. At the end of the short leg an open porch and a big white door obviously led into the working side of the house. Several pairs of mud-caked boots were lined up beside the door. A big rusty triangle hung from an overhead beam. One of the classmates saw me looking at the triangle and laughed.

"Old man Kronk likes to keep this part of the place the way it was. You're looking at what's left of the house built after the original homestead shack was abandoned. The porch and that end wall were all they saved after the tornado in 'forty-seven. That triangle was used to call the family to meals. It's kind of a sentimental touch," the man chuckled. "Only sentiment I ever saw in old man Kronk."

Filling in the space in front of the two legs of the house was a big concrete-and-tile swimming pool with an apron of bright green artificial turf. I whistled under my breath. The pool seemed a bit ostentatious for this part of rural America. Or maybe not.

Across the pool was a low white building–every building on the place seemed to be white–with several doors. Probably an acre or two of well-watered, neatly trimmed grass surrounded the whole complex of buildings. Not that I have any experience gauging how many acres or square feet a piece of land might be. In the shade of the long porch that held the sun away from this side of the house, the ubiquitous podium and microphone had been set up. Dick Borken was once again trying to get our attention.

I recognized him right off, by now. I recalled he was the present owner of Martin's Implements. I looked around. There seemed to be a whole lot of new people I didn't know and didn't recognize. Apparently they hadn't been present last night at the banquet.

"Okay, folks, this afternoon is strictly fun in the sun. There's extra sun block on the table for those who forgot it. The dressing rooms are over there." He waved at the building on the other side of the pool. "You'll find plenty of suits in various sizes if you want to take a dip. The barbecue pit is already running and we've laid on a selection of picnic goodies. Edith and her daddy brought in a couple of nice gentle horses to add to his stock just for this occasion, so several people can ride if you've a mind to do that. There's a man in the tack room to help you saddle up. Enjoy. We'll also have an old fashioned hay ride a little later in the afternoon.

"I just want to say a couple more things. We asked Dolores Holbrook to supervise the barbecue, so I'm sure you'll have another great feast. Dolores has been a big help all along. You might want to thank her whenever you see her. Now, here's our host, George Kronk, who most of you know, and of course Edith, back from California for this reunion. Let's give 'em a nice round of applause." We did that.

I looked at the couple who came out to the podium from the shadows of the porch. George Kronk was a short, round-shouldered man. His gnarled hands and weathered, seamed face marked him indelibly as a man of this land. Except in this anachronistic setting, he would blend in anywhere in the county and hardly be noticed. He wore a pair of faded jeans over stained scuffed work boots and a white shirt with a black string tie. His head was covered with a sweat-stained John Deere cap, pulled low on his forehead. Next to him his daughter Edith, one hand lightly on his shoulder, smiled at the applause. Taller, her mane of teased and managed hair flowed to her bare tanned shoulders. She was wearing a white tank top and white shorts. Her I definitely remembered from the night before. California chic. Edith waved, and when the clapping died down, the crowd began to disperse to its selected pleasures.

"This is quite a place. The Kronks must have something going besides farming."

Beside me, Lori nodded. "Mr. Kronk—George—married money. Lots of people in the county envied Edith, but she was generally pretty easy to get along with. Everybody knew she had more money than anyone. But she never made an issue of it that I remember. We were in choir together. Let's check out the barbecue."

* * *

After demolishing heaping plates of mixed salad and a shared, nicely grilled steak, we wandered over to the stable. We were discuss-ing—not to say arguing over—whether Lori was going to get me on a horse. I was reluctant. A couple of eager riders were already cantering around out in the pasture. Most of the box stalls, ten of them, held docile-looking horses, or had the tidied look of stalls that had not housed any animals in a long time. Redolent of hay, straw, and well-used leather, the cool stable was still and dim, in contrast to the scene outside. We turned into the tack room and looked at the tack, as Lori called it. Saddles I recognized from watching western movies and television. On the wall hung a couple of complicated items that could have been what are called bridles. They all looked well used and well cared for. The Kronks' stableman had apparently stepped out.

In the west end of the place, five spacious box stalls lined each side of a wide central aisle. At the far end, large double Dutch doors opened into a white-fenced paddock. Through the open upper half I saw two colts frolicking in the sun, muscles rippling under their shiny brown hides. We turned to go back and Lori put her hand on the nearest stall gate. It wasn't latched and swung silently open.

"Oh!" Lori gave a soft, involuntary exclamation.

I turned my head and looked in the stall at the woman we had just startled into immobility. Georgina Maxwell was sitting on a straw bale. She was wearing tan riding pants and boots and a white silk shirt undone to the waist. She wasn't wearing a bra. Her dark hair was mussed and I noticed bits of straw stuck in her hair and on one shoulder. She was alone and I wondered what had happened to the other person. If there had been one.

"Excuse me, Georgina," Lori said and turned away. "I didn't real-ize…" The woman clutched at the front of her shirt and brushed by us without a word. Lori canted her eyes at me with a hint of a smile and we walked away, back down the aisle the way we had come.

I persuaded Lori I wasn't going to get the first riding lesson of my life on this day and we left the building, to be immediately swept up by Terry and Ada Worckowski. Terry I remembered easily, he'd been Lori's good buddy in high school. His wife, whom Lori said she'd known slightly, was a couple of years younger. I hadn't met her at the banquet the previous night. Slight, with a generous sprinkling of freckles on her nose and upper chest, Ada Worckowski had the aura of what I supposed to be your typical farm wife. Her hands were strong and hard. Her gaze was direct. Ada was laughing loudly when we met and, I remembered, even long after that weekend, that she seemed to laugh a good deal. It was almost as if she were making a serious effort to have a good time, something that might have been missing recently in her life.

"C'mon, guys," said Terry, "we've got a table over here."

I snagged a couple of bottles of beer from a nearby tub of ice and followed Lori and the Worckowskis to an empty table at one end of the pool. Lori and Ada immersed themselves in what Terry fondly called girl talk. From someone else it would have sounded conde-scending. Terry caught my expression and began to explain to me the farming enterprise he and Ada were building.

"You seem to be a pretty tight team, Terry."

"Yeah. Farming isn't a one-man operation anymore. Oh, there are still some around who seem to think the women don't contribute as much as the men." He leaned forward and lowered his voice. "Old Kronk is a good example. He only had one kid. Story is, when he found out the baby was a girl, he went into a funk for a week. We've got one of each." He grinned at me. "I'm basically your small busi-nessman. Crops or seed and animals are the inventory, I follow the markets pretty closely, we have a computer, and I'm always reading about new farming techniques to get the most out of the land. These days we talk a lot about sustainable agriculture and organics."

He switched topics abruptly. "So, Mr. Investigator, what have you learned about Riverview so far?"

I raised an eyebrow. "I'm not an investigator. I'm a mid-level administrator in an urban college for adults. Where'd you get the idea I was an investigator?"

Terry laughed and drained his beer. "Apparently somebody in town checked you out when Lori answered the reunion letter. They must have turned up your stint in the Navy as a criminal investigator. Word gets around, you know."

Behind Terry, the woman called Dolores Holbrook, back straight, tight smile on her face, passed through the crowd. I rose to get another round of cold beer from the ice-filled washtub and bumped into someone. When I turned around there was the tall redhead with the long legs, the same woman Lori and I had seen in the alley in Riverview. Stacy Frommer. She was talking to someone whose face I couldn't see at first. Stacy shifted to one side and I recognized Georgina Maxwell, her head thrown back in laughter. Maxwell had buttoned her shirt and combed the straw out of her hair. Her eyes flickered over me with no particular expression.

13

"Terry, forget the second amendment. Do you seriously believe the government in Washington is going to sweep down and cart you off because of a gun registration law?"

"No, Lori, I don't, actually. It's just one more regulation we don't need. Taxes are high enough. Adding more bureaucrats in Washington to keep track of all the paper that law will generate certainly won't lower my taxes."

Lori laughed in fond exasperation. Their conversation had the tone of a long-running argument both pursued as much for the argument as for their cherished beliefs. I knew it was frequently like that with good friends who have known each other for most of their lives. Even though they hadn't talked for more than fifteen years, it was as if time between those two had taken a holiday.

"Oh, Dolores," said Ada, looking over my head. "Lori and Jack, I want you two to meet one of the best additions to Riverview in the past ten years." She stood up and shoved her chair back.

Dolores Holbrook, the woman she was talking about, turned to look at Ada.

"Hello, Ada. How are you today?" Holbrook's voice was low, with just the tiniest trace of an accent. I couldn't place it.

Ada took Dolores by the arm and pulled her toward our table. "Meet Dolores Holbrook," she said, "owner of Ralph's Cafe on Main Street."

"Ah," I said rising, "the bringer of espresso coffee to rural America." It didn't come out as witty as I'd thought it would and Lori cocked an eyebrow at me. The Holbrook woman took it with good grace, smiled, and extended a firm handshake.

"Dolores is active in lots of local things, aren't you?" Ada said.

The woman nodded and responded, "In a town the size of Riverview, I think everyone should do their part. I don't have many skills outside of the kitchen, and running my little cafe takes a lot of time, but I do what I can. And you've made me welcome. Where I come from, Chicago," she slanted a quick look at me almost as if acknowledging I'd been trying to place her accent, "it is hard for people to get involved." She backed up a step and said, "I must check on the kitchen. Excuse me."

I watched her walk away.

"I've never seen anyone move here and be accepted so quickly," said Terry around the neck of his beer bottle.

"She's just great. Even though she's taken over some things that in the past other folks have always done," Ada said.

"She seems nice. Is she married?" Lori took out a handkerchief and dabbed at the sweat on her face.

"A widow," said Ada.

"Was she married to somebody local?"

Ada shook her head. "No, I guess her husband died before she moved here. She doesn't talk abut him."

Interesting, I thought.

The party around the pool got louder as more people returned from their diverse pursuits. They'd started out in a somewhat somber mood. The awful fact of Elroy of Guteman's death was still fresh, but almost three hours of hot sun, cold beer, wine, and good food had their effect. The scene was more like an upbeat wake than a funeral. It was, after all, a reunion and some of these folks were trying hard to remake old ties.

My own thoughts kept returning to the hay rake and the body of Elroy Guteman leaking blood onto the warm ground. I knew I'd have that image to contend with for a long time.

Tessa Larson walked to our table and stopped. She held a sweating can of beer in one hand and she swayed slightly. She was the one who'd made that crack about Lori at the banquet. "Well, hello, Lori dear."

"Tessa. It's nice to see you again. I was sorry to hear about your husband, about Ron's death."

"I'll bet." Tessa's voice was even, but there was an undertone of dislike. I had forgotten to tell Lori about the remarks the widow Larson had made to me the previous evening at Georgiana's 40-Mile Club.

"Been doing any swimming this trip? Or maybe you and Marge are planning a little slumber party for tonight?" She smirked nastily and walked away, her fingertips white on the beer can. I glanced at my table companions. Ada Worckowski wore a polite frown as if she'd just heard a mildly salacious joke. Terry was a study in befuddlement, his mouth hanging open. Lori had slipped on her mask of studied unconcern. It was the look she wore when she was seething at a recalcitrant client, or a student at her massage school who'd made a basic error, but determined not to reveal her true feelings. She watched Tessa go.

"I have a feeling that woman doesn't like you," I remarked.

"Oh, very astute observation. I'm surprised. I can't imagine why she feels that way."

"Didn't you guys sing in the choir together?" Terry asked.

"Yes," responded Lori, "and she got all the alto solos, not I."

"Did you know her husband? Ron Larson, wasn't it?"

"Not well, Jack. He was only here for our senior year. Then I went away to college. I don't understand her anger, but I'm sure not going to lose any sleep over that crack."

I wondered what real or imagined past hurt Tessa Larson harbored. I returned my attention to the conversation around me.

"Well, I've heard a few things." Ada's voice was so soft, I almost didn't hear her. We all leaned closer. "Her folks lost their farm, you know."

"Really? That's a shame," said Lori. "I didn't know the Petersons well. I met them at concerts and school stuff, of course. Peterson is Tessa's unmarried name," Lori explained to me.

"It was about six years ago when it happened," Terry said.

Ada looked at her husband and nodded. "More like seven. Foreclosed. But it wasn't the bank. Peterson got into trouble with Joshua Martin. The implement dealer? Tessa's dad bought some machinery and couldn't keep up the payments. Martin took his farm. There was a lot of talk about it. People thought Dick Borken would make it right when he bought out Martin the next year. But he didn't. Tessa's been pretty bitter about it ever since."

"And then, a couple of years later, Ron got killed," said Ada.

Terry shrugged and took a sip of beer. "Some people thought that with the Petersons havin' a son-in-law at the bank, he could fix things for them."

"I thought you just said it was Martin, not the bank," said Lori.

"Well, yeah, but Johnny Houck and Borken are, you know." He held up two tightly crossed fingers and took a long swig of beer.

Ada gazed at Terry with no expression on her face. When he took the beer away he noticed. "Well, it's true. Everybody knows it. All the talk was that Ron would fix things for Tessa's parents, but he never did." He shook his head. "I never got to know Ron Larson hardly at all."

I was having trouble following the conversation. Seemed like my table companions were consciously avoiding gossip about the deceased.

Lori smiled briefly. "Worckowski seems to be protesting something."

"Terry, everybody knows you helped Ron load his pickup that day. People saw you." Ada said, frowning at him.

Terry shrugged. "Well, sure...."

"You were with Ron that day, the day he got killed?" Lori leaned forward as she spoke.

"Well, yeah, but..."

"Excuse, me," I said then. "Will someone fill me in here?"

Lori reached a hand over and touched mine. "Sorry. Ron was only in our class our senior year. He went away to college, but then he came back and worked at the bank. Tessa and Ron got married and they lived in town."

"Marge?" I said. "You mentioned Marge."

Lori looked at me and I looked back blankly for a moment.

Then she said, "Marge McMenny. We met her on the street yesterday. Dark, tall, smoking?"

I nodded. "Right, I remember." I opened my mouth to say more, thought better of it, and closed my mouth.

"Ron and Tessa were married somewhere else," Ada chimed in. "Everything was apparently fine between them, although I guess the Petersons were disappointed they didn't see any grandchildren right away. Then what, five years ago?" Terry nodded. "Five years ago this fall, Ron packed some stuff in his pickup and drove off to the dump."

"The dump?" said Lori. "That's it? He never came back?"

"Nope. Week later a deputy sheriff found the red pickup on a side road nobody used any more, all burned up. Ron's body was in it. Real mess, apparently."

Lori was frowning. "What happened?"

"Sheriff said Ron musta been driving too fast, ran off the section line road, over near the old Coleson place. Hit a tree, they said."

"An abandoned homestead. The Colesons left the county before I went to college," Lori told me in a quick aside.

"Was Brad Arnason sheriff then?" I asked.

Terry and Ada shook their heads. "Nope. Anyway," he continued, "the pickup was burned up, all kinds of junk lying around and the body in the cab. They figured it happened the same day, right after he drove off. I musta been the last one to see Ron alive."

"Was the body Larson's?" I asked, intrigued in spite of myself.

"Sure, who else? It was really burned though."

Ada made a grimace of distaste. "Anyway, Tessa was just devastated and took a long time to get back to normal. Then there were those stories that kept coming up every so often. Not much to talk about in a small town you know. Except about the weather, the crops, the government, and the neighbors." She smiled at the cliché. "Sitting around at circle or a sewing bee--yes, we still do that some--or after church, you'd hear people talking."

"What about?" I said.

"About missing money or missing records at the bank. About how

Ron Larson was maybe stealing from the town. For several years." She paused, flicked a glance at Lori. "And...other things."

"Ahh," Terry waved a big hard hand in disgust. "Just talk. Nobody never proved nothin'."

"What was he loading in the pickup?"

Terry adjusted the cap on his head to better shade his eyes and thought a moment. "Nothin' much, a rolled up rug, some busted tools, several boxes, I think. Buncha junk. I thought he was just clearin' out the garage or somethin' like that."

"Boxes," echoed Lori.

"Yeah, you know. Boxes. Cartons. Some of 'em were old and real dirty. He said thanks, see ya, and drove off east, toward the town dump."

A high keening sound lifted over the hubbub, stilling the conversation around the pool. The scream went on and on, louder. It burned through the air around us. The temperature seemed to rise. Louder, on and on, hardly pausing, the scream continued. There was a freeze, a cessation of all movement, like a still frame from a video, for just a moment. Simultaneously, Terry Worckowski and I bolted out of our chairs and raced toward the stable. Toward the sound of the screaming. That broke the spell and others surged after us. The scream continued, pushed against us as we ran toward whatever it was.

Worckowski and I slammed into the stable at a dead run. The central aisle was empty. I looked toward the tack room, but the stableman wasn't there. We ran down the barn to an open stall on the south wall. The screaming abruptly changed to huge, wracking sobs. Elaine Tomlinson, red faced, eyes streaming, was crumpled on the floor of the aisle against a stall gate. I knelt in front of her as Terry skidded to a halt beside me on the slippery straw. I heard his sharp intake of breath. Behind us others were bunching in the aisle, shouting, heaving toward us.

I looked into the stall from my position beside the sobbing woman and my stomach lurched. "Don't touch it," I snapped at Terry. He stopped reaching for the gate, stared at the figure against the stall wall. "Just step back and don't touch anything."

Edith Kronk sagged against the back wall of the box stall, in the mussed straw. Her long, tanned California legs were askew and slightly bent at the knees. Her wide-spaced eyes stared at us from under half-open lids, but she couldn't see us. She was pinned to the wall by the four tines of a pitchfork that were jabbed through her neck and upper chest and into the barn wall behind her. Blood stained her mouth and breast and had dripped down her white tank top onto her shorts. Her eyes were vacant, staring at nothing I would ever know. I knew she was dead, but I gingerly stepped into the stall and checked for a pulse anyway. I remembered thinking whoever had used the pitchfork was carrying a lot of rage.

"Terry," I said. He didn't react. The rest of the crowd was getting closer. "Terry!" I hollered. "Keep them away from here!"

He tried, but there were too many of them, and Worckowski kept glancing over his shoulder at the body that had been Edith Kronk. A few eager souls slipped by. One woman, I never knew who, took one look at the body and promptly lost her lunch. After that, the pungent acid-smell of fresh vomit helped keep the crowd back.

Lori forced her way through the others and took charge of Elaine. It would have been better if we could have kept everyone else away altogether, but at least we kept them out of the stall.

A woman somewhere in the milling, crying crowd wailed over and over, like a mantra, "What'll we tell Mr. Kronk? We've got to tell her father."

After things calmed down a little, Terry, Dick Borken, and some of the other men gradually pushed the crowd back out to the pool.

At the stable door Ed Tomlinson took my shoulder. "Somebody better stay in the barn to be sure nothing's disturbed. Seems like a good job for someone with your experience."

I looked at him and started to say something about my experience, then decided, what the hell. If people were going to persist in reminding me I was an investigator eons ago in the Navy, I'd start acting the part. I could play a walking cliché as well as the next person.

It's a big county to patrol. Twenty minutes later, a young deputy I hadn't seen before showed up. He strolled into the cool barn in his aviator glasses, his tight, form-fitting gray uniform, and his creaking leather holster belt. He had a toothpick stuck between his lips.

"Jack Marston?" I admitted my identity.

I noticed his pointy-toed cowboy boots were dusty. "Yeah, Sheriff said you was here. Said you could be useful. You wanna be a deputy?" He laughed and side-stepped around me until he had a clear view of Edith Kronk. He stared at her for a long time. Then he took the toothpick out of his mouth and shook his head. "Wheeyou. Good lookin' chick, that. What a waste." He turned and looked at me again. "Anybody touch anythin'?"

"The outside of the stall, that's all. No one went in after Terry Worckowski and I ran in here. Mrs. Tomlinson found her first and started screaming. She was lying just outside the stall gate." I indicated where I'd found the Tomlinson woman. "I stepped into the stall to check the woman's pulse." My voice was low and hoarse. Keeping company with dead bodies was not on my list of uplifting experiences. The smell of the vomit in the straw just outside the stall was getting to me as well.

"Good. That's good." He nodded and returned the toothpick to his mouth. "Okay. You're relieved, Mr. Marston. I'll take over now and you can rejoin your friends. But don't, as they say, don't leave the ranch without checkin' first. Okay?" He hitched up his belt on his slender hips and took his toothpick and his pointy-toed boots to a bale of straw on the other side of the aisle opposite the door to the stall.

I went back to the pool after a stop in the tack room to wash my hands. The stableman was still among the missing. Things were subdued, but the beer and the sun were still having their way. A nervous crack of laughter, abruptly stifled, greeted me from across the pool as I sat down beside Ada Worckowski. Her hazel eyes were wet and red-rimmed. The low murmur of conversation and the movement of the crowd projected an uneasy restlessness.

"Reminds me of a herd of cattle," said Terry, "when they know a storm's comin'."

"We'd all like to be gone from here," I replied. "Even when it's expected, death is hard for us to deal with. I expect that's also true for rural folks who have to deal with animal deaths on a frequent and personal basis. But murder. Murder only happens to other people, people who live across town somewhere, or in another county."

Abruptly I shut my mouth. I was talking too much. Must have been nerves.

"Lori just went inside to check on Elaine and poor Mr. Kronk," Ada said softly. She looked at me sadly. She opened her mouth to say something, then just shook her head.

I nodded. There was nothing to say. Even the people around us, talking in low tones, weren't saying anything. From across the rolling fields, faintly at first, I heard the wailing of distant sirens.

14

Sheriff Arnason leaned forward, elbows on his knees. He was sitting on the edge of an overstuffed wingback chair in the Kronks comfortably cool living room.

"Hell. We got us a real mess. It's Saturday afternoon and most everybody from out of town was planning to be gone by this time tomorrow. First Guteman, now Edith. I dunno." He scrubbed his face with one big hand.

"Do you think the murders are connected?" Lori's voice was steady, carefully controlled.

I looked at her sitting rigidly beside me. For the past two hours Arnason and his people had been examining the crime scene and interviewing people. Lori and I were among the last. Arnason shrugged a non-answer.

"Sheriff?"

"Yeah?"

"Can I make a suggestion?"

"Marston, I'll take almost any help I can get at this point. The BCA is sending a team in tomorrow first thing, an' the state police will make people available, but we got too many out-of-towners in here right now. There are just too many possibilities."

"Have you eliminated anybody from suspicion about Guteman?"

"Jack." Lori put her fingers on my forearm.

"Yeah, you two and at least half of the rest of 'em."

"Isn't it likely the two murders are related as Lori suggests?"

"Jack, please." Lori's voice was an intense whisper across my conversation with Arnason. They both looked at her. "Brad, you don't want Jack getting involved, do you?"

"Well, he was a trained investigator. And I sure to hell am short-handed. I can't even remember the last time we had a murder in this county."

"Brad, this is different. These are my high school classmates. This is just too close."

I twisted on the couch where we were seated side by side and took Lori's hands. Her skin was cool, but not clammy. "I understand how you feel, but if we can help solve these murders, we can get home that much quicker. Do you see?"

She looked me in the eye for a long silent moment. Then she said, "We, huh?" And leaned back, pulling her hands from mine. Damn woman was entirely too quick for me at times.

I turned back to the sheriff, who had been silent, watching us. "I think the murders have to be linked. Probably something to do with this specific class. Face it, Sheriff, the school has had lots of reunions in the past twenty years, am I right? So, if I am right, you can safely eliminate everyone from out of town who couldn't have had anything to do with Guteman's murder. That alone will reduce your complications."

He nodded. "Yeah, that makes sense. But what if they aren't connected? First I have to prove your theory. I don't know how to do that, yet." He sighed and rubbed his face. "Jack, I'm gonna take you up on the offer of help. You can do a little pokin' around. See what you come up with." He looked at Lori. "Whole town thinks you brought him along to do some investigating, anyway."

"What?" Lori stared at Arnason. "Why would they think that? Is there something here to hide? I'm beginning to think this isn't the same place I grew up in."

It never was, I thought.

"I don't know, but ever since word got around you were bringing Jack here, there's been talk. Not so much gossip, you know, but it was like you were coming back for the first time with some sort of an agenda, and Jack was gonna help you with it."

Lori snorted. "That's ridiculous!"

Brad looked at the floor and then sat back and looked at me again. "Listen, no word of this to my deputies or anyone else. I can't do anything official, you understand, and you watch out. Whoever is responsible isn't squeamish about gettin' close to his victims."

"Sheriff? You in here?" A deputy appeared in the living room door. Arnason stood up.

"What?"

"They want you out to the stable."

"Okay." Arnason hitched up his toolbelt and hurried out of the room, leaving the impression he was glad to get away.

"Jack, are they sure Elroy was murdered?"

"It is nearly impossible to imagine he could have slipped. I can't think of any reason why he'd be climbing around on that old rake in the dark, can you? The autopsy will confirm it, but I'm sure it's murder."

She sighed and shook her head. "Dammit, Jack."

I looked at her. "Honey, Guteman's body was jammed down on the tines. That took some strength. He couldn't have just fallen on them. It was a deliberate act."

"Oh, Jack, how did we get into this situation?"

"As to how we get into situations like this, babe," I said, leaning closer, "it must be our karma."

"Folks?" The same deputy who had called Arnason away reappeared. "They're loading the buses to take everybody back to town."

Lori stood abruptly and, without looking at me, went outside. I trotted along close behind. Walking through the door into the heat was like being smacked in the face with a bucket of hot water. Sweat started immediately at my hairline and in the small of my back. Two of the buses were loaded and rolling. We climbed aboard the last of the yellow monsters and had to sit separately. Nobody gave up a seat for us. Nobody would meet my eyes, either. I sat in a jump seat behind the driver. It faced the side of the bus so it gave me a chance to watch my fellow passengers. It was not comfortable.

The ride back to Riverview was made in almost complete silence.

People stared out the windows. A woman two seats behind Lori sniffled quietly into her handkerchief. I noticed a man in the wide seat at the very back of the bus, tear tracks on his face, just staring up the aisle. Not the ride back most of them had envisioned. I knew what they were thinking. They were all wondering the same thing. Was one of us sitting next to a murderer?

* * *

LORI AND I TALKED over iced tea in the motel restaurant. It was late afternoon but the sun still retained its searing power. Richard Borken had circulated word of the cancellation of the final dinner and the planned Sunday outing. The twentieth reunion of Riverview High's class of 'eighty-nine had collapsed under the weight of two brutal murders.

With no more reunion activities to occupy us, we made other plans. First I went to the desk and canceled our departure. Then we sat down to lay out a plan.

The prospect of investigating former classmates was unappetizing to Lori. "I'm still not comfortable prying into this. Either of us."

"We'll give it a day or so and if nothing turns up, we'll split, all right? One of the things I've noticed, by the way, is that you haven't introduced me to a girlfriend."

"That's because there wasn't one. I had a lot of casual friends, but no special girlfriend. Terry filled that role, I guess."

"Got it. Do you have any suggestions about how to start?"

Lori nodded and took a sip of her tea. "As a matter of fact I do. I think we should talk to Georgina."

"Good idea. People in service positions frequently hear and see a good deal."

"After that, let's talk with Marge McMenny."

"At Martin's Implements," I said.

"Right."

"Martin's will close pretty soon."

She glanced at her watch. "All right, we'll go there first."

When we entered the door to Martin's Implements no one was

visible behind the counter. One side of the room was an open expanse with several shiny machines standing as silent sentinels on the floor. One was a complicated-looking affair with pipes and hoses. I had no clue what it was used for.

Lori noticed me looking at it. "New style milk separator," she said.

"Cool." I tried to act like that meant something to me. The north half of the building was cut up into offices and a long counter. In front of the counter were floor displays of tools, racks of pegboard hooks holding plastic bags of small stuff, and bins of oddly shaped machine parts. The place was air conditioned.

"Hello," called Lori. "Marge? Anybody?"

"Just a minute." The male voice came from somewhere back among the tall shelves that stood in deep ranks behind the counter. A squat, fat, darkly tanned man of about fifty, with wispy blond hair, appeared from an aisle between the shelves on the other side of the counter. "Help you?"

"Hi. I'm Lori Jacobs and this is my friend, Jack Marston. We're looking for Marge. Is she here?"

"Hi. I'm Randy." He stuck out a hard callused hand. "Marge? Yeah she's here somewhere." I heard the staccato sound of hard heels on the tile floor of the store and Marge McMenny came swiftly from between two of the high shelf stacks. She wore a shopkeeper's smile pasted on her face until she recognized us, then her smile faded so rapidly I was afraid she'd injured her cheek muscles.

"Well," she said. "Look who's here. I guess you two aren't looking to buy some tools, are you."

"Marge, can we talk to you? Is there somewhere private we can go?"

Marge just stared at Lori for a moment, then shrugged and said. "Okay. Come on back to my office."

Her office was a small cubicle at the very back of the building. It contained several file cabinets, a big old well-scratched metal desk, and three chairs. The walls were cheap wood veneer with darkly stained, grooved joints. They were mostly covered with unframed posters of flowers, a seascape, and a shot of the Golden Gate Bridge bathed in warm late-afternoon light.

When we sat down, Marge ran her fingers through her short dark hair without a word. Overhead light picked up deep reddish highlights. I wasn't entirely sure why we were here, but Lori had suggested it and she knew the neighborhood better than I.

"Marge, did you know George Hermansonn was arrested last night?" I thought it was an abrupt beginning.

"Again? Where this time? How do you know?"

"I heard Dick Borken and Ed Tomlinson talking about it at Kronk's. He was drunk, out at The Junction."

"Poor Sarah. She's had a helluva life with that man." Marge looked down, picked at a cuticle. "He always drank a lot, remember, Lori? Even in high school, he could be counted on for a beer or three."

"Excuse me," I said. "Hermansonn?"

"A classmate. We saw him at the bar with his buddies at Georgina's on Thursday, remember?"

"Was he at the dinner last night?"

"No. At least, I didn't see him."

Marge sighed. "He's been getting really bad this last year." She stopped and didn't appear inclined to say any more about George Hermansonn.

After a pause, Lori said, "Marge, I want to know about my pa's farm." She leaned forward and speared Marge with a look. I knew that look. I was surprised. This seemed way off the reason we were here. On the other hand, maybe not.

"Marge," Lori went on, "when my mom died and Pa sold the farm, they expected the sale to leave us a quite a bit of money. But it didn't. Turned out we owed Martin's a whole lot of money. I knew about the mortgage at the bank, but none of us kids knew about Martin's loan to Pop. How could that be?"

Nor did I, I thought, watching Marge fade under the weight of Lori's questions and her stare. Lori was acting like an experienced interrogator. Depths I never knew she had.

"I'm not just a secretary, you know. I kept Josh's books, at least his regular ones. Joshua Martin," Marge looked at me. "You know, Martin? Name on the building?"

I nodded. "Yes," I said flatly. She wasn't going to get a good cop-bad cop routine here.

"After Dick took over Martin's business, he kept me on, doing the same work." There was an undertone of eagerness in her voice. Her rate of speech picked up. I got the impression she was relieved to talk to somebody. "Josh made loans to some of his customers. You know about that, Lori. Anyway, he was pretty good about letting people have credit and helping his good customers, but when somebody stiffed him, or lied, or didn't pay on time, he was completely different. Josh hated a liar. George was bad news. He was a liar and a drunk. He didn't pay on time. And he wasn't straight with Josh later on. He wasn't straight with Dick, either."

"What happened, Marge?" Lori watched Marge intently, sort of like a cat stares at a trapped mouse.

The other woman stirred and looked down at her desk. "Dick called in Hermansonn's notes. Mr. Martin told him to. He owed a lot of money. He couldn't pay."

"And?" Lori prompted when Marge stopped again.

"So he, Dick, took the farm. Hermansonn's." She shrugged. Her fingers started a nervous tattoo on the desk. "I argued with him about it." She blinked rapidly. "God. His mother is still alive and she still lives out there with them. It'll kill her when she learns George lost the farm. Just kill her."

"So George, in his frustration and anger, drinks and fights," I said.

Marge shrugged again. "I guess."

"If Martin, or Borken, foreclosed on the Hermansonn's farm, why are they still living there?"

"State law. You can't kick a farmer off his place until a year goes by after the foreclosure."

"But it wasn't exactly a foreclosure, was it?" Lori's voice was soft.

"Well, they had the notes," Marge responded. "Sheriff said it was legal."

"I suppose so, but there were stories about Josh for years. I heard he walked a pretty fine line."

"Yeah?" Marge flared. "Josh wasn't so bad. And Dick is okay too, mostly. Not like some I could name. At least he tells you right up front what can happen. What'll happen if you screw up and don't pay. You oughta talk to some of the others about what's really goin' on."

I leaned forward. "What do you mean, Marge?" said Lori, putting a warning hand on my arm. "Was Pa's farm part of that? Part of what's really going on? Do you know when Martin loaned my pa the money? Did John Houck know? The banker," she said to me in a quick aside.

"I don't know nothin' about that. It must have been before I started working here. I don't know nothin' about Banker Houck. Either one. Johnny or his old man, J.L. Not before Borken took over." Marge stopped, apparently realizing she was talking out of turn. I'd just reached the same conclusion. "Please," her tone turned beseeching. "Leave me alone, I don't know nothing else."

For a moment we were all silent, staring at each other.

"Marge," I said, breaking the weave of silence. "You said Dick Borken took over. What did you mean by that?"

She looked at me and narrowed her eyes. "Mean? It means Dick bought him out. Martin. This business. All the business. What else?"

"But I suppose Josh Martin still has a lot of influence on how things operate around here, doesn't he?" I said.

Marge shrugged. "I suppose so. After all, he built this business from the ground."

"Do you know if he still owns part of the business?"

"No," she said flatly. "I have no idea about that. Nobody ever said so."

"All right. Do you have any idea why Elroy Guteman and Edith Kronk were killed?"

"No. None. It's crazy. Edith didn't even live here any more. And I never heard a bad word about El." Suddenly, with no warning, she started to cry. Tears ran down her face. "He..." She gulped, groped in her desk for a tissue. "He was a good friend. He knew...he knew about me, about what it was like to be alone. He said he didn't care. He was always nice to me." She laid her head in her arms on the desk and sobbed quietly.

Lori stood up and put one hand on Marge' shoulder. "Marge."

"Oh, goddamn it! Get away." She sat up and flung Lori's hand off, spinning away from us in her chair. "Just get out of here."

So we did.

On the way out, Lori said, "Josh Martin and Dick Borken. Interesting."

"Is Josh Martin still living here in town?"

"I don't know." Lori had a slight frown on her face. "We should have asked Marge." She stopped and then said, "We'll ask Georgina. She'll know. And what was that all about 'took over'?"

"Just different from 'bought out', that's all," I said. "Probably doesn't mean a thing."

15

"The supper hour ends pretty early here. Then things will quiet down. How's your salad?"

I shrugged and tossed Lori a small smile. "It's all right. I'm getting a little tired of meat and potatoes and gravy, that's all."

"Well, you should have tried the ham and potatoes." Lori flicked a finger at me from across the small table. We were sitting in a corner of Georgina's 40-Mile Club restaurant. Two-thirds of the tables were occupied. I didn't see anyone I recognized from the reunion. Georgina Maxwell, from all appearances a cheerful hard-working proprietor, had greeted us at the door with a big smile, but there were circles under her eyes that her artfully applied makeup didn't entirely conceal. We went through polite commiseration about the two deaths while she showed us to a table. We avoided labeling the deceased as murder victims. As she turned to leave us, Lori stopped her.

"Georgina, will you be around all evening? When you have a few minutes, Jack and I would like a little talk with you, if you don't mind."

Georgina was silent for a moment. "Sure, okay. Why not? I don't think I can tell you anything, though. About Edith or Elroy, about their murders, I mean."

* * *

"Well, that was certainly filling," I said, half an hour later, pushing my plate away. "I wonder what Georgina *can* tell us about."

"What?"

"She specifically qualified herself. No information about the murders. I wonder why she automatically jumped to the idea we want to talk about the murders."

"Under the circumstances, it seems like a reasonable assumption. But now I suppose there's an implication in your devious mind that she can tell us about other things."

"Years of jousting with the agile minds of students sometimes leads me to devious thoughts. As it happens, I'm becoming more and more interested in those other things."

"Really? Why?"

"Something is going on in this town. Remember what Marge said? About Borken taking over from Martin? As I said earlier, an interesting choice of words. Didn't Borken buy the business from Martin? Now there are two murders in the same weekend. It's not just coincidence."

"I assume Dick bought the implement business when Mr. Martin retired. You are thinking perhaps Borken was installed by Martin? Why would that be?"

"I'm not sure what I'm thinking. Maybe whatever is going on is connected to the murders, maybe not. After what Brad said out at Kronk's about my investigating people in town, I guess the dormant skills I learned in the Navy have kicked in. I have a feeling there's something out of kilter here. I think Brad knows it too, but probably not what it is. Whatever it is. Several people seem to have assumed I came here with you for reasons other than that you just want me with you. My presence in Riverview seems to be making a few people nervous. I'm starting to wonder why."

"There's also the question of our farm," Lori said. "I think perhaps I'll talk to Johnny Houck about that."

"Okay, but be careful. Your place may be part of whatever it is that's going on."

Lori nodded slowly and blew out her breath in a gusty sigh. We were on our second cups of coffee when Georgina appeared from a back room, where her office likely was located, and came to our table. I wondered if there was a way to get a few moments alone in that office. Probably not tonight.

"Debbie. Bring another cup over here, please." The same waitress who had been working the bar at the reunion hurried over with a pot and a cup. She gave us a cursory smile and poured for Georgina. She placed the carafe on the table and turned away, flipping her long blonde hair over her shoulder. Georgina pulled out a chair and sat down.

"Well, now. How was your meal? Everything all right?"

"It was fine, Georgina."

"Mrs. Maxwell," I said. "How's business these days?" She turned her gaze on me for a moment.

"It's okay. Fine, in fact. Pay my bills. Set a little aside. Take a weekend off now and then. Why?"

"I understand you recently bought the club and motel."

"Me and my partners. So? I thought you wanted to talk about the murders."

"Why would you think that? Did we suggest that?"

"Well, no, but, what else is everybody talking about?"

"Anything you can tell us will help. I'm just trying to get a complete picture of Riverview and its citizens. And maybe a little bit of recent history? Lori's memory is a little fuzzy on some things." I smiled. Ingenuously, I hoped. Since I didn't have the least bit of clout I was going to rely on guile. Besides, honey was more enticing than nettles. Or something like that.

Georgina didn't smile back. "Yeah, sure. Looks like somebody's been talking out of turn." She took a pack of cigarettes out of the pocket of her dress and lit one. She blew a plume of smoke high over our heads. "Look, this place, or one like it, was always my dream. My old man made me keep all his books for the farm, ever since he discovered I had a knack for figures. Lori, you know. I never had much social life in school. If it wasn't chores, it was taxes, or my regular school books. Even after I graduated.

"After I moved out and got my own place here in town, I still did dad's books. I wanted him to pay me. It took a while but we finally came to an understanding why I wanted to save as much as I could. He wouldn't front me any serious money unless I got a job. So

I started doing office work for some of the local businessmen, a little bookkeeping, filing forms, paying bills, the usual. Showed 'em how to save a little here and there on their taxes. Nothing illegal, just real careful record keeping.

"Then I started doing the books for Don Carmichael. He owned the 40-Mile Club back then. One day, after I'd been working here about a year, I found his other books." She stubbed out her cigarette and looked at me.

"You mean the account books for the silent partners. With the other business."

She looked away. "Yeah. Turns out what went on was kind of an open secret around town. Oh, only a few people knew about everything. We had a little illegal gambling, a Saturday night high-stakes poker game, pull tabs, sports betting, stuff like that."

"Payoffs?"

"God," she shook her head. "Lori, this guy must be some kind of investigator. How'd you get all this so fast?"

I didn't respond. I also didn't let her compliment distract me. "Do you know who Carmichael's secret partners were?" I pressed.

Georgina looked at me. "You sure know a lot," she muttered. "No. Not for sure. Just that there were several, maybe five or six. Oh, I got some ideas."

"Local people?"

Georgina shook her head and refused to answer. She examined the curling smoke of her cigarette. "I thought we were going to talk about the murders,"

"You said you didn't know anything about that."

"Well, I don't."

I leaned forward a little in my chair. "Look, my only interest in your backstairs operations is what it may have to do with the murders."

"There isn't any connection."

"How can you be so sure, Georgina?" Lori murmured. She eyed a couple at a nearby table who looked like they were trying to listen in.

"It's all over. Has been for a while, I'm glad to say. But nobody believes me, I guess. Damn gossips! Back then there was always too much cash around that I couldn't account for. Don kept saying not to worry about it, just keep the books balanced. So I did. Finally I told Dad 'cause I didn't know what else to do an' I was getting nervous about it."

"What did he say?"

"It was funny, he didn't seem surprised. He just said not to talk about it to anyone else. Then one day a month or so later the banker, Houck? He comes in big as you please and plunks down across from my desk where I'm doin' the books. 'How much will you take?' he asks. 'For what,' I says. 'For what you got on Don Carmichael,' he says.

"I really didn't know what he meant, but I looked at him and I could see he was offering me some kind of deal. So without even thinking about it I says, 'half this place.' Old Man Houck just looks back at me and says, 'I'll bring the papers tomorrow.' That was it."

"That was all?" I exclaimed? "When was this?"

"That was all. It was nineteen ninety-four. The next day he shows up with Eddie Tomlinson, fresh outa law school, and a bunch of papers. There was the deed and a note. A contract for deed. 'Here,' he says. Tomlinson laid it out and showed me where to sign. I became the owner of record with a half interest and Tomlinson and the bank owned the other half.

"Carmichael had left that morning for a business trip to the Cities, he said. He never came back. He called me a couple of days later and just said he hoped I'd make a go of it. He wouldn't say anything else, but he didn't sound mad, or anything."

"You shut down the gambling?"

She nodded, drew sharply on her cigarette. "Not right away, but soon. Every time there was a group in I'd show up and just tell 'em Carmichael was gone and I was changing things. I started charging for drinks." She blinked and drew on her cigarette again. "I told my dad about the deal an' he didn't say much then, either. All he said was, I shoulda asked for the whole place."

I stared at the tablecloth. In spite of my academic background, I was not wholly ignorant of how some things worked in the real world. "And you never found out who Carmichael's partners were?"

Georgina shook her head. "Not for sure."

"Local law know about the gambling?"

Georgina took out another filtertip cigarette. She took her time lighting it. Thinking. "Brad wasn't sheriff then."

"But he was a deputy in the next county."

"I don't think he knew. One or two of the others, well, maybe."

"Did the sheriff know?"

"Hard to say for sure. Sheriff Clemens used to come around couple times a week. Talked to Don privately. After Don left town, the sheriff, he quit coming around."

Lori smiled. "Georgina, do you think he was collecting a payoff?"

A shrug. "Seems likely, but I really don't know."

"Is he still around? Could we talk to him?"

"He died. About a year after Brad won the election. Cancer, I heard." Georgina looked at the glowing ash on her cigarette and stubbed it out. "I should quit these things. Well, what else do you want to know? Do you think all that stuff has anything to do with whoever killed Elroy and Edith? I mean, how could it?"

I rubbed my nose. "I don't know. We'll just have to see. Georgina, thanks for talking with us."

"Sure, but you already knew most of it." She smiled at Lori as if she was relieved and left our table.

"Clever you," said Lori after Georgina was out of earshot, "leading her to think you already knew what she was going to tell us."

"Educated guesses, built on shaky bits I've picked up since we got here."

"Why does this seem so weird to me?"

"Maybe I'm more cynical." I reached for her hand on the table, put a finger in her limp palm. "Fresh eyes. I don't know these people, I'm not making the same kinds of assumptions you are."

She nodded. "I'm beginning to think I don't know these people at all. Maybe I never did."

16

"Look. Heat lightning," said Lori, pointing past my nose at the western horizon. The sky was overcast with heavy clouds and, except for the few street lights, it was very dark. All around Riverview, twinkling like fallen stars, shined the hard white mercury-vapor yard lights REA had sold to nearly every farmer in the land.

When we parked our vehicle outside the motel, I noticed a county sheriff's car near the entrance.

"Want to stop in the bar for a late drink?"

"I'm bushed after all that's happened today. You go. I'm for bed."

"Good. Me too." I took her hand and we walked up the stairs. A teenaged boy with long straight hair floating out behind him bumped down the carpeted steps three at a time and caromed into the lobby, hardly glancing at us as he flew by. I opened the door at the top of the stairs and immediately heard the murmur of voices coming from down the hall. Our room was around a corner so there was only the empty hall, but the voices got louder as we walked along and turned the corner toward our room.

"Jack, what's going on?" Lori frowned at the small knot of people standing outside an open door. Our door as it turned out.

"Excuse, me, can we get through here?" I made a path and pulled Lori with me to the room. There were two deputy sheriffs standing just inside. One of them was the older man we'd encountered at the Kronk farm. Brad Arnason stepped out of the bathroom and gestured us in.

"Okay, guys, let's pack it up. We seem to have a simple case of breaking and entering here."

"A burglary? Whoever it was made a bad choice. There's nothing here. No jewelry and we're carrying the small amount of cash we brought," I said.

"Good. There's no real damage. It looks like the door might have been left unlocked. A guest called the night manager to complain about a loud TV. She called your room on the house phone. Somebody picked up this extension but didn't say anything. So she came up. By then, the TV was playing to an empty room. Whoever was in here was gone."

"The night manager didn't see anyone?"

"Naw. Said the door was open a crack and that window over there was wide open. We think the guy went out the window and over the roof of the pool to a ladder."

Lori prowled through her things and confirmed that nothing was missing.

"If that's it, we'd like to go to bed, Sheriff." Arnason nodded at me and began to shoo the corridor crowd away. In a moment he was back, standing at the door to the now silent hallway. I checked my watch. It was after midnight.

"Just one more thing." I looked at him.

"Whoever broke in was probably looking for something specific. He moved furniture and rifled the drawers. Any notes you're keeping on your interviews, you'd better not leave 'em lying around." He touched the brim of his hat and went out again.

"Thanks, Sheriff. We'll take precautions." I closed the door and turned to Lori. "So, he already knows we've talked to people. Does everybody in town know?"

"I expect so. Everybody who wants to."

"Do they also know what we've been talking about?"

"Some will. The others will be guessing hard. Incidentally, what have we been talking about?"

"You mean to Georgina?" I unbuttoned my shirt.

"Primarily."

"What we've been talking about, I suspect, is some gambling," some greed, some fast dealing and quite possibly some graft right here in quiet little ol' Riverview."

"Seems inconceivable." Lori stood in the middle of the room, arms crossed, staring out the window gently shaking her head.

"Hey," I said. "Are you okay?"

"I don't think so. Not entirely. It feels rotten. Knowing some creep was in here, poking through our stuff."

"I'll get another room." The night manager was very accommodating and we moved to a room on the top floor with windows that looked out on the prairie, three floors below. The manager herself helped carry our luggage. She was very apologetic. I hadn't bothered to button my shirt. The manager sneaked a quick oblique look at me and thereafter ignored my bare chest. After she left, Lori quickly divested herself of her clothes and slid naked into bed. I soon followed and put out the lights.

"What was going on, do you think?" Lori murmured.

"I think Carmichael's partners saw it was time to bail so they dumped the whole gambling operation, cut their losses. It's a little surprising since greed is usually the primary motivator for this kind of thing. I'd have expected them to hang on longer."

"Think Tomlinson and Banker Houck were part of the original group?"

"Can't say for sure. Probably. Except Tomlinson is too young. I suspect your Johnny Houck was brought into the game by his father. They could have involved Tomlinson after he finished law school. I have the feeling both those classmates of yours knew a lot about whatever was going on, back in them bad old days."

"Jack, don't do that." She paused. "This is just great. We've apparently got second-generation criminals following parental footprints. Is this attempted burgle part of it?"

"Most definitely. But it probably wasn't a burgle." I felt Lori's head turn toward me. When I looked over, the dim lights from the parking lot glistened in her eyes.

"Play that again, please."

"Not a real burgle. More like a warning."

"What led you to that conclusion?"

"Loud TV, intruder picked up the phone when called, things mussed and moved. I think somebody's telling us they can get to us anytime and to quit while we're still healthy and ahead."

"A threat. Imminent, you think?"

"Not tonight. Whoever did this will wait to see if it has the right effect."

"Are we ahead, as you put it?"

"Now you've got me. Seems as if somebody thinks we know more than we do. I still can't say for sure if the murders and the rest of it are connected."

"And you neglected to mention your suspicions to Brad just now because you aren't sure about him."

"Ninety percent sure he's on the side of the angels, but less sure about some of those he associates with. I don't know how much of what I might tell him will travel through his department."

"Nuts. Sleep on it."

I leaned closer and saw her eyes droop as she puckered her lips. One hand came up to rest lightly on my bare chest. We kissed gently.

Abruptly Lori sat up in the dark and hugged her knees. "Jack. There is something else."

I rolled over and reached for the lamp beside the bed.

"No, please don't turn on the light. I'd rather say this in the dark."

I rolled back and looked up at the side of her head.

Lori's low voice was quiet in the dark. "You know I've had mixed feelings about this reunion all along. About coming back here to Riverview. I know you've been wondering why."

I had. I still was, but what I said was, "You know I'm pretty good at reading people."

"Including me, by now."

"Yes. The time we've been together gives me more experience at it, so I can read your moods, mostly. Some of them. I figured you'd tell me when you were ready, if you think I need to know."

She sighed. "It's about Tony Litvek. I already told you I was there the day he fell into Wilson's Creek. Until today, though, I didn't realize the guilt I was carrying. All these years, I've been feeling like I was responsible. Oh, not directly, I guess, but I should have done more, should have taken Tony's side. Tried to protect him or something. Told him he didn't have to jump the creek. I don't know. Subconsciously I guess I've blamed myself. That's why I wanted to stop there at the creek. I finally had to go back there again. Do you know that's the first time I've been there, since it happened?"

I didn't know that but I wasn't surprised. I reached out a hand and laid it gently on her bare back.

She turned her head to me. "You've been good with me, out here. Patient. Helped a lot. I'm getting past it. Thank you." She slid down on the bed and her arms came around me.

In the silence that followed, I realized a weight I'd been carrying all weekend long was going away. I'd been afraid I was losing her, losing her to her memories, to Riverview. To the past. To something I wasn't able to deal with. Now I sensed that wasn't happening. Lori squirmed closer and my arms tightened around her. She lifted her face to mine and her lips touched the tear on my cheek.

We murmured together for a while longer, saying consequential things from our hearts until we drifted into the arms of that guy, Morpheus. Outside the heat lightning flickered and distant thunder muttered far away over the prairie.

17

"Ooh, nice, very nice."

It was difficult to say anything because my mouth was filled at that moment. I just hummed at her.

"Um. Much better than a wake-up call from the desk." Her fingers drifted over my naked body, teasing, fondling. She shifted slightly and brought her left knee up, one of her signals that she was ready. She already knew I was.

I raised my head from her breast and our open mouths came together, tongues flicking at each other. Her eyes gleamed into mine. "Now, babe," she whispered.

I slid up her body. Lori arched her head back, breath hissing from parted lips. Her legs clamped around me and we fused together in a long curling upward ride on the horses of our mutual desire.

    * * *

"I plan to go to church this morning. So shift over and let me leap up," she said a little later. "Will you join me?"

"In the shower yes; at services, no, thank you."

We share a liking for hot, steamy, intimate showers. This motel had a good one with lots of water pressure. Water beat down loudly while we carefully soaped each other all over with big, soft washcloths. One slippery caress led to another and it became a long shower. So long that we had to pass up breakfast to make it to the ten o'clock service. Lori had intended to walk the few blocks to the United Methodist

Church. Instead, I drove her there and parked down the street after dropping her off. By unspoken agreement, we avoided the one topic uppermost in our minds. The day promised to be warm.

It turned out to be a useful wait. I planned to read the *Sunday Star Tribune* I'd snagged as we left the motel, but instead found myself watching the parade of passing church-goers. Several people went by on the sidewalk and in the street. A few nodded when they noticed me. Most never realized I was there.

At the other end of the block was the Presbyterian Church and across the corner, the stone-faced Roman Catholic edifice. Only the Catholics had a parking lot, although it wasn't a large one. There was lots of traffic and many people walking by from more distant parking spots or from their homes.

I looked at the entrance to the Presbyterian Church and saw Stacy Frommer mounting the steps. Her mane of red hair flashed in the sun from under her hat. She nodded to a man at the door and passed into the dark interior. I'd noticed her at Kronk's ranch, but not to talk to. I wondered again about her relationship with Elroy Guteman.

"Hey, Marston."

I turned my head. The toothpick-chewing deputy was talking to me through the window of his patrol car from the opposite side of the street.

"Good morning, deputy." I realized I didn't know his name.

"If you're working here in Riverview, we'd appreciate a courtesy call."

"Working? I'm just waiting through the service for a friend. Anyway, my job as a college student services administrator hardly qualifies me for investigative work."

"Yeah? That ain't the way I heard it."

Sheriff Arnason said he was keeping our discreet arrangement to himself, so I assumed this was just more gossip. I had no other answer that wouldn't get me in trouble so I just smiled and shrugged. Sometimes silence brings its own rewards. Services were starting and the street cleared of pedestrians. For the moment we were alone, two men in our machines. Organ music drifted by on the breeze and blended with the twittering of birds in the leafy elms that lined the boulevard.

Dutch Elm disease had not yet made serious inroads in Riverview. I opened and refolded a section of newspaper, hoping the deputy would leave. Finally, he did, driving slowly up the sunlight-dappled street. The temperature continued to rise.

I read for a few minutes. Traffic picked up slightly. Catholic Mass apparently started thirty minutes later than services at the other two churches and another congregation was gathering. Along the street an old, bent, white-haired man slowly and carefully maneuvered his way toward the church. He wore a dark blue suit with a white shirt and red-figured tie. Even from across the street, I could see his clothes were too large for him. The aluminum cane in his left hand branched into three legs at the bottom so it would stand upright by itself and give him more stability. Several people greeted him as they went by, or hesitated a step and nodded. From my vantage point they appeared to accord the man a certain deference. Who was he, I wondered. Some relic of the town founders still clinging desperately to life? Like me, too curious about what came next to let go? I thought he must be hot in that suit.

It took him a long time to climb the several stone steps to the Catholic Church entrance, but eventually he made it and disappeared inside. I went back to my newspaper.

Protestant services ended and the sidewalks and street filled with people. Having made their periodic homage to God, the good people of Riverview were now ready to enjoy a pleasant summer Sunday afternoon. I wondered how many of them concealed evil beneath the Sunday façade.

I got out, stretched, and stood by the car, looking up the block trying to spot Lori. A husky voice at my back said,

"Jack Marston?"

I turned around. Stacy Frommer had taken off her hat and the dancing flame of her hair swirled around her face. The sun flashed and sparkled in her curls where she stood on the sidewalk beside the car.

"That's right. You're Stacy Frommer, I believe."

She smiled slightly. "Lori and I spoke briefly in church. She invited me to dinner. She'll be along in a minute."

People going by on the street turned their heads to look at us. It was apparent many of them knew who she was. It was apparent as well that several of them knew who I was.

I started around the car, prepared to open the door for her, but Stacy didn't wait. She leaned down, opened the passenger door, and climbed in, shutting the door firmly behind her. Well, if that's the way she wanted it. The thing about Lori's Miata is it's really a two-person automobile. There was a tiny jump seat and I could fit it okay, but it wasn't what you'd call comfortable. I hoped dinner wasn't located too far away.

I looked toward the Methodist Church, still spilling its crowd onto the sidewalk. I had a glimpse of Lori as she came down the single step, before she was swallowed up in the milling throng.

A few minutes later, Mass concluded and the Catholic Church disgorged its parishioners. Methodist, Catholic, and Presbyterian merged together in ecumenical good will on the streets of River-view, smiling, nodding to friends and acquaintances, shaking hands. I supposed that this might be the only time all week when some of these farmers encountered each other. Lori appeared again at the edge of the crowd, leaning over, walking slowly. The old man in the blue suit beside her was the same man I'd seen entering the Catholic Church thirty minutes earlier. I could tell by her gestures she was telling him about me and nodding affirmatively at the same time. After she walked him across the street into the next block, she returned to where I stood.

"Feel better?"

Amusement glinted in her eyes. "The sermon was about forgiveness of sins, past and present. Appropriate, it seemed to me."

"Learn anything interesting in temporal matters?"

"Possibly. Stacy found you, I see." She looked down at Stacy Frommer sitting in the front seat.

"Stacy, I'm sorry we haven't had a chance to really talk yet, but we'll make up for it at dinner." Lori opened the car door, grimaced to let me know she understood about cramped seats, and ushered me into the back. I scrunched around so I wouldn't be breathing down Stacy's neck.

Lori got behind the wheel and started the engine.

"Where to?" I asked.

"Not Georgina's." I heard a quaver in Frommer's voice. I wondered if her control was cracking.

"Our motel is okay, and it's close."

Stacy turned her head to look over at Lori. "Can we go out of town a ways? I don't mind being seen with you guys, but a little more privacy would be good."

"Can we get noontime dinner at the Junction?" I asked.

In answer, Lori just snorted. "I have an idea. I think there's still a small restaurant at the intersection of Highway 7 and the Interstate. We can make it in less than half an hour. That's enough time."

She drove west past our motel. The Interstate was closer to Riverview down here, running at an angle toward the northwest.

"Enough time for what?"

"To eat and talk and make it to our next appointment," responded Lori.

Stacy had been silent for several minutes, looking through the window at the passing country.

"What appointment is that?"

"With the old gentleman I was talking to after church."

"You mean old man Martin," said Stacy.

"Yes. He's invited us to have a drink this afternoon at his home. To talk a bit, he said."

"Interesting."

"Jack, he was looking right at you and Stacy when I came up to him on the sidewalk. I think he was really watching Stacy."

Stacy snorted and muttered, "Sure he was, randy old goat."

The restaurant was open and not busy, so we had a corner table with a fair amount of privacy. I felt the onset of a crick in my neck from bending my head in the car.

Stacy Frommer seemed to relax and hold herself under better control during the meal. Today I had roast turkey with potatoes and gravy, and fresh peas on the side.

"Stacy, you knew Edith as well as anyone while we were in school. Did you keep up afterward?"

She shook her head. "I went to what was called beauty school and got my license. She went off to wherever. When did she go to Hollywood?"

"I think she worked in Minneapolis and Chicago first," Lori responded.

"Yeah. Anyway, we were pretty tight in school, but not after. Does he know about the RVs?"

"Reluctant Virgins," I said. Stacy's mouth twitched.

"Right. We had quite a time. Marge, Tessa, a couple of others. I remember once in ninth grade we caught Tony Litvek outside the girl's locker room window. We teased him a lot that winter. Anyway, I hung around some with those girls. Later when we were seniors and the RVs didn't do many school things, we hung together a lot. But I never thought some of us were completely frank. Even after we took that crazy pledge." She looked at Lori.

"You were never a member, Lori, so maybe you don't know. We swore we'd tell the other RVs when we went all the way the first time. I never did. Tell, I mean."

"Stacy, what did you think when you first heard Georgina had purchased part ownership of the 40-Mile Club?"

"I thought it was about time she got something of her own. Her old man was a kind of a skinflint. Remember, Lori? Georgina almost never had money to buy a nice sweater or blouse. Not that any of us had a whole lot, but he was pretty well off. Of course he bought the place for her."

"Really? That's not the way I heard it."

"What did you hear?"

"I heard she was doing a good job and the people who owned the club offered her a share."

"You mean after they forced Don Carmichael out? Listen, Lori, there's lots of ways to buy things, if you know what I mean. And there's lots of reasons to pay for things too. I should know. Georgina's old man knew something, or he found out something, maybe, about what really went on at the club, or…" Her voice trailed off and she stopped. "Shit. I'm talkin' too much. Let's just forget it, okay?"

We passed on dessert. I paid the bill and we left. As we pulled out of the restaurant lot Lori leaned closer to Stacy and said, "Stacy, I'm sure it's difficult right now, but I do want to know about Elroy, if you can talk about him so soon. What was going on with you two?"

Stacy didn't answer right away. I saw her fumble with a tissue and dab at her eyes. She glanced back at me. "Listen, I don't want to cause any trouble, okay? I mean, El is dead and I'd just like to go back to Fargo and forget all this."

"I sympathize, but maybe you can help us figure out who killed him, and why." Lori reached across and pressed Stacy's shoulder.

She sighed and nodded. "Elroy was a good friend. During our senior year, I used to work at the club sometimes. When they'd have big poker games. There'd be a few out-of-town guys there and they wanted some girls around. Sometimes they'd bring a couple of hookers. I didn't do that, but we served drinks and danced with the guys. Once some guy from out of town wanted me, wanted me to go to bed with him. I wouldn't, so he got mad and threatened to leave."

"Who were the locals who were there?" I asked.

"This night I'm telling you about, none. None of the regulars. The crowd was all from out of town."

"So local men came to the club on a regular basis, right?"

"Sure. Old man Houck the banker, Martin, and the county superintendent of schools. A few others.

"Anyway, this night I'm telling you about, Carmichael called my old man. It was late in the winter, probably March. My dad was drunk. What else is new? First he tried to order me to go with the guy. When that didn't work, my old man dragged me to a room somewhere in the motel and whacked me around."

"The bruises I saw on you at the swimming hole," Lori murmured.

"Yeah. That was from another time. I didn't dare tell you everything. Anyway, Elroy happened to be at the motel delivering meat to the kitchen from the locker. He heard me screaming. He charged into the room an' cold cocked my old man, with a frozen pork shoulder, I think it was. Before he knew who was beatin' on me." She sniffled and wiped her nose.

"I never worked for Carmichael again. And I never told my old man who hit him. El and I started sneaking around. We never really dated, you know? But we found out where all the good haymows in the county were." A smile drifted across her face. "So after high school I moved away and went to beauty school, and he got married. We never broke up, you know? We just…stopped. Then one day, he showed up in Fargo, outside my shop."

She shrugged. "I took him home and we've been seeing each other a couple times a year ever since."

"We saw you in the alley behind your old place on Thursday."

"Was that you in the car in the alley? I saw you stick your head out the window when I turned into the back entrance. Thought you looked familiar."

"We ran into Guteman coming out the street door later," I said. "Before the door swung shut I saw your silhouette."

"Yeah, that's the last time I saw him." Her voice was low and wistful, full of unresolved sadness. "He never really loved me, you know. But we couldn't seem to stay apart. Once I called him and we met in Wahpeton. A few times, I came here, to Riverview, so we could be together. Sometimes I thought he had other women besides me."

"What did you do when he left?"

"Thursday? I didn't want to go to dinner alone, so I bought some snacks and went back to my room at the motel."

"Georgina's?"

She snorted again. "No way. I'm staying at the same motel you are."

"Stacy, you weren't at the banquet Friday night."

"And you want to know where I was, right? Makes me a suspect. No alibi. Listen, I know it sounds crazy, but I got cold feet. I figured Elroy would be there with his wife. I was bummed, you know? I was afraid she'd notice something." She gestured with one hand. "I drove to Junction for a sandwich. Nobody knew me there. God, it looks bad. I haven't got an alibi."

I didn't look at her. "Can we drop you at the motel?"

"Sure," she said morosely.

After we dropped Stacy off, I moved to the front seat and said, "I have the feeling she knows more than she's telling."

18

"Things get more convoluted all the time," Lori said.
"Do you think Stacy killed Guteman?"

"I think that's very unlikely," Lori's tone was firm. "Kill someone? Probably. You know that I believe we all have that capability, given the right circumstance. But unless Elroy was physically threatening her, no."

"Besides, she hasn't got the strength to lift him off the ground without help."

Lori nodded. "She cares–cared–a lot for the guy. Funny, now I know about those two, there are things I remember from school, things I only half-noticed about them. Do you know what I'm saying?"

"Yes, I do. It's unfortunate she apparently has no alibi. It's still possible she might be skillful enough to fool us."

"Well, yes, but I doubt it in this case. Turn right here. Martin lives in that recent development between the high school and the river."

We turned and drove another block. We found the address and parked. The house was a modest, solidly built rambler. It looked spacious enough for three nice bedrooms over a full basement. There was an attached garage. I rang the bell but no one came to the front door.

"Over here, I hear something," said Lori. We followed the concrete walk around the side of the house to an unlocked gate in a tall wooden wall and discovered this rambler had a bit more to it than appeared from the street.

Lori walked ahead of me through the gate, into a large yard with an impressive in-the-ground swimming pool between the long left arm of the house and the fence encompassing the pool and its attached patio. On two sides the pool was protected by the house, on the gate side, by a nine-foot-high cedar plank fence. At the back, facing the river, an eight-foot wire cyclone fence provided an open view. The lawn outside the fence, speckled with a few bushes, ran down a long green slope all the way to the river's edge.

"Well hello, here's Lori Jacobs come to call on an old man. How nice. Do come over here and sit."

One might have thought from his greeting that Lori and I had just dropped in instead of being invited. I realized Martin's comment was directed at the others on the patio. I'd assumed we were joining Martin for a private chat. This had the appearance of something else, maybe the proceedings of a court. Or maybe it was to be a star chamber session. My bullshit antennae began to quiver as I went forward with Lori.

Josh Martin sat wrapped in white terrycloth. His skinny legs stuck out below the robe. It was apparent from the way his hair was plastered to his skull that he'd just gotten out of the pool. Beside him in bathing trunks and a short-sleeved shirt that hung over the beginnings of a slight paunch was Ed Tomlinson. He looked a lot less buttoned down than the last time I'd had seen him. Standing opposite those two was Richard Borken in long shorts and an open shirt that showed off his hairy chest.

I looked at the pool. Sitting on the far edge, dangling her feet in the water and wearing a two-piece suit too small for her was Elaine Tomlinson. The suit would have looked all right if she hadn't gotten overweight, probably from too much booze and not enough exercise.

"Hey, Lori, lookin' good." Elaine raised a plastic glass in greeting. "C'mon in, the water's great."

The other woman at the pool was Tessa Larson. A different picture altogether, she was wearing a shiny black single-piece strapless suit cut high on each thigh to accentuate her lean, taut legs. Water streamed off her flanks as she flipped out of the pool and merely glanced toward us.

"Hi, Elaine, Tessa. I'll take a pass for now if you don't mind." Lori smiled at Martin.

The men nodded at Lori and me, and indicated vacant chairs. Dick Borken smoothed his glossy black hair and said, "Can I get you folks anything to drink?"

"Thanks," I said, "I'd like a short gin and tonic if it's available. Lori?" She nodded and Borken turned away.

Josh Martin had been watching the small group dispose of the social amenities in silence. Now he entered the conversation in his gravelly voice. "We understand you are investigating events in River-view, Mr. Marston. But I think your scrutiny is aimed at more than just the two recent murders."

"I beg your pardon?" I decided to play it cautious and ignorant.

Tomlinson stirred and punched the air with his fingers. "Look, Marston. We know about your career in the Navy as an investigator in NCIS. We know you have connections with law enforcement in Minneapolis. I checked you out. Your cover is blown."

There was an edge of contempt in his voice. In other circum-stances I might have taken umbrage. A line from Romeo and Juliet came to mind; *The day is hot...we shall not 'scape a brawl; For now, these hot days, is the mad blood stirring.*

"Excuse me, gentlemen." Lori's scornful voice cut through the heavy atmosphere. Borken pressed a cold glass in my hand and gave Lori another. Then he sat down. "You seem to be operating under false presumptions here," she continued. "When I got my invitation to the reunion and decided to come, I asked Jack to accompany me. That's why he's here. That's the only reason."

I smiled and saluted with my glass. I thought sourly that right about now Lori was probably wishing I hadn't been so persuasive about our coming to this reunion.

"Oh c'mon, Lori." Tomlinson leaned forward and stared at her. He'd probably hoped she'd show up alone. I couldn't decide whether that tone in his voice was sarcasm or rueful realization that no mat-ter how rich and locally powerful, he was still small potatoes in many circles. "Why would someone like Jack here want to spend a weekend at your high school reunion in Riverview, for God's sake?"

I took a small sip from my glass. Either Borken hadn't blended the ingredients or he'd made my drink awfully strong. "Because she asked me to," I said, looking fixedly at Tomlinson. Martin was paying close attention to the wordplay. Neither of us told them I'd been the one who persuaded Lori to return to Riverview.

Tomlinson backed off. "All right, I can accept that. I guess we all can." He blew out his breath and glanced around at the others. "But now, what's going on? I mean, why are you talking to people like Georgina Maxwell and Marge, for God's sake?" His voice was becoming petulant.

"What Ed here means," said Borken evenly, "is you seem to be sticking your nose in all sorts of places. Acting like an investigator, not a visitor. Why can't you just relax and enjoy your weekend?"

"For one thing," Lori snapped in the icy tone I had learned to associate with simmering anger, "we don't take kindly to being burgled, and seeing our classmates killed."

"Burglary? Goodness, I hope nothing significant was taken," Martin commented. His voice rattled in his throat.

"Only our peace of mind."

There was a squeal from the pool and a great splashing as Elaine Tomlinson slipped off the side and began thrashing clumsily through the water. I caught Tomlinson's look of resigned disgust while he took a long swallow and watched his wife through the thick bottom of the glass.

I turned to Josh Martin. "I wonder, Mr. Martin, if I may ask, do you have any idea who is murdering the class of nineteen-eighty-nine?" I used my most deferential tone, the one I employed when I was trying to wheedle some favor from the president of City College.

"No, Mr. Marston, I certainly haven't. I'm surprised you even ask me. I'm an old man and I don't get out much any more." He sighed and shook his head. "It must be a madman. I really can't imagine who would want to kill Elroy Guteman. Of course Edith, living out there in Los Angeles…." He pronounced the city's name with a hard g. "She could have made any number of enemies, don't you think?"

"I guess so. It's odd that someone from LA would wait until she traveled all the way to Riverview before sticking her with a pitchfork." They all nodded, wisely, sagely, or wearily. I took another sip of gin. "You know it's sort of a cliché to suggest there may be other things going on, under the surface, so to speak. But that does appear to be the case, doesn't it?" There was hardly a ripple of reaction to my gentle sally.

Martin looked steadily at me out of faded greenish eyes and said, "Other things? Oh, I think you exaggerate, Mr. Marston. You've been here what, a little over forty-eight hours? What can you have discovered beneath the placid surface of our small community? Especially if, as you suggest, you didn't come here looking for something." Martin's court nodded. I nodded. The heat, heavy with humidity and mixed with the booze, pressed down, making everyone lethargic. I thought for a moment we might all just nod off. It wasn't an unattractive idea.

Dick Borken stirred in his chair and said, "Still waters may run deep as they say, but I bet you've found we're just a pleasant, if somewhat boring, middle-American community. Apple pie, Fourth of July, all that."

I didn't say anything, but Lori did. She sat up straight, eyes wide, and stared at the men. "Discovered? I'll tell you what we've discovered. Racism! Oppression! Payoffs! Murder! That's what!" She had their attention, all right. So Lori told them about the incident on Main on Thursday with the old Asian gentleman and about the stories she was hearing of payoffs to a former sheriff to avoid raids for illegal gambling.

"Of course you have proof of all this?" asked Martin spreading his spotted, gnarled hands.

"Well." Lori stopped and looked an apology at me. "Actually, I haven't."

"I see. So what you really have is just a lot of gossip, rumors. Old stories. I'm sorry my dear, I never put a lot of stock in old stories." Martin stretched his thin lips in a sort of smile.

Tomlinson and Borken looked at each other. I wondered how much of Lori's narrative was old news to this trio. I was glad she'd not said anything about bank records or about foreclosures on debt-ridden farmers. That would have been impolite. Possibly even dangerous. Lori seemed about to go on, so I stirred in my chair and gulped at my drink. She glanced at me and subsided. There was a long silence no one seemed anxious to disturb. It wasn't my place, being a mere out-of-town guest at the gathering.

Finally Martin looked up and said, "I am pleased to have met you, Mr. Marston. And to have renewed my acquaintance with Lori." Martin inclined his head. "I well recall her as a lovely young lady coming into my store with her father."

I just bet he did, I thought without flinching. Martin nodded slightly. He reached forward and gently patted her hand. "Such a young beauty, she was. Now, forgive an old man. I'm forced to take a short nap each day, you see. But do stay a while longer. I'm sure we can find suits if you'd care to use the pool." Borken stood and helped the old man rise. Martin fumbled for his cane and I got to my feet. Martin turned and took my hand in his dry fingers. "Do take care, Mr. Marston, during the rest of your stay in our little town." He went off slowly with Borken to the patio door while the others silently watched him go.

When I turned back to the rest, Elaine Tomlinson had disappeared, apparently also into the house. The sun was a little farther west in the sky and the back yard had gathered heavy soft shadows from nearby oak trees. Tessa Larson, alone now in the pool, swam back and forth, back and forth, quietly, almost effortlessly, a dark form slicing through the clear, pale water.

19

"Do you have a feeling we just successfully made it through an interview with the local Godfather?" Lori laughed shortly as we got into the car outside Joshua Martin's modest-appearing home. The heat seemed more oppressive than ever.

"It was a curious meeting, wasn't it?"

"I'm sorry for shooting off my mouth, Jack. We're supposed to be gathering information, not giving it."

"It's all right. In fact, your outburst may just allay their worries somewhat."

"Thanks for that. I'm getting a distinct impression that your being here with me is bothering them a whole lot. It makes me wonder about the sale of dad's farm. Is there something about that sale that won't bear closer inspection? When the farm was sold, we were surprised about dad's note to Martin, and the size of the obligation. I think I'll have a talk with Johnny Houck about it." We drove off toward the motel. "What now?"

"Be careful what you say to Houck. Now, how 'bout calling Terry Worckowski? If he's available, I'd like to talk to him some more about the life and times of Riverview. Since he was your good friend, I assume we can rely on his discretion. For supper, what say you introduce me to that place we passed coming to Riverview–Junction?"

"Really? Hope you brought along ear plugs and some Rolaids. The food's not the greatest and the music gets pretty loud. Anyway,

Friday and Saturday are the big nights at Junction. Or were in my day. Sunday is usually pretty quiet."

"Well, it's either tonight or not at all."

Lori smiled and we headed toward the highway.

"Remind me about the players at Joshua Martin's court," I said.

"Dick Borken, implement dealer, class president. Then there's Ed and Elaine Tomlinson."

"Right. He's the big time lawyer in town, wife thought to be a frustrated writer."

"Yep. Elaine. Overweight, a little drunk and careless, apparently. Did you notice she wasn't at the pool when we left?"

"I did. She went into the house just before Martin ended our little conference."

Lori nodded. "Right. Sort of odd timing."

"I intercepted an impression that Tomlinson cued her. Maybe he thought she was drinking too much."

"She did act a little tipsy."

"Or maybe she was expected to go inside."

"Elaine? Isn't Josh Martin a little old for such stuff?"

I looked around at Lori. "I don't know, what do you think?" We drove in silence for a few minutes.

"And finally, Tessa Larson. Widow of Ron Larson."

"She didn't seem to fit. I mean, I thought of her as an outsider, sort of like us. Can't say exactly why, though."

"She's a classmate, of course, but she didn't seem to be having a good time."

"Maybe she's looking for something," I said.

"But what could it be?"

The answer to that question would have to wait. The late afternoon sun sent long shadows across the highway as we drove north to our destination.

* * *

WE STOPPED AT the motel to freshen up. Then it was back in the Miata and off to The Junction, with the air conditioner cranked high. There were a surprising number of cars and dusty trucks scattered across the bumpy paved parking lot when we drove in. The neon sign over the door winked 'JUNCTION' in a nervous non-rhythm, indicating the place was open. A thick vaporous atmosphere greeted us when I hauled open the big, dented, wooden door.

"Ah, there's nothing like the odor of stale beer," I remarked, "unless it's many odors of stale beer mixed with all else."

"Another low-class roadhouse. Your kind of atmosphere, right?" Lori grinned.

"Exactly."

The music system was apparently on break, because there wasn't much noise, just low conversation, clinking glasses, and the sounds of metal on metal from the kitchen area. Over the bar hung a big paper banner that proclaimed 'Don Bruns & his Last Flight Out Blues Band'. They were appearing this weekend, apparently, to be followed by something called 'The Honeydogs'.

"God," smiled Lori, wrinkling her nose, "I don't think it's changed a bit in twenty years." She led the way across the cavernous dance floor that dominated the center of the place. Along one end stretched a bar long enough to require two or three bartenders during busy times. Tonight there was only one that I could see. He was a medium-sized fellow with big arms, a big gut, and not much hair on his head.

"Let's take a booth. This one," she said. We were about midway along the wall opposite the door. There were two exit signs on different walls. It appeared they led to different ends of the parking lot.

"Okay. Anything special about this one?"

"No, but in a booth it's easier to see and not be seen. Unlike the tables."

I raised an eyebrow at that. Was she a little embarrassed to be here?

A waitress appeared out of the gloom and took our drink order. I usually made it a rule to drink beer from the bottle in the rare times I patronized places like this, but Lori ordered scotch and water before I could say anything. The waitress made it back in double time. She was wearing tight blue jeans and a loose, black off-the-shoulder blouse that revealed most of her bosom when she put down the drinks.

"You guys want menus?"

"Please." I nodded and watched her walk away.

"Cute ass," commented Lori. She got up. "I'm going to the little girl's room. Watch my purse." She took her billfold and went away toward the bar, hips swinging just a little more than usual.

Cute ass, I thought, watching her go.

The sound system started up while Lori was absent and three or four couples swayed onto the dance floor, clutched in each other's embraces. Most of the people still sitting down were men. A lot of them were sitting alone, some at the bar, others at small tables. We'd noticed a sheriff's car in the lot when we arrived, but I didn't see a deputy in the bar. Perhaps he wasn't in uniform.

"I called Terry. He'll be happy to see us. I told him we'd be out after supper and chores." Lori slid back into the booth. "Did you decide what you want to eat?"

"I think I'll go for the California with a side of refried beans. There isn't much they can do to ruin that."

Lori smiled and ordered a small chicken-fried steak and home-fried potatoes. We were just finishing up and having a cup of coffee when someone approached the booth.

"Deputy Miller, isn't it?" said Lori resting her cup back in its wet saucer. She looked up and held his gaze where he stopped just behind my right shoulder. I looked to my right to see the man's belt buckle. It would have been awkward to crane my neck to see his face so I returned my gaze to Lori.

"Well well, how you folks doin'? No big final get-together for the reunion folks?" It was the voice of the toothpick chewing deputy.

"No, Deputy Miller," Lori responded in a quiet voice. "Events of the weekend have put a damper on the reunion. Any progress in finding the murderers?"

"Wal, of course the details are confidential, you understand, but yes, I'd say the sheriff and I, and the rest of the department, are making definite progress. Definite progress."

"How long have you been a deputy sheriff, Officer Miller?" I asked.

"'bout two years, Mr. Marston. Yes, just about two years." He was too young looking in any case, but only two years on the job meant he hadn't been around during the gambling days and possible payoffs at the 40-Mile Club.

"You're not from around here, are you?" asked Lori.

"Nope, I moved here from Pierre. I understand the sheriff is releasing you out-of-towners. I s'pose you'll be headin' back to the Cities right soon?" It was more a statement than a question.

"Probably tomorrow. We want to stop and see a few friends before we go." Lori sipped her coffee.

"Wal, you take care, now. An' don't worry none, we'll nail those killers real soon." Deputy Miller sauntered away toward the bar. I paid the bill and we left.

"Do you suppose Brad's office really thinks there's more than one killer out here this weekend?" Lori was behind the wheel, pulling the Miata out of the lot and back onto the highway, south toward Riverview.

"Doubt it. I also seriously doubt he's put Miller in charge of the case. I don't think he's Brad's fair-haired boy in town."

The sun was setting in the west, glowing over the far horizon. We could see a long way under the darkening, nearly cloudless sky. The highway was empty. About a mile north of town, Lori slowed and turned east on an unpaved county road. The road had a slight crown of gravel that rattled against the undercarriage. Weeds grew sparsely along each side. Like most county roads in this part of the country, this one had deep grassy ditches. Lori had explained that the deep ditches held the snow in winter so it didn't drift as much on the road itself. These particular ditches rose to mostly old, rusting, barbed wire fences marking the fields we passed. We saw corn and soybeans, something that Lori identified as sorghum, then a crossroads at a section line.

Darkness was falling faster. I could see the lights of town in the middle distance, here and there the glow of a yard light signifying a farmstead. The tires crunched on the gravel. We smelled the dust we were kicking up. Lori switched on the headlights. She drove slowly enough so the low-slung Miata never bottomed on the roadway.

Two miles off the highway we reached a weather-beaten stop sign with several bullet holes in it, and turned right onto a narrower gravel-and-dirt road. Here the ditches were shallower and overgrown with weeds and tall grasses. The hot sun-glow in the west cast dimming light over the plains and fields. The heat was oppressive.

"There's the Worckowski place," said Lori. We lurched and bounced over ruts in the road. More stones kicked up by the tires banged against the insides of the fenders. Lori didn't slow down. Sure-handed, as if she'd done this hundreds of times, she drove down the narrow road until we reached a break in the fence-line on the east side of the road. A one-lane dirt track led at right angles into the dark toward the bright glow of Terry Worckowski's yard light, a quarter mile distant. On the right, opposite the entrance, a sturdy post held a big rural-style mailbox that flashed dully at us in the headlights.

As we drove up a slight rise into the yard, there was just enough light to see the outlines of a big barn, two round, dark blue silos, and several smaller outbuildings around an open square. Lights glowed from many small windows of the barn. The other buildings were dark.

A little way away on the left a high-peaked roof over the two-story white farm house stood out against the sky. Lori swung that way and parked beside a dusty pickup. Most of the downstairs windows of the home poured yellow streams of light into the night. Although the sky was still light, the land now rested in hot breathless darkness. I opened the door and got out. A loud snuffling sound and hot air blowing on my leg made me stop.

"There's a dog here."

"She doesn't bite," said a quiet male voice from the direction of a big oak tree–Terry Worckowski.

"I'm surprised she didn't bark," said Lori, walking over to Terry. A light over the back porch door came on.

"She would have, if I hadn't been out here." We shook hands and started toward the light. The door banged and Ada Worckowski came through the screen to greet us. She stood with her feet apart, hands on hips, waiting.

"Evenin'," she said and turned away when we reached the step. "There's coffee or iced tea in the kitchen."

Inside, the big kitchen table where the family took all their meals, had been cleared and a fresh tablecloth laid out. Its creases were sharp ridges across the plane of the table top. Terry leaned the rifle he'd been carrying against the wall beside the door. As we all sat down, a door banged somewhere upstairs and Ada looked up.

"Brian, our oldest. He's gettin' ready to go out," Terry said. Ada smiled at Lori and brought iced tea in tall sweating glasses.

"I have coffee too," she said.

Everyone declined.

"How are the kids?" Lori asked.

"Good, good. Brian's saving money to go to technical college in Detroit Lakes. We'll help some, if we can. It's gonna be tough to go back to farming without another man around the place. Louise is just about a straight-A student. Graduates high school next year."

"Where will she go to school then?" asked Lori. I smothered a grin. Assumptions.

"Oh," Terry rubbed his big hard hands. "Maybe we can figure out a way to help her go to secretary school up in Watertown. We'll just have to see." He dismissed the subject and Lori let it go. I sensed she knew now was the wrong time to start an argument with Terry about fairness to the children. Ada watched and listened, sipped her tea. There was a loud clumping on the stairs and a dish in a cabinet close by settled with a musical click. A door banged and a tall, muscular young man came into the kitchen.

"Dad...oh." He stopped short, seeing strangers.

I recognized him immediately. He was one of the group of young men we'd seen harassing citizens Thursday afternoon when we arrived in Riverview. I saw Lori watching him. She also remembered.

His father introduced us. We shook hands. I couldn't tell if the boy remembered our encounter.

"Listen, Dad, I'm a little short right now. Can I borrow a couple bucks for gas? Just until payday?" Ada rose and went to the counter beside the sink. She fished out a ten-dollar bill from a drawer and handed it to him with a small smile.

I looked up at the boy, he was a man, really. "Hey, Brian, your dad tells me you're thinking about studying robotics up in Detroit Lakes." Worckowski hadn't actually said that, but with other technical colleges closer and robotics being the specialty at Detroit Lakes, it wasn't a difficult deduction.

"Yeah, I guess so."

"Robotics are big in Asia. Maybe you'll go to Japan and study with the developers."

"Yeah, that would be somethin'." He smiled again, white teeth a flash in his tanned face. I didn't think he'd got it, but then Lori spoke.

"Ada, are the Fongs still living here? I thought I saw Mr. Fong on Thursday afternoon in town, but I wasn't sure." All the while looking past Ada at Brian.

"Oh, gosh, I think so. I'm sure we'd have heard if they left."

Brian looked quickly from Lori to me and back, then his gaze dropped and he turned toward the door. "See you guys later," he muttered and fled into the hot night.

20

Ada offered a tentative smile that wavered in the overhead light. The house was air conditioned, but the atmosphere seemed stifling, close. For a moment we all sat in the oppressive silence. A badly mufflered car roared out of the yard, gravel spitting from its tires. Ada sighed and wiped tiny droplets of perspiration off her upper lip. I could feel sweat gathering in the small of my back.

For a few minutes we all traded social pleasantries and sipped iced tea. Terry said, "So, Lori, you said you two wanted to talk to us? Something specific?"

I interrupted "Excuse me. Before we get to that, I'd like to ask you something else, and believe me, I know these are sensitive areas. So if I seem to be prying, please understand we're just trying to get a full picture of the situation."

The Worckowskis looked at me and waited. I wondered if I wasn't already overstepping a social barrier. The lights flickered, dimmed, and began a slow crawl back to full.

"Ah, damn it," said Terry softly and reached to the wall beside the door. He flipped a switch and we sensed rather than heard a change in the atmosphere. "Air conditioner. There've been problems on the power line. Needs more capacity, I guess. Hot nights, everybody's air conditioner's running full bore, draws down the power. Low power will damage our compressor, so when the lights dim like that, I have to shut 'er down for a while. Sorry. Some people on the system have had to buy gas-powered generators as backup. Keep the milk coolers runnin'."

"Doesn't the co-op know? Why don't they build more capacity?"

"Lori, who knows?" His voice was a tired sigh. "They say they don't have the capital right now." Terry shook his head and looked across the table to me. He shrugged. "We own it, but they run it." The temperature and the humidity began to rise.

"When Dad was farming, the milk was picked up every day, sometimes twice." Lori looked at me. "The co-op had a fleet of trucks and they came around more often in the hot weather to keep the milk from spoiling."

"Not anymore," Ada said. "Once a day, that's it. Farmers have the responsibility. That's one of the reasons we got out of dairy."

"Are you carrying a mortgage?" I asked.

Terry grunted. "Don't waste any time, do you?" He nodded. "To the hilt. We took out a second coupla years ago from Dick Borken when I bought that quarter section off Georgina."

"You own a piece of the Maxwell place?" questioned Lori. I took a big slug of iced tea. It tasted good. Cooled off my insides, if not my skin. I pressed the sweating glass to my forehead.

"Yeah, when Georgina's dad died, she broke up the place. Nobody made an offer for the whole spread. I was first in line, 'cause she needed some quick cash, I heard. Something about the motel, I think it was." Terry shifted in his chair and scratched his chin. "Matter of fact I was coming from making a payment to Dick when I saw you guys on the street Thursday." He shook his head. "Man, I been payin' off that note for an awful long time, seems like."

Lori nodded. "I know. So much has happened. But we wanted to ask you about something else, about Ron Larson, Terry. About the day you last saw him. Would you go over that again for us?"

"Sure, but there wasn't nothing to it. I was driving through town. I don't remember where I was coming from." He looked at Ada who was gazing intently into her glass of brown tea clasped in her fingers on the table. "Anyway, just as I went by, here comes Ron out to his truck with a box in his hands. I didn't have anything pressing so I stopped to talk."

"Was he glad to see you?"

"Jeez. I don't know. He was just the same as he always was. We'd got to know each other some from doing bank business, you know? Anyway, upshot was, I gave him a hand, hauling some stuff to the truck."

"What kind of stuff?"

"Just stuff. An old musty roll of carpet, I think. A broken window frame maybe. Some more boxes."

"Boxes." I frowned in thought for moment. "Can you remember, describe the boxes?" I took another swallow of tea and waited for his answer.

"Gosh, just a stack of cardboard boxes. They were full of old papers. Smelled musty. They were just brown boxes, with covers. Holes in the ends."

"Holes."

"Yeah, like where you put your fingers to carry 'em."

"Anything written on the boxes? Labels maybe?" I asked.

Terry frowned. "Gosh, no, I don't think so. Can't remember anything, anyway"

"What color were they?"

Terry shrugged and now Ada was looking intently at me. "I don't remember. Brown, maybe? They were just boxes."

"Anything else?"

"Some other trash. I said I thought it was an odd day to be hauling junk to the dump. Most everybody goes to the dump on Saturday."

"Some Saturdays there's even a line at the dump," said Ada softly, still staring at me.

"What happened then?"

Terry thought some more and shrugged. "Nothin'. He said thanks, see you, something like that, and drove off. I got in my truck and followed him out of town. I turned off to come home. Last I saw him, Ron was on the road to the dump."

"Are there turnoffs on that road? Could he have gone somewhere else after you saw him?"

"Sure, Jack. The dump is a couple of miles east of town. He coulda gone most anywhere. Between town and the county road over east, there's two or three farms along that road."

"But only after you go by the dump road," said Ada, her heavy-lidded eyes now fixed on her husband.

He nodded. "Or he coulda turned off on the lake road. Well, he must have," Terry finished.

"Why do you say that?" I asked.

"Because his truck was found way south of town, not far off the lake road."

"Did you see the truck? Later, I mean. After they found him?"

"Nope. It was a total wreck, I heard. Burnt out completely."

"Tessa was pretty broken up," said Ada, leaning her thin elbows on the table, one hand still around her sweating glass of tea. "She didn't want to ever see that truck again, she said. I heard the insurance didn't want to pay up. Said there was something funny about it. About the accident. Ed Tomlinson put a stop to that, got her her money right quick." She was watching me carefully again. Assessing whether what Terry had told us meant something significant. I struggled to keep my expression as neutral as possible.

Lori piped up, "Did you guys ever hear anything funny about the 40-Mile Club while we were in school?"

The Worckowskis glanced at each other. "Funny, how?" From Ada.

"I don't know," Lori replied. "About parties there or anything?"

"You mean the gambling and the girls?" Terry looked over at his wife and shrugged again. "Yeah, some of the guys knew. We never talked about it much, even when Brad said he saw Marge McMenny coming out of there real late one night."

"Brad Arnason?"

"Yeah," said Terry. "There'd been an out-of-town football game and the team got back late. He stopped to see his girl. Who was that, Ada?"

"Yolanda Parsons, that year," she supplied. Her voice had gotten softer, almost whispery. The heat was taking hold, sapping all our energy and deadening her interest in the conversation.

"Yeah, that's right. Anyway, he claimed he drove by and there was Marge in a party dress, sorta weavin' across the parking lot at the motel. She was laughing and hanging on to some guy," he said.

"Thing like that must get around town pretty quick. Did lots of people talk about it?" I chimed in.

"No. Brad, he was pretty looped too, I guess, and wasn't clear on just what he did see. And he said he only told me and Dick Borken. Borken just laughed and said Brad musta been drunk or seein' things and to shut up about it."

Terry looked over my shoulder toward the clock on the kitchen wall behind me. I looked at my wrist watch and saw it was getting late. Ada sighed tiredly, shoulders drooping in her thin dress.

"I expect we'd better be running along," said Lori. "Ada, are you all right?"

"Oh, yes. There's just so much…" Her voice trailed away and she gave her husband a look that said much and so little. She raised a hand off the table, palm out as if she was trying to push back old unwanted memories or new pain. "It's just…the murders and all. I can't think anymore." Tears came and trickled down her damp cheeks.

Lori stood up and bent over Ada, handing her a tissue, pressing her fingers into Ada's bowed shoulder. Terry and I rose also. There was a look of concern on Terry Worckowski's face as he watched his wife fight back more tears and begin to straighten up. With murmured goodbyes, the scene broke up. Terry came into the yard, reached down, and petted the dog. The night was hot black and still. Insects hummed around the yard light that struggled to push back the blackness, succeeding only in illuminating a small cone in part of Worckowski's yard.

"It's been a tough summer, drought and all. Crops'll do poorly this year. We had trouble finding the money for the mortgage. Ada never was very strong, you know. And now this reunion and these murders. She's taking it real tough."

"Thanks for talking to us, Terry." I shook his hard callused hand; Lori reached up and pecked him on the cheek. He stood in the fringe of the light watching the car as Lori drove slowly out of the yard.

After a few minutes of crawling down the driveway, Lori said, "What do you think? Was it the boxes?"

"What do those boxes sound like to you?"

"They sound like transfer files, Jack. Like the kind of banker's boxes I store old patient records in. But what does that mean?"

"It might just mean that Ron was cleaning out his garage, took a load of trash to the dump, and then drove off south where he ran off the road and died."

"I don't believe that's all it is. I don't think you do either." In the reflected light of the headlights, I saw her turn her head to me. I leaned across the front seat toward her and the door window on the passenger side of the car blew out in a crackling explosion of safety glass.

"Jack!"

"Go!" I shouted. "That was a gun shot! Go! Go!" Lori slammed her foot down on the accelerator and the little car leaped forward, swaying crazily on the gravel. Suddenly sweat poured off my face and my hands turned clammy. I looked all around. There were no lights to be seen except from Riverview far ahead on our left.

"Seat belt," Lori cried. The words were harsh in her mouth. The car was doing about sixty on the uneven road and I could feel the Miata starting to float a little off the bumps.

"Hang on," she said. She stomped on the brakes and wrenched the car to the right. We skidded into another gravel road in what felt like a perfect four-wheeled drift.

"Jesus! Do you know this road?" My voice sounded louder and higher than normal.

"Not very well," Lori yelled back. We went over a small dip in the road and for a moment the car was air-borne. Then there was a horrible grinding sound when the bottom of the car scraped the road surface. I had a vision of a torn out oil pan. Lori immediately eased off on the gas and slowed down.

I peered back into the moonless night. Now I saw moving lights, a pair on the road behind us, and another pair that seemed to be running on a parallel road to the east.

Lori flicked off our lights and drove forward slowly for a quarter of a mile.

"Don't touch the brake pedal," I said. "Use the hand brake."

"Okay. My mouth is dry, but my hands are sweating."

"Could that have been an accident?"

"Not likely," said Lori. "I've heard of cars being hit during deer season, but not out here in the open on section lines, in the summer. At night. God, Jack. Someone tried to kill us!"

I was watching the two sets of lights and said, "Or tried to warn us off again. We'd better get back to town."

"There's another road just up ahead here somewhere that will take us back to the highway on the north side."

Lights of the following vehicle flashed over us. "Are you okay to drive?" I wondered.

"I'm a little shaky, but I can handle it." Lori put us in gear and ran the Miata quickly up to speed, switching on the lights only when it became necessary. A moment later we swerved into a narrow, bumpy crossroad that was more dirt than gravel. We headed west toward Highway 75. This road was apparently little-used and not much better than a field road. The car banged and floated over the uneven surface. I looked past Lori and saw that one pursuer had also turned west on another road about half a mile away. Now it looked like we would both reach the highway at about the same time, but they'd be between the Miata and Riverview. The second vehicle seemed to have disappeared. I wondered about that. It could mean pursuit had been abandoned or it could have more ominous implications.

Lori gasped, spun the steering wheel and the car suddenly lurched to the left, but not fast enough. The road made an abrupt detour around a large tree. The right wheels skidded off the dirt into softer ground. We tilted right. Lori wrenched the wheel back to the left. The Miata hit bottom, went into a groaning skid back across the road.

The car bolted over the edge of the road and down into the ditch. Only the seatbelts kept our heads out of the windshield. The poor Miata buried its nose in the soft bank of the ditch and came to a sudden stop. One headlight went out. Steam rose from under the crumpled hood.

"Shit!" said Lori and bent her head over the steering wheel. "Are you okay?"

Suddenly the stars seemed to be a lot closer, and for a moment there was only the sounds of a dying automobile.

"Yeah, nothing's broken. C'mon, Lori, we can't stay here. They'll find us if we do. We'll have to hoof it back to town before it gets light."

We unhooked the seat belts and scrambled out of the passenger-side door, into the hot dangerous night.

21

A three-strand barbed wire fence barred our way almost immediately. It was an old fence and the wires were slack. I pushed the
loose top strand down and started to climb over.

"Wait. Wait a minute," whispered Lori.

"What's the matter?"

"Let go the wire and let me feel it." She took the wire and shook
it. The rattling noise sounded loud to my ears. "Okay. This is really
loose so there probably aren't any animals in there."

"What animals?" The lights of a vehicle drew closer, although
they were still more than a quarter of a mile away. I tugged at the
wire. It screeched. I held it down and climbed over, then held it in
place for Lori. "C'mon, let's go. We'll have to take our chances with
any four-footed animals. I don't hanker after a close encounter with
those coming up behind us."

We started walking fast across the field, stumbling on the uneven ground. "Some of these fields are used for pasture after the grain
is combined. And not all the animals people hereabouts keep are
friendly," Lori said.

"I get it. Right now it can't be helped."

"Nobody would turn animals into a field without mending their
fences. So the animals don't get loose." Lori's normal sounding voice
helped keep panic at bay. I was thankful for that.

"I'm starting to get royally teed off. Those guys behind us are enough to cope with right now." I stumbled over a large hummock in the field and fell to one knee. I risked a quick look back toward the wrecked Miata, The vehicle whose lights we'd seen had stopped on the road a few yards behind it. We crouched in the stubble field and watched. The stubble wasn't high enough to conceal us, but we didn't want to be seen against the horizon which was still a few shades brighter than the ground. The sliver of moon I noticed rising in the eastern sky provided no significant light. For a minute nothing happened. Then a figure got out of the idling vehicle. When he stepped into the headlights and walked slowly toward the empty car, it was apparent he was holding a rifle or a shotgun at his side.

"Anybody you know?" I whispered.

"Nope."

Whoever it was also carried a flashlight. He stood by the rear fender and played the light over the interior, holding the flash to one side so the reflected light didn't blind him. When he turned his head, his words floated faintly across the field.

"Empty, but the engine's still hot. I c'n hear it ticking."

The unseen driver must have asked a question.

"Nope. Prolly walkin' out to the highway." The man waved the beam of the flash over the area around him. Then he killed it, turned, and walked back to the car. The driver put it in gear and drove slowly past the Miata toward the highway. As they passed, the spill from his headlights bounced off the side of our car. The silhouette of the emergency light bar fastened to the top of the vehicle flickered in the reflection. It was a police squad.

I stood up after our pursuer passed and looked south across the fields. There were no other headlights to be seen, only the glow of the town.

"We'd better get moving. It's a long walk to the motel," said Lori. "Was that a police car?"

"Yeah. Sheriff's Department, I bet. This is getting deeper and deeper."

We joined hands and started across the field, tripping occasionally on the stubble, sweating profusely. The ruts between the rows didn't help. Eventually we came to another fence.

"We can keep cutting through fields," Lori said, lifting the top wire. "Or we can stay on the road, which will be easier, but longer."

I went under the top strand and felt a barb prick my shoulder. "I vote for the road."

We started south along the gravel road parallel to the highway. The walking was easier, but it was still hot, sticky work. We kicked up dust from the track. It coated our hands and filled my nostrils. More sweat dripped. Great, I thought. Nice night for a stroll in the weeds.

"Jack, the only reason I can think of for Terry to be driving by Tessa and Ron Larson's during the day like that would be to see the Larsons, or because he was coming from Parsons. Steve and Yolanda live a block or so down the same street."

"Why would he be doing that?"

"I don't know and that bothers me. Both Steve and Ron would usually be at work in the middle of the day."

"Normally."

"Normally. Yolanda frequently worked at the store, too."

"Lori, suppose Terry has been to see Yolanda, and leaving he realizes that Ron recognizes his truck going by."

"And what? He stops to chat and then help, to make Ron think his being there is just happenstance?" she said.

"Or he stops because it really is happenstance," I said.

"Or he and Ron had arranged to meet at Larson's and the boxes in the garage are the coincidence."

"But what reason would they have to meet away from the bank? Except to load the trash? Nobody has mentioned, even in passing, that the Larsons and Worckowskis see each other socially."

"Jack, if they were meeting away from the bank, why not say so? This is a small town. Everybody sees everybody else once in a while. Consider the possibility that Ron Larson's mysterious boxes don't have anything to do with the murders."

I thought about that for several steps. "Maybe the boxes were the reason for Terry to meet Ron Larson on that particular day at that particular place."

"But why?" Lori flapped her hand in exasperation.

"I don't know. If that's true, it's also possible that after Larson disappeared, Terry was too frightened to say anything to the sheriff."

"Frightened of what? And how does this all tie to the recent murders?" said Lori. We walked on in silence, each busy with our separate thoughts. Lori was walking a step ahead of me on the narrow strip of grass beside the gravel. When she suddenly stopped in her tracks, I almost walked her down.

"Lori..." I started, but she grabbed me. Her fingers squeezed my arm. I stopped talking and looked carefully along the road. Then I too saw what had pulled her up so abruptly.

We were in a shallow dip in the track that rose just about twenty yards ahead. In front of us was the next intersection. It wasn't empty. A vehicle was parked there, and I saw two silhouettes leaning against the front fender.

What had saved us from walking right up to them was the gentle rise in the grade and that we had been coming from the darker east. The two waiting men and the vehicle were faintly outlined against the starry night sky. I squinted and could just make out a light bar across the top of the car. Another patrol car. This solved the question of what had happened to the other pair of following lights.

We crouched at the edge of the road. The glowing end of a cigarette flared briefly and then was covered. Lori put her lips against my ear. "I smelled that cigarette," she breathed.

"Man, we must have missed 'em."

"They can't have walked all the way across to town yet."

"Mebbe they went the other way, back to Worckowski's," said a voice I thought I recognized.

"Sure, or maybe they're still walking to the highway. From here we can see the highway and intercept anybody out there. But if you keep bitchin' and smokin' an' they're coming along the section line, they'll hear you or smell you."

I squinted and thought I could make out that the one at the front of the car was holding what appeared to be night glasses. He scanned slowly along the highway, a half mile away. He was slender, and over the sounds of night creatures around us, I thought I heard the leather of his belt creak when he moved.

"Hey," said the other, the older man. "Somebody's comin'."

"Okay, okay. Relax. Just put your shotgun on the seat. We aren't doin' anything illegal."

I looked back toward the Worckowski place and saw what had attracted the man's attention. The glow of headlights moving slowly west cast an aura over the road from the dust that hung in the still air. As the car topped a rise, the sharp-edged beams came into view. I returned my attention back to the two men and in the light of the approaching headlights, identified Deputy John Miller.

"Jack," Lori whispered. "Let's get off this road. There's a shallow ditch over here." We used the gravel-crunching noise of the approaching vehicle to slither into the high grass at the edge of the road and partially hide ourselves. The car pulled up beside the patrol vehicle.

Lori turned her head and looked at me. I nodded, silently mouthing Miller's name to her. She nodded. She'd recognized him too.

"Problem here, Deputy?" asked an unfamiliar voice.

"No sir, just takin' a short break. Everything all right with you?"

"Sure thing. See ya." The car slowly drove off, leaving Deputy Miller and his companion on the road and us crouched a few yards away. I was tempted to stand up and yell, but I had no guarantee the man in the second car wasn't part of whatever was going on. I stayed put on the warm dusty ground.

Miller's companion, an older man with a big belly, watched the car go down the road for a moment. Then he said, "Let's go. If those two are close by, they know we're here now and they'll just go around us." He climbed into the passenger side of the patrol car.

Deputy Miller swore softly under his breath. He hawked and spit into the gravel, then got behind the wheel. The two men drove away, leaving their quarry lying ten yards distant in the dusty grass at the side of the section line.

22

"Did you recognize the older guy, Lori?" I stood up and brushed off my pants, stabbing myself in the thumb with a small thorn in the process.

"I recognized the deputy, John Miller," she said, "but not the other one. I wonder how deeply Miller is involved."

"I wonder how much of law enforcement out here is corrupt," I muttered.

We started walking again, following and watching the disappearing tail lights. We walked in silence for what seemed a long time. Eventually we reached the dark outskirts of town, dusty, tired, and more than a little irritated.

"I'm liking my reunion and this town less and less. Murder, burglary, gun shots, possible corruption. I didn't know about any of this stuff when I was growing up here, but maybe some of this was in my subconscious. Maybe that's why I haven't been back until now. I sure don't think I want to come to another reunion. Let's go home as soon as we can."

"If it's any consolation," I said, "I'm sorry I talked you into coming after you rejected the idea the first time." She squeezed my grimy fingers in response.

We stood on a quiet side street. Because we'd come in from the east side, we were now walking west across town on a dark residential street. There was no one else about. Not even a roaming cat or dog.

I took out my now-soiled handkerchief and wiped the dust-filled trickles of sweat off the side of my face. As we approached the main street and the highway, I slowed and we stopped beside a concrete block building that still radiated the day's heat. I checked back the way we'd come once more.

"Why are you stopping?"

"That's a very wide street. I just want to look things over before stepping out," I said.

"High Noon in Riverview, Jack? Do you think someone is waiting in the shadows to gun us down?" Lori's lame attempt at relieving the tension didn't hide the tiny tremor in her voice.

"Hit-and-run vehicular homicide would be more likely," I said sourly. I looked both ways up and down the street. There were no cars parked at the curb. The two widely spaced street lights closer to the center of town didn't penetrate the night in this section. I stared off into the night, trying to see a little farther, trying to see if someone was waiting in a truck on the edge of the road out there with their lights off.

Lori looked over my shoulder at the street and shrugged. She took my hand and we walked briskly across Main without hesitation and down another dark street in the direction of the lighted parking lot of our motel.

There was no one at the front desk, but I found one of the two room keys in my trouser pocket so we went upstairs. I inserted the key card in the lock. The light blinked green. I put a hand on the knob and then I stepped back.

I looked at Lori.

"Would they risk waiting in our room?" I shook my head. Tired, hot, and dusty, I decided they wouldn't. "Maybe I don't care if they are," I said and re-inserted the card. When the green light blinked again I twisted the knob and pushed the door wide open. I walked into the room beyond. Nothing. I reached around and switched on the light. The room was empty unless someone was hiding under the bed. Lori went to the bathroom for a drink of water and rinsed her face. I followed with a similar idea.

She plopped down on the bed and kicked off her shoes. I checked the time. It was after one in the morning. Lori took a long drink and reached for my hand. I sank down on the bed beside her.

"Oh, God, Jack. I'm really frightened. That shot wasn't just a warning. I think somebody's trying to kill us."

We sat there a long time, holding each other. There was no real tenderness in the embrace, we were hanging on for dear life, reaching out and giving support and strength to each other.

"We'd better call the sheriff," Lori said huskily after a few minutes. She let go, rolled over and reached the phone, punched an outside line and the number. It seemed to take a long time for someone to answer.

"Good morning, is this the county sheriff's office? This is Lori Jacobs. I ran my Miata into a ditch on a section-line road east of the highway and north of Riverview. Out toward the Worckowski place. No, I'm okay. Yes, I walked back to town. No, you don't have to do that, just tell the sheriff when he calls in, please. Yes, Sheriff Arnason. He'll want to know. Do I need to come in to make a report? I see. No, I'll arrange for a tow truck in the morning. Thank you."

"Why'd you leave the impression you were alone out there?"

She sipped a little water. "I'm not sure. Just suddenly thought it might confuse somebody a little."

I nodded. "Good thinking." I chained and double-locked the door. I looked at it a minute and then jammed one of the side chairs under the knob. If there was a fire, I realized we'd be slower getting out, but nobody was going to get in without waking one of us. I decided I felt a little safer. We showered, turned out the lights, and slipped into the queen-sized bed, but sleep didn't come right away, tired as we were.

"Jack," Lori's voice whispered across my hearing, "what's going on?"

"Wish I knew. A complicated question with no simple answer. I think whatever is going on is connected to a number of events, old and recent."

"Yes. I can't get those transfer file boxes out of my head."

"Yeah. Suppose they were records that revealed some illegal transactions at the bank. They could have been the cause of Larson's death," I said.

"Do you think Larson was murdered?"

"It's a definite possibility, Lori."

"Do you think Terry might have killed him?" She rolled away from me onto her back. "God, I don't want to believe that."

"It's also a possibility, but that seems even more unlikely, unless he was working for someone."

"Maybe he was having an affair with Tessa." Lori's voice was flat, devoid of expression. She rolled back toward me.

"Tessa Larson," I said. "How would you describe your relationship with her?"

"In high school? Ordinary, I guess. We weren't close, but we certainly weren't enemies, either." Lori paused. "Oh, Friday night, you said she told you I asked her about going to the river later, right? What else did she say?"

"What makes you ask that?"

"Your last question. I think she and Terry dated occasionally, but Terry always said it wasn't serious."

"He told you that?"

"Sure. I told you he and I were best buddies."

I reached for Lori's hand. "She called you `our tight-assed little Lori'." I waited for a reaction. For a long moment there was only the silence of our breathing and the sighing of the air conditioner.

"Well, I'll be damned. I wonder if…" Lori took her hand away and sat up in the dark, pulling her knees to her chest and curling her arms around them. "I told you she was a Reluctant Virgin and I wasn't. I didn't tell you some of those girls asked me to hang around with them anyway. This was before they thought up that silly name for the group. I never did. Not because I didn't like them or anything, but I was busy with studying and chores and stuff. And I liked school dances and events. Funny, the things that come back once you start thinking about that time. I heard that a couple of the girls were mad at me. Said I was stuck up. Maybe Tessa was angrier than she ever let on."

"And maybe, when she was dating Worckowski, she resented the time you two spent together. Did you ever criticize Tessa to Worckowski?"

"Not that I remember. Do you think this has anything to do with the murders?"

"Dunno. Just considering all angles." We rolled together and, with our arms protectively around each other, fell into exhausted sleep.

23

Monday morning Lori and I again took breakfast with the sheriff of Cobb County in the coffee shop attached to the motel. "I had your car towed in. It's over to Tedvedt's shop," he said. "Tedvedt told me they'd either replace the smashed window or cover it. Car doesn't look too badly banged up, so you should have it back sometime tomorrow. I noted that the report you phoned in didn't mention how the window got smashed. The superficial damage from going off that road isn't enough to have caused the window to go like that. They've got to order a new window out of Sioux Falls."

When there was no response from either of us, Arnason took a drink of his coffee and then said, "Another item you forgot to mention. The slug that took out your window was in the back of the back seat. Almost made it to the trunk. I dug it out. A big one. It coulda done a lotta damage, even though it musta been nearly spent."

I shuddered, remembering how close it had been. No Shakespearean quotation suggested itself.

Arnason went on in a flat, almost matter-of-fact tone, staring at us across the table. "I keep asking myself why you neglected to include that little detail. The slug is big, could be from an elk or a buffalo gun. Several of the men around here go to Montana every other year or so. They use scopes and they're pretty good shots. I don't think this was an accident. Looks to me like somebody set up to get your attention." He didn't say that the shooter might have been trying to kill one of us.

"And another thing. Where were you, Jack, while all this shootin' and runnin' was goin' on? The report I read, the one you phoned in early this morning, Lori, sounded like you were alone in the car." He looked a hard question across the table at her.

"That was kind of an afterthought," I said, summoning a disarming smile. "We were both in the car; drove out to see Terry Worckowski."

"What is this all about, Brad?" said Lori. "Do you think someone was really trying to kill us or just scare us off?"

"I don't know, yet. Anything else about last night you left out?"

"A squad car pulled up right after we went in the ditch," Lori said.

Arnason sat back abruptly. "Who was driving?"

"Deputy Miller."

"Yeah? I guess he didn't file a report yet. What'd he have to say?"

"We didn't talk to him. About fifteen minutes later we saw him again on another section road about a mile away while we were walking back to town. He was with a big heavy-set man holding a shotgun or a rifle."

"We overheard part of their chatter," I chimed in, "and that's how we know it was Miller who checked out the Miata after we had to abandon it."

We were at a table near the windows and I surveyed the room. The restaurant was less than half full. Several people were going through the buffet line. The waitress brought coffee refills to our table.

Brad sighed. "All right, you better tell me the whole thing, and don't leave anything out this time."

When Lori finished, Brad sighed again. "Dammit. Miller, huh? We've had a few problems with him. Just small stuff, like pushing people around when he didn't have to. I've warned him a couple of times, but never suspected he was dirty."

"Brad," I interjected. "It might be wise to say nothing right now until the murders get sorted out. There are too many questions."

"Yeah, you could be right. Burglar in your room, shooting, two murders, now Deputy Miller somehow involved, apparently on the wrong side." He wiped his face with a big white handkerchief. "Jesus, I sure don't need this."

"I have a question about the 40-Mile Club, Brad."

He looked across the table at me. "You mean Georgina's? You think Georgina is involved in this?"

"No. I don't know, but I was referring to an earlier time, before she bought in. Before you became sheriff."

There was a pause during which Arnason looked at me and then down into his coffee cup, possibly searching for answers. When he didn't find any he looked up again, this time staring across the restaurant toward the window as if he wished he could be there, out in the sunshine. "All right. I was a deputy in Deuel County, just over the line in South Dakota. I'd passed the peace officer licensing test here in Minnesota, but there weren't any jobs. Then I went into the service. When I came back to Riverview, I got my old job back over there and started working up through the ranks. We heard things from time to time about the local law here. Nothing concrete, just talk, you know? No reason to check it out. Out of our jurisdiction, anyway."

"What kind of talk?"

"Oh, the usual stuff. You could have a good time over here, poker, girls, stuff like that. Word was the law looked the other way 'cause it was good for business in Riverview. It all seemed to center on Don Carmichael's place, the 40-Mile Club."

"And of course, you had some personal knowledge, didn't you?"

Arnason turned his eyes on me. They had grown hard, flinty. "Exactly what do you mean by that, Jack?"

"Wasn't there a time, it would have been the fall of `eighty-eight, I think. After a football game, you drove by the club and found Tessa Larson in the parking lot, drunk?"

His gaze didn't waver or soften. He just said softly, "Yeah, you're right. I'd about forgotten that. She told me a little of what was goin' on."

"Go on."

"That's it. It was a long time ago. But I remember. Anyway, just about the time I heard Georgina had bought a piece of the club, old

Jim Clemens was up for re-election. There was talk he wanted to retire. And some folks weren't too happy with his service. So I put myself up to run against him. I had enough experience by then and a pretty good rep. I moved back across the line to Minnesota. It wasn't much of a contest and I won going away."

"And you've been sheriff ever since," smiled Lori.

"Yep. I was prepared to go face down Georgina. Didn't relish the thought. She 'n' I had a couple of dustups in high school. But I overheard one of the deputies I inherited grousing one day that the new owner was talking about shutting down the party.

"I called a meeting of the deputies and the office staff. We only had six people then. I told them I wasn't interested in prosecuting anyone, but we were going to have a clean operation, top to bottom. I said anyone who didn't like it that way had better move on." He lifted his lips briefly at the recollection.

"Within a month or so I'd lost all three deputies and the clerk. Folks were starting to wonder if they'd elected the wrong man. But it all worked out." He stretched then and called the waitress over for yet another refill of coffee.

"Brad, did you ever talk to Georgina about the activities at the club?"

"Not officially, Lori. After my first deputy resigned, I did have a conversation with her in the dining room one evening. I just told her that I understood it had been Sheriff Clemens's habit to drop by every week, regular like. I told her I didn't know why he did that. I wasn't going to follow a regular pattern like that. She might see me twice a week sometimes or maybe once in a particular month. It would be just like my visits to other businesses in town. Or in the county. With no local police, my department is responsible for the towns as well as the rest of the county. I also told her I was sorry about the talk that went around about her and the club and that I expected it would all go away in time."

"What was her reaction?"

"She just smiled and said she'd voted for me and she expected the talk would die down eventually. She hoped it would. That was it. I learned later she'd already cut out most of the gambling. And she wouldn't let the guests bring hookers to the few games that did go on. 'Course, she couldn't stop small private games in the rooms. Now, of course, everything's changed. Gambling's legal in Minnesota."

"But only under certain conditions."

"Sure, but the fact that we have it in the casinos and pull tabs are everywhere means we'll likely have it in other forms pretty soon."

"You against gambling, Brad?"

"No, Marston, I don't much care, one way or the other. It's the other stuff that usually comes with it. People losing their shirts, their land, drugs, organized crime, maybe."

"Speaking of losing their land, let's talk about Dick Borken for a minute."

"Borken? How about old Josh Martin in the bargain?"

I nodded. "So you consider those two a single problem?"

Arnason shrugged and took a sip of coffee. "Like peas in a pod. Always been close, those two."

"Based on what we've learned from Marge, Dick is a lot harder than Josh Martin ever was," put in Lori.

"Don't you believe it. Martin and old J. L. had a good cop-bad cop routine going. Everything I've learned over the years about a lot of the land deals in this part of the state tell me that Houck and Martin were in cahoots."

"I don't get it. How does it work?" asked Lori.

"Let's say your dad gets encouragement from the bank to borrow money to replace an old tractor, Lori. After a while, your dad begins to think it's the right thing to do. It's pretty easy, the bank is cooperative. Then Houck suggests your dad put up a certain piece of land as collateral. Your dad agrees, even though that wasn't his original idea. Remember, he trusts the banker. Known 'im all his life.

"Later, the loan committee at the bank turns down the deal. The turndown is set up by Houck, who encouraged your dad to apply in the first place."

"Ah," I said. "I see where this goes. Of course, Lori's dad doesn't know the banker persuaded the loan committee to reject the loan application. If he's subtle, even the other committee members won't realize Houck has turned them against the loan."

Brad nodded. "Sure. Then, having been disappointed by the bank, Mr. Jacobs goes to Josh Martin at the implement company, 'cause now he really wants the new tractor."

"Why does my dad go to Martin?"

"Initially, he probably heard about Martin's deals from a neighbor. Sometimes he gets a nudge from his friendly, helpful banker. The one who's so sorry the bank can't lend the money Mr. Jacobs needs for that new tractor." Arnason took a sip of his cooling coffee and leaned back in his chair. The wide black leather belt at his waist creaked.

"Okay," said Lori. "The banker has psychologically softened up my dad so the disappointment of being turned down makes him just that much more vulnerable. 'Sure, this is a good loan,' old J. L. would tell my dad. 'I can just see that new tractor in your shed, Mr. Jacobs.' Then later, great disappointment, fed and manipulated by Houck. Puts my dad on an emotional rollercoaster so his good sense is submerged. With some people, it wouldn't take much. Next thing you know, here's Josh Martin at just the right time offering a bad deal. Only now my dad's natural good sense is depressed for just long enough. Those rats. But I don't see how Houck gets anything out of it."

Arnason frowned and said, "See, if Houck makes the loan and it goes sour the bank forecloses. Houck has to sell the land. The bank makes out, but Houck doesn't get any more than his salary. But if the loan is made by Martin, when he calls in the loan, he can sell the collateral, the land, and pay Houck under the table. Everybody but your dad makes out, and if they're careful, they can run this scam for years."

I nodded. "And just to weight things even more to their side, sometimes Banker Houck is right there if your dad gets behind in loan payments to Martin."

"Only now, the deal is tighter," nodded Lori. "Because of his increased debt, the deal is for more interest or a smaller loan on another piece of land."

"I'll bet Banker Houck is careful to say all the right things about hard-hearted Martin ruining some farmers with his deals the bank couldn't touch," I said.

"And if the deal comes at a time when Martin is a little short of cash," Arnason continued, "he just gets a loan from Houck's bank for some other reason."

"At a favorable rate of interest no doubt," said Lori bitterly.

"Sure, you've got to figure the implement company is a good long-term commercial customer."

"Um," I said. "It probably wouldn't be too hard to get a loan from a different bank, with a reference from Houck, if they wanted to be particularly cautious. Just to muddy the waters a bit."

Brad nodded. "Anyway, when Martin sold the land they somehow split the profit. They don't move a lot of land real fast. In fact, I know that some farmers have continued to farm the land they lost on a lease-back arrangement."

"Brad, how do you know about all this?" asked Lori.

"I've been watching these guys operate for years. Building a record of bits and pieces. I think I've got a handle on most of it. They don't confine themselves to Cobb County, either."

"I just had a thought. Deals like these need an attorney, don't they?"

Lori looked at me. "Oh no. Ed?"

"Oh, absolutely," responded Brad. "Tomlinson has been the attorney of record for nearly every one of their deals. Sorry, Lori. Looks like a bunch of our classmates are up to no good. It's illegal of course, or close to it, but proving it is really difficult without records of some kind."

"Which they'd be careful not to keep," Marston added. "Sheriff, is this connected with Elroy Guteman's murder?"

"I can't see how. Or Kronk, either. At first I figured it could have been Elroy's wife, or one of her brothers. On account of Stacy."

I looked at him and he just looked back.

"So you think it's true? About El and Stacy?" said Lori.

"Yep. None of my business, of course, until somebody put a knife in poor Elroy."

"A knife." I echoed.

"Yeah, doc called me with preliminary findings this morning, early. Somebody stabbed Guteman twice, right above the gut. Might have used an ice pick or a boning knife. Either one would have killed him. But then, for good measure, whoever did it slammed him down on the tines of the rake. Funny, the state extension service has been sending out circulars about safety with farm machinery. Pointing out that stuff like that old hay rake Elroy was hung on can be dangerous."

"Any ideas? About his murderer?"

"Well, Stacy is clear and so is Elroy's wife. We're gradually checking everyone else as fast as we can. Concentrating on out-of-towners from the reunion. Long way to go, though."

"And Kronk?" I asked.

"Nothing yet." He glanced at his watch and sighed. "You two might want to think about heading back to Minneapolis. Somebody thinks you know something or are getting close to something. Either way, gettin' more dangerous out here in rural America." He smiled mirthlessly and rose. "Gotta run. You two take care."

24

"What do *you* think was in those boxes Ron Larson was loading in his truck, Jack?"

"Don't know." I shrugged.

"Don't know a whole bunch, do we?"

"Well, we're getting somewhere. You know everything I know."

"I do?"

"Yep. One of the rules of the detecting game, so I hear. Keep the assistant up to speed."

"Sure. So, now I'm your assistant detective?" Lori raised her eyebrows. "Sounds like you're making a career change from academic administrator to private eye."

I smiled. "I never expected to be labeled a private eye out here, but I seem to have been, so now you get to be number one assistant eye, although it's more like *ad hoc* nosey parker. Any ideas? At the moment I'm non-directional."

"Let's go see what progress has been made on my car. The garage said they'd get to it first thing." We walked the few blocks through town to Tedvedt's garage. It was the identical route we'd taken the night before, running away from an unseen shooter.

The white-painted concrete block building had two working bays, one for automobiles, the other for trucks and heavy machinery. The red Miata was up on one hoist. Three overweight older men were working when we walked in out of the sun. The garage was cooler and smelled of old oil and grease and machinery.

One of the men turned and looked at us. He wiped his dirty hands on a filthy piece of rag and came forward in the shadows. "Marston?" he said. He had yellow eyes and he seemed to be paying more attention to Lori.

"Right. Just dropped in to see how long it will be until her car is ready."

The man didn't bother to introduce himself. His deep-set eyes roved over Lori from head to toe. He took his time about it and he didn't care that I saw him looking, but when she turned her head in his direction, he looked away.

"Yeah," he said. "We don't have a window that fits. I called a supplier in Sioux Falls. They happen to have a truck comin' this way and they had the right window in stock, so we should have the glass in a few hours. Won't take but a few minutes to install it. What happened anyway? Sheriff's guy just said you ran 'er off the road. But that window couldn't have broken like that from running off the road. Leastways not with the little front-end damage you got. An' there's a hole in the seat back. Looks like somebody dug something out of the upholstery."

The man's mouth continued to work. He was full of questions and his odd yellow eyes were never still, flitting about like a bee looking for a likely blossom.

"Are you saying the car is ready to go except for the window?" I interrupted the river of his voice.

"Naw, not quite. Len'll pull out the fender that's rubbin' on the tire, an' we still have to check the linkages and the tie rods an' the wheels. Realign her. Replace a blown tire. Looks like you need new ones in front anyway."

"Can we rent a car somewhere?"

"Well, I don't have anything, but Ken Johnson might. He's the Ford dealer."

Lori picked out new tires, agreed to the other repairs and we walked out of the garage back to the sunny street. "He was there," Lori said in a low voice when we were out of earshot.

"What?"

"That…mechanic. The one working at the bench in the rear was the man with Deputy Miller on the road. I'm sure of it. I'd be absolutely positive if I could hear his voice."

"How did you decide that?"

"It was his profile. When I looked into that dark corner he was just pulling down a piece of exhaust pipe from an overhead rack."

"A shape sort of like a rifle, or a shotgun."

Lori nodded.

"Interesting. We'll find out who he is and keep him in mind for a little tête-à-tête. I have this thing about people who shoot at me, especially when you're involved."

"I never knew that," said Lori.

At Johnson's Ford, we rented a small blue Escort. Lori elected to drive. "Where to now?" she asked, buckling her seatbelt.

"Let's take a ride in the country. Let's go to the dump."

Lori wrinkled her pretty forehead briefly, but didn't ask the obvious. She headed east on the county road leading to the town landfill, two miles away.

"Okay." I leaned back and stared at the ceiling of the car. "It's five years ago and it's a weekday morning. You're Ron Larson in your little red truck and you're taking a load to the dump. Somewhere along here, you are persuaded to change your direction."

"Couldn't Ron have gone to the dump first?"

"No, because remember Brad Arnason mentioned that the fire that burned up Larson's body left remnants of carpeting and other things in the bed. That description sounds like the stuff Terry Worckowski says he helped load into Larson's truck."

"So your hypothesis is that Larson was persuaded–"

"–or forced–"

"–to go to that gravel road south of here where his truck was found." We rode in silence until we arrived at the entrance to the dump. Not a crossroad the whole way. Just one or two field gates. There wasn't any evidence there'd ever been a cross-road, abandoned, say, five years ago.

"We have a problem," Lori said, stopping opposite the gate, which was closed.

"Yes. I guess he had to go to the dump first."

"At least he had to get here," Lori pointed out.

We thought about that for a few minutes. "This road goes east a couple miles further to a county road," Lori said.

"Any crossings between here and there?"

She thought another moment and then put the car in drive. "Let's find out." There were a couple of intersections, but there was no one home at either of the two farm houses we checked. At the county road intersection we turned south, away from town.

"All right," I said, "here's another possibility. If Larson was hiding bank records, suppose the trip to the dump was a cover. Suppose he drove out to the dump and finding himself alone, went past the entrance. He kept going, to a place where he'd planned all along to hide the records."

"Makes sense. If he stopped at the dump first, somebody there might wonder why the old boxes weren't being thrown out with the rest of his trash."

"Exactly. So he follows the route we're on, going to that hiding place. This assumes he had some reason to hide whatever was in the boxes."

"If it was evidence of illegal dealings at the bank, why didn't he go to the sheriff in the next town? Or all the way to Montevideo?"

"I can think of several possibilities," Jack said. "He's not sure enough of everything yet. He wants to collect more evidence. And he isn't sure how far Houck, Martin, and Carmichael can reach. He's probably worried about the safety of his family as well"

"So, you think the banker, the lawyer, and Georgina's ex-boss started all this?"

"I think they're in it. Or were. I won't be surprised to learn that J. L. Houck, the old banker, not his son, your buddy Tomlinson, and probably some others, had a piece of Carmichael's action. I have a hunch they decided to dump Carmichael, or more likely, they paid him off when Georgina blew the whistle on the club operation."

"They maybe saw the end coming and cut their losses. So," Lori went on, "if your theory is right, Ron Larson somehow learns about their chicanery and decides to seek justice or reward by building a case against his employer and the others. But why bank records?"

"Banker Houck has no legal problems holding a mortgage on a place that's doing illegal business on the side. But suppose Mr. Larson has an ethical problem with the club and in trying to sort out the bank's connection, he happens on other transactions that cross the line."

The little Escort had by now brought us a few more miles south and Lori pulled over on the grass and gravel shoulder of the road. Crickets and other unseen critters stirred and twittered in the heat. Otherwise it was very quiet. The wind for once had gone elsewhere.

"Is that serious enough for murder?" Lori's voice was solemn.

"Can't say. It could depend on the amount of money involved." I looked away to the west. "See that clump of trees over there? Is that where they found Larson's truck?"

Lori looked out where I was pointing. "The old Coleson place. Yes, that's it. I think there's a crossing just ahead so we can cut over there. Coleson's was already abandoned five years ago when Larson died. Must have happened right near those trees. He'd know about that empty farmstead, of course."

"All right. We have Ron Larson collecting files and storing them at home. He decides to move them and uses a trip to the dump as cover."

Lori nodded. "Where would he go? Someplace no one would ever think to look. Someplace no one would associate with him. So it wouldn't be a friend's, especially if he thought the records were dangerous."

"Which is probably the reason he decided to move the files in the first place. He'd look for someplace secure but not too far away. Let's go to the place they found his body." I sat forward and peered through the windshield. Lori turned right and drove slowly along the bumpy little-used road until we came to a row of old trees, poplars and cottonwoods, the aging remains of an untended shelter belt. She stopped by the side of the road.

It was easy to see where the buildings had been. Foundation stones stuck up through the weeds and grassy depressions identified other sites. Rotting wood scraps, broken glass, and pieces of rusty metal poked their way out of several bald sandy spots. There were no remains of Ron Larson's red truck. Prairie grass and golden rod and other weeds had long since returned to obliterate what must have been an ugly black scar on the land.

"Do you think he ran off the road here, Jack?"

"No, I don't. Not unless he'd been drinking that morning. This road is narrow, there's hardly any gravel left, but it's straight and pretty smooth. Apparently he got here sometime around noon. I think he drove out here. He was probably followed. I think if he was killed, he was murdered here, and his body burned, along with the evidence he'd collected that he was trying to hide."

"Why didn't the authorities discover he was murdered?"

Marston shrugged. "Don't know. But consider this. If he was killed in a way that wasn't obvious, the fire and five days out here could hide a lot of evidence. Remember, Larson was missing but not under suspicion, so there may not even have been a thorough autopsy."

Beyond the forlorn disintegrating farmstead at this remote corner was a field of corn, ripening in the sun. Tall corn. The planting ran parallel to the road we were on, so there were no discernable rows. I looked over a tight sea of dusty green leaves hanging silent in the hot still air. I scanned the scraggly tree line on the far side of the corn field that once had probably been another neat shelter belt, groups of trees planted by the government all over the rural states in the nineteen-thirties to protect homesteads from the miserable icy winter winds and snow.

I thought I saw a faint track leading straight through the brush between the rows of the shelter belt across the field.

Years of neglect had turned the rectangular grove into a thick, overgrown mess of trees fronted by what appeared to be almost impenetrable bushes. I examined the corn field again, thinking that's how the tall corn grows, realizing that if I walked two rows in, I'd be totally concealed and probably lost in the bargain.

"Lori, is that a building over there?" She looked where I was pointing and shook her head. "What? I don't see–. Oh, yes. I do see the corner of some kind of shed in that clump of trees."

"Now I don't see it. Well, I'm sure there's a building over there.

Maybe the next farm?"

Lori shook her head. "No. It's too close to the Coleson home-stead." She looked at me. "If there's anything there at all it's probably just a big shed. Some farmers keep hay or straw in remote locations. When they have scattered fields, it takes too long to bring the crop all the way back to the farm. So they store it elsewhere until they need it."

I thought about that for a moment, standing there in the sun. "Let's go see if there's a way in to that barn, or whatever it is."

25

"What are you thinking?" Lori steered the car slowly along a bumpy road that was hardly more than a pair of ruts. She concentrated on the edge of the track.

"I have another hypothesis. We assume Larson was murdered for those files. We're also assuming he was caught here at the Coleson place where, possibly, Borken and Martin killed him and burned the evidence, right?"

"Right. What's changed?"

"Suppose the sequence of events is wrong?"

"Hunh. There's got to be a way in somewhere along here. It wouldn't make sense to have the only track in go through the farmstead past the main barn. Of course, we could just park under those trees where Ron's truck was found."

I looked at Lori. We were thinking the same things, recalling the scene we'd heard described. Ron Larson's body, horribly burned in a blackened, wet, stinking hulk. "Let's not," she whispered.

We found a way in. It took two passes along the road before Lori spotted an unused, heavily overgrown, track that led through the trees and bushes. The track was blocked by a rusty, sagging, barbed-wire gate.

"This track hasn't been used in years. I don't know how far in we can drive. We'll probably scratch this car."

I got out and stood looking at the tangle of growth. The barbed wire gate had seen better days. "I'll open that gate. We should be able to drive in far enough to hide the car." I struggled with the gate for a minute before pulling open the loops of rusted wire so Lori could drive through. I closed the wire gate again and followed the car.

After driving into the weeds and brush about a hundred yards, the wall of an old building blocked our path.

"It's an old barn. I bet no one's been here for years," Lori commented when she'd shut off the engine and got out. "Most people probably don't even remember it's here."

Insect songs hummed and buzzed loudly in our ears as we approached the small weathered structure. A multitude of disturbed grasshoppers sprang up in all directions. A faint breeze rustled the dusty corn close by on the right. It was hot and breathless. I stopped a few yards away and looked at the weather beaten wall. A large double door hung across the near end. Walking around the corner I found a smaller door that appeared to be falling off its hinges. I touched it gingerly. It creaked.

"Be careful, Jack. It looks as if this whole thing could come down around our ears."

I pushed gently on the small door and it fell to one side with a clatter in a shower of rust from the hinges. The floor inside was thick with dust, animal litter and other stuff I didn't want to examine too closely. The planks sagged alarmingly when we stepped inside. I could smell it, dust, rot, the odor of mold and decay. I bounced lightly. The planks held.

"There's a small loft. Probably some hay up there," Lori pointed. Numerous cracks in the walls filtered dim afternoon light into the single space. There were no stalls, no interior walls. The ceiling was low under the loft floor, which covered only part of the space. This was no bright sunlit barn like the paintings of happy farm scenes on the old calendars of yesteryear. Even the loft was not much higher than an ordinary man's head. It was gloomy in this barn. Surprisingly the roof appeared to have only a few holes, which might have accounted for the lack of greater deterioration. Except for the big pile of redolent straw or hay filling the back of the structure almost to the loft floor, the barn appeared to be empty. Midway down the wall on our right, pieces of two by four had been nailed across the building studs to form a crude ladder leading straight up to a dark square hole in the loft flooring. I pointed at it and looked a question at Lori.

"Ladder to the haymow. On a big barn there'd be a door on one side, maybe a track overhead where they'd have taken the hay in. That's also how they'd get it out again when they needed a big load. If they'd had animals in the barn, the farmer would go up the ladder, like that one, and fork the hay down to the animals. The hay might be loose, or it might be in bales. Mostly bales nowadays, I guess. Straw would be loose, Timothy for feed, straw for bedding. Probably not here. This is really just an overgrown shed. The haymow is too small.

"Haymow," she said again, and looked at me. Stacy Frommer's voice from yesterday came back. "We knew where all the best hay-mows in the county were," she'd said. Was this the secret she'd been protecting?

"Suppose Elroy was here with Edith Kronk that day? Stacy said she thought he was messing around with other women," said Lori.

"Could they have seen something?" I wondered aloud.

"That could explain why they were murdered."

"I think we'd better talk to Stacy again before she goes back to Fargo. See if she knows about this place," I said, walking over to the ladder. I shook one of the two-by-four pieces and banged on the studs with a fist. The studs seemed solid.

I stepped up and the first rung took my weight with no protest.

"Careful, Jack. You could have a nasty fall."

Testing each step, I went all the way to the top and stuck my head up into the loft. Holes in the walls made it easy to see that the loft floor was covered with more bird dung and a thick, dusty carpet of old hay. Dust filtered into my nose. I stifled a sneeze. The place did not smell sweet and fresh like the songs said. When I thrust my shoulders farther through the access, a small covey of pigeons warbled and flut-tered out of the loft with a thrashing of wings through a large gap in one wall. The skin on the back of my neck crawled. Slowly, carefully testing each step with my weight on the boards, I walked across the floor to the north wall. When I looked at the east wall, I saw the door Lori had mentioned. In this small loft, it was right at eye level. I turned and looked out through a large crack in the north wall where a piece of siding had fallen away. From inside the concealing shelter belt, the crossroad was laid out before me . I could easily see the poplar and cottonwood trees and the intersection of the two township roads. The place Ron Larson died.

"Jack!" Lori called. "Come look at this!" The edge of excitement in her voice sent me back to the ladder and I clambered back down.

Lori was standing knee-deep in the edge of the straw pile at the back of the space. A rotting smell assailed my nose. She pointed at the corner, where the heap of straw leaned against the back wall. A piece of raddled carpet protruded. "That rug is covering something."

I grunted an affirmative and waded gingerly into the straw. We pushed the prickly stuff aside and the rodent-ravaged carpet slid to the floor. Five years of neglect in an almost open barn would make most paper items disappear. Even those tightly packed in file folders and metal-cornered banker's transfer cases.

The stack was a mess. There'd been at least three cases stacked against the wall and covered with carpet and concealed under the straw. Now they were mostly collapsed into a large untidy stinking pile. In spite of the damage inflicted by weather and varmints, we could read the name of the Riverview Bank on the side of one case and on some of the file folders Lori fingered out of one box.

"Ron Larson's secret files," Lori said in a whisper. She picked up another damp file folder and looked at it.

"From the loft there's a clear view of the intersection," I said. We looked at each other. Suddenly the quiet afternoon turned silent. The golden sunlight dimmed just a little, and isolation surrounded us, coiling mysteriously like snakes on the head of a Gorgon.

26

Hastily we threw several armfuls of straw over the exposed file cases and got out of there. Lori rubbed her shoulders as if she felt a sudden chill in the air. She backed the car down the path while I went to the wire gate and once more wrestled it open. Again without gouging myself on the rusty barbs. A quick glance around confirmed no one was lurking in the immediate vicinity unless they were well concealed. I peered at the crushed grass tracks from the car wheels. Short of starting a grass fire, I had no idea how I might erase the evidence that somebody'd driven through that fence recently. A few minutes later we rolled north, toward Riverview.

"I think a visit with Stacy is on the immediate agenda," I said. I used a clean handkerchief to wipe the rust from the wire off my hands.

"Do you think somebody caught Ron Larson hiding the files?" Lori said. "They must have. They surprised him at the truck and never realized he'd already carried the boxes to the barn."

"Or they found some boxes and didn't check the barn for others. If they caught him there and had figured out what he was doing, they might have killed him on the spur of the moment. But if he hadn't finished unloading files, who covered those three boxes we found under the straw?"

"Maybe that was all the files he had. Larson covered them, then he was killed and no one found them, until now."

"Maybe."

Silence. Then Lori said. "Seems unlikely. Whoever killed Larson would have searched if there were no records in the truck, because somebody must have suspected that he had some records or had stumbled onto whatever was going on."

"Why didn't they look in the barn?"

Lori thought for a minute more. "They were focused on Larson, on eliminating an immediate threat, and then on getting rid of the body. I think they found some files in the truck, probably had no idea how much he'd stolen, and just assumed they had everything." She looked over at me with a question on her face.

"Works for me. Under stress, and this was a heavy situation, people often forget or ignore obvious things. I figure we spotted that barn by chance, or because in five years, maybe trees died. Even after we saw it we had some trouble getting to it"

"I'll bet there have been people in and out of there. Hunters, kids. But no one looking for anything, especially boxes of files. Over time, that straw pile would have compacted some. So maybe it was easier to spot the carpet by the time we came along."

"The only one who would have a reason to search that barn would be Larson's murderer. If he, or she, assumed he'd recovered all the files Larson took, he'd have no reason to go back there, and wouldn't want to. But there might be someone else in this, someone who figured out exactly what happened that day." We stared at each other.

We entered Riverview on a side street. I looked up, along the main street. Two blocks away, I noticed people gathering and cars blocking the street.

"Look at that," I said. "Quite a crowd for this time of day." Lori slowed and I cranked down the window. "What's going on?" I yelled at a kid running past.

"It's Brian Worckowski," he replied. "His ma has a gun." The boy skipped around us and took off into the press of people.

Lori double-parked behind a mud-splattered pickup and we pushed into the crush of folks standing along the curb and spilling into the street. Slipping back and forth, we worked our way to the front of the crowd of murmuring citizens.

In the middle of the hot, wide, sun-blasted street, we discovered Ada Worckowski. She stood spraddle-legged on the baking pavement. Beside her, sprawled on the concrete, was her son, Brian. There was a trickle of blood on his cheek and a bloody smear on his upper lip. He had one hand over his eyes.

Ada Worckowski was holding a double barreled shotgun. She didn't act awkward with it. She held the weapon as if it was familiar. One hand rested over the trigger guard. I zeroed in on her fingers. I couldn't be sure from my angle, but it didn't look as if she had a finger on the triggers.

The people of Riverview formed a large circle around Ada and her son, three and four deep. More came down the street, pressed into the crowd between the store fronts. Citizens spilled out onto the street. Men, women, children were there in the surging, murmuring crowd.

No one stepped forward. When she swung that shotgun in their direction, they surged back a few feet. Then they swayed forward while others, behind Ada, moved the other way. There was an avid anticipatory feel to the scene. I could almost hear what many must have been thinking: *I don't want to get shot, but I don't want to miss whatever happens next. Maybe the shotgun isn't loaded.*

"What's going on?" I said to a weathered farmer standing next to me.

"She clouted him up 'side the head," the man said laconically. "Thought she'd killed him at first."

"What was he doing?"

The man never took his eyes off the pair. "Brian? Him and Ed an' his buddies 'er doing what they allus doin'. Hasslin' people."

"Ed Olson!" It was Ada's voice, raised in a high shout. "I see you standing over there! Don't think you can hide from me! Get out here where I can see you better."

The crowd shifted, murmuring. They opened a ragged lane between the agitated woman with the long black shotgun and a young man backed against a store front.

I looked to my right and picked out the faces of three more young men standing in the shade of an awning over the hardware store window. They were some of the same boys I'd seen on the street our first day in Riverview.

"Well? Not so brave now? C'mon boy. Get out here," Ada spat, standing there in the sun, holding the shotgun at port arms. There were silvery tear tracks on her cheeks. Ed Olson didn't move. The crowd surrounding Ada murmured and pulsed; watched and waited for what would happen next. Heavy conflicting emotions swirled through them.

I looked across the street, scanned the crowd through the heat vapors rising from hot concrete and asphalt. My eyes met those of the sheriff. He'd taken off his hat and was easing his way through the people with hardly a ripple, working his way entirely around the edge of the crowd toward Ada's left. I assumed he was moving as far out of her sight as he could get. But close enough so he wouldn't miss if…. I didn't finish the thought.

Brian muttered something and made as if to get up. His mother whirled and jabbed him in the chest with the barrels of the shotgun. I saw she still didn't have her finger inside the trigger guard. "Stay down there, you disgusting worm!" she snapped. She raised her voice again. "C'mon, Eddie, show yourself. You can't hide anymore. I saw you today, you and your buddies, pushing people around. Can't you face me? What's the matter, Eddie, 'fraid to own up to what you've been doing? Can't come out here in front of your mother's friends? Your mother was alive, Eddie, she'd be down here in the street with me." Ada's voice rose and fell. She swayed a little and now her finger caressed one trigger of the shotgun. I hoped the weapon wasn't loaded.

"I saw her standin' over there by Parsons," said someone behind me. "Then Eddie and Brian started hoorah'n people on the street. She practically called him out, and when he met her in the middle of the street, she just hauled off and whacked him. Knocked him right down."

He heard a nervous chuckle from a man on his left whom I couldn't see. "Boy went down like a pole-axed steer," the voice said.

"Got a mouth on him, that kid," someone else said.

Lori stirred and pressed her way around me, stepping into the clear before I could restrain her. "Ada," she called "It's Lori. Lori Jacobs."

"Lori," I murmured, my heart in my throat. "Where are you going?" I knew where she was going, all right and it scared me. Guns, hand guns, long guns, machine guns or howitzers. They're all made for killing. Mostly people, and sometimes they go off unexpectedly.

Lori made a pushing movement toward me with one hand behind her back, "Ada? I'm over here, Ada." Lori started slowly forward, directly toward Ada Worckowski, talking normally as she went. Ada swung her head and her attention to Lori.

After that, it was just words, the sound of Lori Jacob's voice overlaying the tension, driving down the blood-lust of the crowd. A constant crooning sound. After, neither of us could remember her exact words. I watched Ada, watched her eyes. I watched the two women draw closer. On the other side of the crowd, Brad Arnason had stepped to the front, exposing himself, if she turned in that direction. His hand was resting on his holster. When he saw Lori detach herself from the ring of watchers and step forward into the clear, he raised one hand and opened his mouth as if to call out. Then slowly, he let his hand fall to his side and he too watched Lori advance. His other hand never left his holster.

It seemed to take forever. Slowly, step by step, Lori walked toward the distraught woman, one hand at her side, the other reaching out, offering support. Ada looked nervous. Her eyes flickered back and forth, back and forth, and her whole body began to tremble.

Lori walked steadily forward. Ada was looking only at Lori. Now they were almost touching. Lori raised her hand and slid it around Ada Worckowski's rounded shoulders. Ada lowered the barrel of the shotgun until it rested on the pavement at her feet. Lori stepped even closer until she embraced her friend. Her friend's wife. There was a collective sigh, a sudden relaxation, as if everyone on the street had been holding their collective breath. I had been.

The crowd began to disperse and I saw the sheriff amble into the street toward Lori and Ada. His eyes flicked over me and he nodded. I went to my right against the flow of people, toward where I'd seen Ed Olson standing with his buddies. When I got to the sidewalk by the hardware store, Olson and his friends were standing together in a tight group. Their eyes flickered toward me as I approached, but none of them moved. A big man in a tan uniform stood leaning against the wall beside the three boys, staring calmly at them. His pose appeared casual, but the trio didn't move. When I got closer, I recognized him. It was Pete, the older deputy we'd met at Kronk's on Saturday.

Whatever he was saying, it held the attention of the three. I went up to them.

"Mr. Marston. Not three of our finest citizens, these here boys."

"I know. I saw them last Thursday in front of the dry goods store. Apparently doing the same stuff that set Mrs. Worckowski off this morning."

"Yeah, she was a mite upset, wasn't she?" His gaze danced to me and back to the three young men. "You willing to come over to the station and make out a statement, Mr. Marston?"

I stared at the three. "Sure, deputy. Whatever you say."

"I hear you was in the Navy. Right?"

I shifted slightly to my left. The deputy and I now had the three isolated from the thinning numbers of passersby, against the wall of the store. Faint alarm was growing in their expressions. They were getting a little taste of their own intimidation.

"Yeah. CID."

"Criminal Investigation, hey. Field work?"

"Sure. A fair amount of physical stuff."

From the corner of his eye, I could see a smile creeping over his face. It was not a happy smile.

"I'll bet you learned a little hand-to-hand there."

"Uh huh. I keep up with it, too. Comes in handy when I have to protect myself against my students." The sarcasm went over the trio's heads.

"When I was a kid 'n I screwed up, my daddy took me out behind the barn." We were slowly easing closer to each other, pressing the boys together. Now they were sweating. One of them looked on the verge of tears. I began to wonder how far this would go. I had a pretty good idea what Lori would think of these tactics. I didn't think she'd approve. On the other hand, sometimes moments occur which make it possible to drive home a point. A teaching moment, an academic colleague called it.

Then the deputy relaxed, just a little. He shifted his stance so he wasn't leaning forward so aggressively. "Well, I really haven't got time to haul these three in, or out behind some barn." He spoke slowly, carefully spacing his words for maximum impact while he stared at the three. "Neither do you, I reckon, Mr. Marston. Not today, anyway. Maybe you boys learned an important lesson here. You go back to the farm. Stay out of town for a few days. Stay outta trouble. You hear me?" We stepped back from the three muscular, bronzed, young men. They looked down at their feet and turned away. I wondered, watching them go, what would have happened if they'd decided to resist.

I looked at the deputy. "Doesn't square with the cliché about small town cops," I said.

"I know," he responded, still watching the trio move swiftly away. "Nightsticks or baseball bats usually aren't the best approach."

I nodded my understanding. When I looked around, my gaze touched a slight Asian gentleman, standing alone down the street under the shade of a nearby awning, looking toward us across the now quiet sun-washed street. He bowed slightly.

27

A hospital ambulance arrived quietly and the attendants loaded Ada and Brian Worckowski into the back side by side.

"Jack, I'm going with Ada. After I've talked to the doctor, I'll go talk to John Houck at the bank. I'll see you back at the motel later."

I nodded and put my hands on her shoulders. "Listen. We have to have some serious talk. I know now's not the time, but soon. All right?"

Lori raised her head and looked into my face. Smiled.

"I think so, too. Be careful."

"Sure," I snorted as she turned toward the ambulance. "Meanwhile, I'll see if I can talk to Stacy again."

I watched her speak to the EMT who came with the ambulance and then clamber inside. She took Ada's hand and bent toward her. Somebody closed the big door and the ambulance moved off down the street, warning lights flashing. I watched it go until it turned at the next block and went out of sight.

Five minutes later, I turned into Tessa Larson's driveway and stopped behind a late model Taurus sedan. I got out and went to the door. When I pressed the lighted doorbell button, a pleasant chime sounded. Before it died away, the door was jerked open. It startled me. Stacy Frommer stared at me through the screen.

"We heard you drive up," she said flatly.

"I want to talk to you for a few minutes, privately if possible."

"So come in. I think Tessa will want to hear this too." Stacy turned away and left me to open the screen for myself.

In the living room Tessa Larson sat on the beige sofa behind a rectangular glass-topped coffee table. Sun flooded through the big windows at the back of the house, but it didn't reach this end of the place. There was an open box of tissues on the table. Tessa, in cutoff jeans and a pale blue, short-sleeved blouse, was sitting very still and erect on the sofa. She held a crumpled wad of white tissues in one clenched fist.

"Tessa, how are you?" I said quietly. She raised swollen, red-rimmed eyes. Her cheeks were wet and her mascara had run.

"How should I be? What're you, the new welcome wagon in town?" Her voice started out in a snarl, but the effect was ruined by her half sob, half hiccup, in the middle.

"Sit down, Mr. Marston," said Stacy. She sat beside Tessa and took her hand. I sat across from them on a hard chair.

"Shit. Why'd you let him in?" Tessa said after a little silence. "So he can go running off to Lori and tell her all the gossip?"

"Look, I'd wait until later, but I have to ask Stacy some questions. We can go to another room."

"No, Mr. Marston," Stacy shook her head. Her hair was like a fire-burst in the dim room. "I think Tessa deserves to be here, if I'm right about what you want to know." She leaned toward me and flicked a piece of straw off my sleeve with her thumb and forefinger.

I thought about how to begin. "Look, you either know or believe that I'm trying to help the sheriff get a handle on these murders."

Stacy said, "But you want to ask about something else, don't you?"

I nodded back. "I've been assuming all along that Elroy Guteman and Edith Kronk were murdered by the same person. I also figure they are linked somehow to something besides this reunion, unless a crazy person is going after the whole class." The two women looked at me steadily. "I remembered something you said earlier, Stacy, something about your suspicion that Elroy might have been fooling around with other women. And your remark about haymows."

Tessa sniffled and wiped her eyes again. She looked away, but I could tell she was paying close attention. The air conditioning didn't seem to be helping and the atmosphere thickened.

"I began to wonder if Elroy was ever involved with Edith Kronk, then I wondered if she might have been here in town five years ago, when Ron was killed."

"Murdered," interrupted Tessa in a flat monotone.

"Murdered," I agreed. "I also began to wonder if those two were together somewhere and saw something connected to your husband's death. That could explain a lot."

"You're right! "Tessa Larson said. She sat up straight and clutched her damp tissue. "That must be the answer!"

"Very good, almost brilliant." Stacy's chin came up and pointed at me. "Except..."

"Stacy! No! Don't say anything!" Tessa flung out one hand and grabbed her friend by the wrist. Suddenly, I knew. I leaned toward the two women and stared at Stacy. Then I nodded.

Stacy pried Tessa's fingers off her arm. Tessa's fingers left white marks on her skin. "Stop, Tessa. It's no good. He's figured it out. Besides, it'd be easy enough to check whether Edith was here then. If we know she wasn't, others will find it out too. Eventually."

"You want to correct me?" I asked softly. "Tell me where I went wrong?"

"You're better'n half right. Elroy did know something, but it wasn't Edith he was with when he learned it. Maybe he had other women when I was up in Fargo, but not when I came back to town." She lifted her chin again, ever so slightly. Stacy appeared more assured now she'd made up her mind to tell me the full story. "Funny, you showing up here now. I've just been telling Tessa what really happened. You might as well have the whole miserable story.

"That weekend, Elroy wanted us to be together for the whole day. Sunday too, if he could work it out. He made some excuse and disappeared from home. I drove in that morning with a cooler and a big picnic basket. We met outside of town. I left my car and we drove to a little barn at the old Coleson farm. It was the only building left standing. Wasn't even part of the original homestead. I guess it was put up after the Coleson's built their place. We'd been there a few times before. I liked it because it was so isolated. You couldn't see it in the summer from either road, and even in the winter you had to look for it. The shelterbelt had grown up really thick. Elroy said most people probably forgot it was there. Anyway, we hid his car way off the road and went up in the loft. It's not a very big barn. No stalls, or anything. Just straw and hay piled up." Stacy sighed.

"When was that, Stacy?" I asked.

"When what?"

"When did you go there? The last time."

"Right after dawn. I remember the sun was just touching the wheat in the field across the road and it was all yellow. The light was. Anyway, El had some blankets and we hauled the cooler and blankets up in the loft. He pried some boards loose on the side part way so more light would come in."

Stacy smiled at her memories. "We fooled around a little, then we made love. We were pretty inventive in those days." She smiled again, a small, woeful, private smile. "Then we had some breakfast and a few beers, some wine, I guess. Some of the details are a little hazy by now, you know?"

I nodded. "What happened then?"

"We made love again and then we must have fallen asleep, 'cause the next thing I remember, Elroy was kneeling over me. He had his hand on my mouth and he was shaking my shoulder. When I was awake he dragged me over to the north side of the haymow. There were a couple of loose boards on the wall that we could push aside to see better.

"There were cars parked along the road, three I think, by the crossroad. And Ron's red truck."

"Was this about noon, do you think?"

Stacy nodded.

"Were they parked where the truck was found?"

"Yeah, on the road by the trees at the driveway to the Coleson place."

"Okay. Go on."

"They seemed to just stand around for a while. I suppose they were talking, or arguing. We couldn't hear anything 'cause they were too far away."

"How many men did you see?"

"Four or five, I think. But somebody else could have been in the cars. Anyway, Ron turned around and walked away toward the open door of his truck. That's when they shot him. Just bang, like that. It was so sudden." Tessa gasped a sob and was silent. Stacy bit her lip, new tears made shiny tracks down her cheeks. "I'll never get rid of that memory," she whispered.

"Who shot him?"

"I don't know, Jack. They all did." She twisted on the couch and wiped her face with a tissue. "It happened so fast. Neither El nor I saw who actually fired the shot. There was a rifle shot and Ron just… he just dropped in a pile. It wasn't like the movies at all."

I looked over at Tessa. She'd obviously heard all this before, but she was taking it hard. "How do you know it was a rifle?"

"Mr. Marston, I been around guns all my life. I've hunted ducks and pheasants. I've even been deer hunting. I have a pistol and I practice with it. I know a rifle shot when I hear one.

"Anyway, two of the men went to Ron and sort of boosted him into the cab. Then those two drove off in Ron's truck. With the…the body."

"The others stood around talking for a while and then they all got in their cars and drove off. We couldn't figure out what was happening, but they were gone so we didn't think much about what they were going to do next. 'Cept we knew one of 'em shot Ron Larson. We were scared. We knew we hadda get out of there. We got dressed and went down the ladder. That's when we found the boxes."

"Boxes?" I said.

"There was a stack of four boxes, banker's transfer files, Elroy called 'em. Ron must have carried them into the barn while we were asleep right above him. Naked as the day we were born." Stacy shook her head. "I wanted to get out of there right then, but El wanted to look in the files. The boxes were old, but some of the file folders were sorta new. We looked in a lot of them.

"I couldn't make much out of them. But Elroy said that was because I wasn't living there anymore. He said they were records used by the bank to keep track of their business for reports."

"The papers were copies of federal and state banking reports?" I couldn't keep the disappointment out of my voice.

"No. Elroy said they were private records of the bank's dealings, and how they handled some real estate deals. See, he said if the bank had a big audit, they'd have to be able to construct a false set of records and the best way to do that was to keep a record of what they had really done and when they did it. That way they wouldn't make mistakes. I didn't quite get it all, but I knew some of the names on the papers."

"Who were they?"

"Same people who shot Ron."

"What names, Stacy?"

"Johnny Houck, the banker and his old man. Dick Borken, Josh Martin, and Ed Tomlinson, the lawyer?" I nodded. I knew who she meant. Classmates of Lori's and the father of one. And one of the town's patriarchs.

"You saw those same people earlier with Ron Larson?"

"Right."

"You're sure who was there. You can identify them?" I didn't want to tell her Lori and I had already been in that barn. I knew she'd watched Ron Larson get murdered from at least fifty yards away through a screen of leaves and a large crack in the barn wall. Identifications would be chancy.

"Well." A small sound of doubt intruded into her narrative. "It was a ways away, but I recognized Ed Tomlinson by his height and I'd know the banker. I sure know Josh Martin's big Cadillac. He's always had a Caddy. I guess we assumed Martin was in the Caddy."

It wasn't perfect, but it might be enough to get one of them to roll over on his playmates. I figured I'd better get the sheriff involved as soon as I could find him.

"After Elroy looked through the boxes, he decided we should hide them, so we dragged them more into the corner and threw a big pile of straw over them."

"How many boxes were there?"

"Four."

I nodded. She'd said that before, but I'd wanted to hear it again.

Lori and I had found only three. So someone had carried one of them off. And Stacy hadn't mentioned a piece of old carpet. All this time, except for an occasional sniffle, Tessa Larson had remained silent. I wondered what she was thinking.

"After you hid the boxes, what'd you do? Why didn't you go to the authorities?"

"I wanted to, but Elroy said we couldn't trust anybody. Besides, we'd have had to tell we were out there. He was worried about his wife and he wanted to figure things out first. He said he'd take care of it. I thought he would, so I went back to Montevideo and stayed in a motel. I was real shook up. I didn't know if Ron was dead. I mean sometimes I did, but other times I thought maybe they took him to the hospital. Then I went home to Fargo.

"Funny, that was the last time we made love. Oh, we had sex after that. But it wasn't ever the same. Even Thursday. It was like this thing was always there between us."

"Did you talk about the murder?"

"Only once before today. I called Elroy a couple of months later and asked him if he'd told the sheriff. By then I'd seen the story in the paper about how Ron's body had been found all burned up at the corner by Coleson's old place. El said he hadn't and he wasn't going to. It was too complicated, he said. I guess I was a little relieved. If either of us told the sheriff what we'd seen, everybody would know about us, about Elroy and me. And Ron was dead anyway." She looked at her friend and sniffed.

"So you let it slide. Until today. When you saw Elroy on Thursday, was everything all right?"

Stacy nodded. "Sure. We went to bed for a while and then he left. That was the last time I saw him." She sniffed and twisted a hanky in her fingers.

"And you don't know for sure who fired the one shot that killed Ron Larson."

"Not for sure, Jack. I told you, it happened so fast."

"Thanks for telling me the whole story." I looked at Tessa. She looked right back through red eyes and puffy lids.

"Ron let a few things slip," Tessa said, "and the last few months before he…before he was killed, he seemed to be more nervous than usual. Nothing I could be sure about. Some of it made more sense after they found him. That's why I been goin' over to Martin's. Only I never knew for sure it was them. They were real careful around me. I figured some day I'd hear something, something that would help me put it together."

I rose to my feet and said, "Don't talk about this to anyone else until we get some things worked out. Will you two be all right?"

"Sure," Stacy said. "We're all right. Shit. Right as rain, you know?" Her lips suddenly twisted in bitterness. Neither woman rose to see me to the door. They didn't ask me what would happen next. They seemed to retreat into their private misery. I didn't have an answer in any case.

I went out and drove back to the motel. I was sure Lori would want to be there when I told Brad what I'd learned about the five-year-old murder of Ron Larson.

28

The bank was locked. I banged hard on the door, but no one came. They were either gone for the day or back in the recesses of the place and didn't hear me. It occurred to me, standing there in the heat, that perhaps some of the people in the bank wanted to avoid me altogether. I stood there, thinking. I still hadn't found Lori and it was starting to worry me. She hadn't been at the motel and no one at the desk remembered seeing her come in or go out. I was sure we'd parted agreeing to meet at the motel.

I looked up and down Main Street. I didn't see Lori or anyone else. Across the street and down the block was the hardware store. Maybe she was visiting Steve or Yolanda and had lost track of time.

Parsons' was a big, old-fashioned place, dark and cool. The aisles between the cluttered shelves were narrow. Some of the merchandise looked as if it had been on the shelf since the store first opened, but everything was well dusted. Steve Parsons appeared from the back of the store.

"Marston, right? You're Lori's friend." He held out a rough hand for a shake.

"Right. Lori was going to the bank while I did some other business. Now the bank seems to be closed. Have you seen her?"

"Lori?" He cocked his head to one side. "No, I don't think so. Business has been pretty slow today so I've been doing some book work in the back."

He must have seen the question on my face.

"Oh. There's a pressure switch under the floor board at the door. I knew it when you came in. We don't have much of a problem with petty theft, so I didn't rush right out. Let the customer browse a bit, that's my philosophy."

"What is that?" I pointed at a black round flat disk that had drawn my attention. It was ornately decorated and it had a pointed rod welded across the flat plane with a curled tapered piece on the other end.

"Stove pipe damper. Nice looking isn't it? Goes into the stove pipe above a wood-burning stove. The point sticks out one side, this handle out the other. By rotating the damper flat, or up and down, you can control the draw of the chimney, make the fire hotter or cooler."

I nodded, feeling the thin coating of oil on the damper. "If it spends its life out of sight inside a chimney, why the decoration?"

Parsons handed me a piece of paper towel to wipe my fingers. He smiled. "I don't know. Maybe the decoration attracts sales. Maybe to give people a little lift in their lives, knowing the damper is elaborate, even out of sight. It's hard out here, you know, most times. Maybe it's a way for some folks to get a little pleasure in their lives."

I nodded.

"They make plain dampers now. I don't stock 'em."

I went out and returned to the Escort and then the motel. The telephone was ringing when I unlocked our door, but the caller hung up before I lifted the receiver. Lori still wasn't there and I didn't see any evidence she had been. Damn it. I was getting a bad feeling. I changed my damp shirt and just as I turned to go out, the phone rang again.

"Marston?" The voice was muffled and hard to understand.

"Yes?"

"We've got her."

"What? Got who?"

"Your lady, the Jacobs woman."

A coldness grabbed me around the chest. Breathing became painful. Lori kidnapped? I looked at the receiver and my hand started to shake. I didn't say anything.

"We want a simple deal here, Marston. A trade. You got something we want, we got your lady friend."

"But…"

"Shut up and listen. You want her back undamaged, you give us the files. Then you both leave town. A simple deal."

I dragged in a deep breath. "All…all right."

"We wanna get this done fast. And we want both of you out of our lives. Permanently. You bring the files to—"

"Wait a minute." My mind started to function again, went into overdrive. "I'll have the files in that barn on the edge of the old Coleson place. Tonight. I don't have them here, but I can get them by tonight."

A pause, then, "Acceptable. Ten-thirty and no law. We'll know if you go to the sheriff." The phone clicked in my ear. They'd know? How? Miller? But they didn't know we already knew about Miller. They also apparently didn't know about the files still hidden at the barn. Pieces were missing. I couldn't stand just sitting around waiting to go to the damn barn and I needed help. There was no way I was going to trust whoever was on the other side to live up to their word. Tessa Larson came to mind. Maybe she knew something. I exploded out of the room and ran downstairs and drove back to Larson's. I watched the rearview mirror constantly to be sure I wasn't being followed. Still I knew if someone was looking they could cover the town quickly. The car I was driving was probably recognizable by now as our loaner.

I parked a block away, in the small lot of the Congregational Church and walked up the street to Larson's. Stacy's bright red car was still in the driveway.

Tessa answered the door. "Again? What now?"

"It's important, Tessa. I have to talk to you right now. Can I come in?" She shrugged and led him to the living room where Stacy was still sitting on the couch.

"Look. I have to trust you two because I need your help. Tessa, I have some more questions." Then I gave them the news that Lori had been kidnapped. While I talked, I watched their faces closely. Stacy was shocked. Tessa sat stone-faced.

I leaned into her space. "Tessa, these are the same people who killed your husband. I'm sure of it. Will you help me? Will you help Lori? Whatever your reason for hating Lori, she doesn't deserve this. Will you help us?"

Tessa Larson stared at me for a long moment, then nodded slowly.

"All right. Stacy, call the sheriff and get him over here. Don't tell him why. And you have to talk to him directly. Don't leave a message. Understand?"

Stacy nodded wordlessly and went to the phone. I listened. Arnason was in his office, came on the line immediately and I began to hope we might be all right.

Five minutes later he rang the bell. "Marston, what're you doing here?" I just shrugged. I had decided to tell him Lori was kidnapped after Stacy told him she'd witnessed Larson's murder.

I turned to the two women. "Tell us what you do know, what you believe. Anything, however insignificant, might help," I urged.

"Help? Help what?" Arnason frowned. He stood in the middle of the room, a dominant figure, waiting for someone to explain why Stacy had called him.

"I never believed Ron died in that so-called accident," said Tessa. "After they found him and nothing much seemed to be done to figure out how he died, I decided to try to find out on my own." Arnason frowned and opened his mouth to protest, but Tessa waved him to be quiet.

"I started visiting Marge at Martin's Implement. I was always especially nice to Dick Borken. And I talked to Johnny Houck at the bank, of course."

"Did Houck ever say anything odd to you?" I asked.

Tessa shook her head. "No, but a couple of months ago I was in his office about some insurance papers and he got a telephone call. I remember because he was upset. We weren't supposed to be disturbed, but he took the call. He swiveled around and looked out the window while he talked. I could tell the call made him mad."

"Could you hear what it was about?" Brad asked, leaning forward.

"No, but he said something like, 'another one? No, not now. We'll deal with it this summer once and for all.' Then he hung up. Slammed the phone down, really."

I looked across at Brad and he shrugged. He was paying attention, but I figured he was still wondering why Stacy had asked him to come over. However he had the good lawman's instinct to remain quiet and listen.

"One day, sort of out of the blue, Elaine called me and asked if I wanted to go with her to Josh Martin's. He'd had a pool installed in his back yard. It was a pretty big party and a lot of our friends were there. There was plenty of beer and food and things got pretty loud. After a couple of hours, Elaine took me aside and practically told me things could be a lot easier for me if I was kind of accommodating to certain people."

"What did you think that meant? Why would she even say that to you?" I thought I knew the answer but I wanted Tessa to say it out loud.

She looked at me. "Well. It's kind of...rotten, actually. She said I was still young and attractive and the men sometimes had meetings where they wanted women around, women who could keep their mouths shut. That's what she said, but I got the idea there was more to it. You see, it wasn't long after Ron died that a few of the men in town started coming to see me, or stopping me in the street to chat. Al Steiger even tried to tell me that Ron had been fooling around. He hinted that a couple of times when Ron had gone to Minneapolis, he'd looked up Lori, and they'd been together." She glanced at me to see my reaction. There wasn't one. I knew it was unlikely and would have been before I met Lori.

My escalating worry for Lori was making it hard for me to focus on anything else. I knew we had to lay out everything for Brad. I wanted Brad to let me make the exchange without interference. I wanted the sheriff for backup, but I was going to make the exchange no matter what. That I had nothing of value to exchange was irrelevant at the moment.

"Anyway," Tessa continued, "he finally said it straight out, said it must be tough for a young widow who was used to getting it regularly. And besides, Ron wasn't...wasn't faithful. I got really mad. I threw him out, said if he was the last man on earth...." Tears ran down her cheeks. Stacy leaned over and took her hand. Brad looked uncomfortable.

Tessa took a long breath and mopped her eyes. "I threw him out of the house, but it festered, you know? I'd get mad and couldn't think straight at times. Sometimes I believed it and sometimes I didn't. Then when Lori came to the reunion, I got mad all over. You know."

I knelt down in front of her and took her other hand. "Tessa, Lori and I have a really good relationship. If she'd been seeing Ron, I know she would have said something to me before we came out to the reunion. I don't believe for a second she ever had an affair with your husband."

The tears came faster and Tessa nodded again. "I realized that after you guys came back here," she whispered. "It's partly why I feel so rotten now." She sniffled and dragged her hands away to pick up another white tissue and blot her eyes.

I stood up and blew out my breath. The room seemed to be closing in. "Stacy, tell Brad about the day Ron Larson was murdered."

Brad started and opened his mouth to say something, but I held up a hand to stop him. After Stacy related her story, Brad shook his head and sank into an empty chair.

"Jesus!" he said. He scrubbed his face with one big hand. "I think it's time to make some arrests. It isn't air tight, but it's close enough, put with other information I have." He took her through the story again briefly while Tessa and I listened. I didn't hear anything new that might help me get Lori back safely.

"I know Stacy is telling the truth," I said. "I've seen the boxes. They're still there, rotting under a pile of straw in Coleson's barn." I explained how we had stumbled on the hidden barn and found the stack of three transfer boxes.

Brad was up and going for the telephone when I said, "Wait, Brad, there's more." After he sat down again I explained about the phone call offering to exchange Lori for the files. Arnason sat quietly enough through my terse recital with watchful eyes. His growing anger seemed to fill the room. He was angry at me and angry about Lori.

"Tessa, Jack and I have to talk. Privately," he said when I'd finished.

"Use the study." She indicated an archway on one side of the living room.

In the small plain study Brad sat down at the desk while I paced and argued. Pleaded.

Finally, "All right, Jack. I'll let you play this out. It goes against all my training, but I'm going to be right there, hiding in the bushes to nail those bastards after you get Lori out of their control."

"Listen to me Brad. Sheriff. I'll do what I have to do, regardless. They've told me I have to bring the files to the barn for an exchange. If we cooperate, everybody has a better chance of getting what they want. But I don't want your deputies anywhere close when I meet those people."

He nodded. "Well ramming around and trying to arrest everybody who may be involved won't help now. We have to out-think them. Knowing that Miller is probably their link, I'll get word to my other deputies by phone and in person. We'll stay well away from Coleson's and from you. Everything will look normal. I want you to have a radio. Once you're in the barn and things look okay, you can signal me. By then we'll control the roads around the place and after you separate Lori from the pukes who have her, another signal from you and we'll move in."

"Just promise me you won't make any moves until we get clear and I signal you."

"Agreed."

I went back to the women in the living room. Brad picked up the telephone to dial his office.

29

In the living room Tessa made me take a cup of coffee I really didn't want. For the most part we were silent, hearing the rumble of the sheriff's voice in the next room, thinking our own private thoughts. It all seemed so placid, so ordinary. So quiet. I wanted to throw something. To break something. Lori was out there somewhere, imprisoned, fearing for her life and there seemed so little I could do.

I tried to focus on the files. Something was missing. I could sense it.

Suddenly Stacy snapped her head up and looked at me. "Jack, didn't you say there were three boxes? That's wrong, I'm sure of it. El and I piled up four of them in two stacks. I'm positive of that, even if it was five years ago."

I shook my head. "What we found was a single stack of three banker's transfer cases. They were under an old rug against one wall, covered with straw."

"Which means," Brad said, walking back into the living room, "somebody else found them during the intervening time and took one box away. Somebody who figured out what they were. Elroy?"

"No!" I said, jumping up. "Bring the files. That's what the man said on the phone. Bring the files. When he said that I now realize he wasn't talking about the files in the barn. He obviously thinks I have some other damn files. But why? The fourth box?"

"Lori told them?" Brad asked.

The two women watched me in silence.

I shook my head. "I don't think so. I think you've hit it. Someone else found them. Probably a long time ago. Whoever it is has been sending them, or copies, to Houck or Borken. A few at a time. Probably demanding money. Bleeding them bit by bit. I'll bet that's the meaning of that phone call you heard at the bank, Tessa."

"Blackmail?" Tessa said frowning.

"Exactly. I know it's a little shaky, but listen. Several people have made a point of commenting on my role in the Navy as an investigator. Borken even wanted to know what I'd found to investigate in Riverview. Why the interest? Something to hide? Lori was beginning to think there might be something wrong with the settlement of her parent's estate. But that's not it at all. Whoever is behind the blackmail scheme, whoever actually found and took some of the files, Houck and Borken must think now that it was Lori, and I'm helping her with the blackmail."

"You think Houck believes Lori brought you out here to snoop around for more blackmail evidence? Pretty far-fetched." Brad looked doubtful.

"Not *that* far-fetched," said Tessa. "If those guys are in this like you think they are and they killed Ron over some missing files, blackmail by one of their little group, or anybody else could make them all paranoid."

The doorbell chimed and a moment later Deputy Pete Olson walked into the room. For a heart-clutching moment I thought he'd come to say they'd found Lori's body.

"I got here as quick as I could, Sheriff," he said.

"I figured we'll need a man here to keep an eye out and relay calls," Brad said.

What he didn't say, I suddenly realized, was that he also had a duty to protect the citizens of Riverview who might be at risk if the exchange went wrong or the kidnappers found out something–anything– to upset their situation. Stacy and Tessa Larson might be in danger. I also knew Arnason didn't want to lose a chance to end the collusion between Borken and Houck and maybe nail Ron Larson's murderer.

I decided right then that I didn't give a rat's ass if they caught the people responsible for Larson's murder. Or discovered for sure why he'd been killed. I was focusing on Lori. For the rest, whatever happened, happened.

I didn't voice my thoughts.

What I said was, "Sheriff, we'd better get going."

Brad stood up. He looked around the room and nodded as if he'd made a decision. "You two," pointing at the women, "are vulnerable. Pete will stay here with you. Nobody goes out, nobody makes any phone calls. If the phone rings, Pete answers. Figure out a reason why you are here, Pete. And the door. Make any kind of excuse. But don't let anybody in. Pete, check for extensions on the phone and unplug them."

Tessa and Stacy erupted in protests, but Arnason ignored the uproar. He just smiled slightly and waved his hands at them. "It's for your own protection, girls. And it probably won't be for more'n a coupla hours anyway. C'mon, Jack." I appreciated his optimism. I clung to it as we went out the door.

Beside the sheriff's squad we paused "We have to be optimistic. Helps keep everybody calmed down," he said. "Me included. You have some idea what we're up against. I don't think those two women are involved, but we have to be careful. One of them could make a comment to the wrong person and give things away." He looked at me keenly. "You okay, Jack?"

"No," I snapped.

"I'll give you my hand-held radio so you can monitor our traffic. The scuzzballs who took Lori will see our cars around, but it'll look like regular patrols so that won't be suspicious."

"All right. But if Miller is involved he'll hear the radio call."

He reached into his car and handed me a portable radio with a short flexible black antenna. "I thought of that too. Use Pete's sign. He's in car eleven today, so when you're ready for us to move in at the barn, press this button and say 'Dispatch, this is eleven. I'm ten-ten at Junction.' Repeat it just once."

"All right, but remember, no move to arrest anybody until Lori gets out. I'm going to make them release Lori before I tell them where the files are. Then I'll tell 'em and we'll run out of there."

"Suppose they refuse to let you go?"

I considered that. "Their arrogance will help. After all, they've been getting away with their schemes for a long time, even though people are suspicious. If they decide to force me to take them to the files, you use your best judgment and take 'em down when it seems right."

"Jack, I just had another idea. I want you to take my car and I'll take yours. This is my personal vehicle, but it's equipped. Use the police radio if you need to until you have to go into the barn. I'll take your car back to the motel and catch a ride to the station. If anybody is watching your rental, they'll be there until after dark. By the time somebody realizes you're not using it, it'll be too late."

I nodded. It made sense unless they were constantly being watched by relays of men. I didn't think we were dealing with a big gang. Brad drove the two blocks to the church where I'd left the Escort and handed me the keys.

"I'll get around to as many of my deputies as I can and give them the word in person or by telephone. I'm gonna contact the State Patrol for some backup. Any of my deputies I miss, I'll call in by radio at the last minute after I get your signal. Oh, one more thing. Try to hide that radio on yourself or in the barn where you can reach it easily. If the situation goes south, just press the send button rapidly several times. It'll make a clicking sound that will tell me to come runnin'."

I nodded again. I got into his car. Brad got out and scanned the street both ways. He leaned down at the window. Arnason looked big, serious and competent.

"One more thing," I said. "Can I borrow a gun?"

For a long moment we stared at each other.

"I don't carry an extra piece and my shotgun won't help." Then he walked away.

30

Arnason's vehicle was a big late-model Crown Victoria. It had a police radio mounted under the dash. There was no light bar so I assumed there was a bubble to stick on the roof. Or maybe there were lights behind the grille. I didn't waste time looking for additional switches. I didn't think I'd need any of that. I switched off the portable radio the sheriff had handed me to save the battery. I adjusted the seat position and fiddled with the mirrors. After I got the car started it took a minute or two of tinkering to adjust the police radio to a low mutter. I realized I was fidgeting, reluctant to commit myself to the plan by driving away. So much could go wrong.

When I put it in gear and pressed the accelerator I discovered there'd been some work done on the mill under the hood. The car had an abundance of pickup. I burned a little rubber at the start. I stopped and tried it again. Better.

I still had plenty of time to get to the barn where the files were stored, where I'd secure Lori's freedom. I refused to think about the consequences if things went bad. If they went really bad, I knew I was going to kill someone. I wondered who'd be at the barn. If Houck and the others were being blackmailed and were suspicious of each other, maybe they'd all show up. That was both good and bad. I had an impression that there was not a lot of love between the operators of the financial game. There could be conflict that would send a tense situation quickly south. On the other hand, more players present provided distractions that could be manipulated.

The sun was rapidly running down the western sky, but some hours of daylight remained. I fidgeted some more and decided I couldn't wait until sunset. After dark, on unfamiliar roads, I could get lost and miss the place. I wanted to reconnoiter the barn in daylight. I drove around town, avoiding the main street and headed east along the road to the dump. It was a longer way, but one I remembered better and if anyone recognized Brad's unmarked car, it wouldn't be seen heading directly toward the Coleson place. Doing something, even just driving was better than sitting still. As I drove I thought about Lori. I ran a stop sign. Great. Fortunately no patrol car was in sight. Having Deputy Miller show up just then to issue a ticket would not be cool. Occasionally the radio muttered with routine police traffic, but I heard nothing of any significance. The jargon and police codes obscured the real meanings of some of the messages.

After I got to the dump road, I pulled over and rummaged in the glove box. There was a county map, well used, with cryptic notes in the margins, along with lint and some candy wrappers. Nothing remotely useful. I continued east for several miles, crossing roads and a paved highway or two, thinking hard about the people involved. Was I right about the blackmail? Who was doing it? Eventually I gave up, abandoning that line of thought. I realized I didn't have enough to go on. So I thought some more about Lori, lovely, bright, auburn-haired Lori.

"Shit!" I knew I was making myself crazy when what I needed was to be calm; calm, focused, and in control. Nothing helped. I realized that if this went wrong and Lori was badly hurt—my mind refused to consider a worse possibility—I didn't know how I'd live with such an outcome. Even in the air-conditioned car I was sweating.

I focused on my surroundings and discovered I was several miles east and north of Riverview. I checked my watch again. It was only seven and my stomach reminded me I'd missed both lunch and supper. I turned right on the pavement and headed south, in the general direction of where I was pretty sure I'd cross the road to the Coleson place. A mile along, I came to an intersection with another paved county highway. There was an abandoned filling station on the corner and beside it a low dark bar that advertised sandwiches. The neon sign over the door glowed that the place was open.

I pulled to a stop on the gravel and checked the county map. The place was marked with a tiny circle in ink on the map. I went inside.

"Don't get many strangers out here. What can I get you?"

The shaggy man in long hair, sandy beard, and beer gut leaned toward me, elbows on the bar. We were the only ones in the place.

"Ham sandwich?"

The bartender nodded and slid a scratched glass of water across the bar toward me. He disappeared into the back room and I heard him moving things around.

"You want a beer or coffee with it?" His light tenor voice floated over the partition.

"Coffee, please."

A moment later the man reappeared with a thick sandwich of ham and mayonnaise and limp lettuce on two slices of soft white bread.

I took a long slug of hot coffee. It tasted freshly made. In spite of the doughy bread and lack of appetite, I managed to down the sandwich and had a coffee refill. The illuminated clock on the wall behind the plain wood bar told me it was time to get on with it. The bartender and I exchanged perfunctory smiles as I paid and I went out. I realized, as the door swung shut behind me that, unlike JUNC-TION, this place offered up no odor of stale beer.

I drove Arnason's car south again, past fields, past farm entrances, and past the road to Riverview's dump. I took deep lung-filling breaths, trying to slow my heart rate. I made a right turn and headed west, back along the narrow section road toward the corner where Larson's truck and Larson's body had been discovered. A mile and a half away I noticed a dull silvery flash in the brush on my right. Was that a parked car? I almost took my foot off the accelerator, but at the last second controlled the impulse. I gave the location only a single brief glance. I didn't see any place where a car could have driven in from the road I was driving on.

Almost immediately the radio came to life. It was clear and undistorted. The sender must have been close.

"Time check, XYZed, nineteen-fifty-seven." I didn't hear any response. Police watcher or someone else? I couldn't decide. I decided it didn't matter.

Just over a small rise I recalled from the time Lori and I had driven this track, there was a break in the fence line on my left. I figured I was about a mile from the old barn, so I pulled off through the shallow ditch and forced the car deep into scrubby bushes and tall grass growing thickly along the sides of the road. I hoped I wasn't scratching Arnason's car, but I couldn't afford to have the wrong people find the vehicle and get spooked. Or worse. In the rear-view mirror I watched brush and tree branches slap back across my path until the road disappeared. I drove another ten yards into the tangled grove, just to be sure.

I took the flashlight from a bracket beside the steering wheel and jammed the portable radio in my back pocket. I locked the car. On impulse, I opened the trunk. There were brackets for a shotgun, but they were empty. When I closed the trunk my eyes caught Brad's license plate. 244-XYZ, it read.

Walking back to the road, I could see the grass already springing back into place. It would take an expert and careful eye to find where I'd driven off the road. I turned and jogged down the road at a distance-eating pace. I was pretty sure I could run to the barn without much effort in about fifteen minutes. I kept to the edge of the road and twice had to slip down into the ditch and lie prone in long, sweet-smelling grass while a car drove slowly past. No bugs. Both vehicles were heading the same direction I was going. There was no traffic from the other direction.

As I jogged along, I wondered where Arnason was. I wondered what the bullies and the manipulators were doing, where they had Lori. I forced myself not to wonder about the outcome of my mad plan. I avoided wondering about other parts of this business, parts much closer to my heart. Focus on your first objective, I told myself, to get Lori safely out of harm's way.

When I reached the vicinity of the barn, I stopped to let my breathing slow to near normal. Except in the far western sky, golden twilight was falling on the land. In the shelter belt it was gloomy. I avoided looking directly at the sky so my night vision would improve. As quietly as possible I walked all around the barn. As I checked out the grove of trees and bushes, I was reminded that it would take Arnason several minutes after he began to move in, to get his men in place to arrest whoever came after me to this lonesome place. Now there were bugs. Twilight seemed to bring out all of them and there was almost no pause to the sound as I slipped along. There were mosquitoes and a whole chorus of chirping, tweeting, and scratching.

I completed my cautious circle of the barn. Unless someone was in there who'd walked in as I had, I was alone. My sense of being alone was almost overpowering. Lori's warm voice and smiling face drifted through my mind. I took two deep breaths, turned, and went directly to the barn door.

After I slipped inside the collapsed door, I checked out the ground floor, still trying to be as quiet as possible. It took me several minutes but I satisfied myself it was empty except for the pile of straw, the three boxes of rotting files, some small silent insects, and me. A few small critters, judging by the slithering sounds, scuttled here and there at the outside edges of the structure. The chorus stayed outdoors. The dusty smell of dry mold from the straw drifted by. I smothered a sneeze. The place felt old, deserted, undisturbed. It got darker in the barn as the sunlight faded so I used the flashlight. I carefully covered most of the lens with my fingers and located the ladder to the loft.

This time, with the unseen rustlings of creatures much closer in the hay all around, the atmosphere in the loft was different from the first time I'd been there. Even the smell of the hay had a different texture. I felt a sense of rot, of dangerous decay. My lips were dry and I couldn't seem to draw a full breath. My palms were wet, the barrel of the flashlight slippery in my hand.

It was difficult to get all around the perimeter of the barn in the deep hay of the loft. The slippery tangled stalks clung to my legs. Timothy, Lori had called it. Timothy who? I heard her voice in my head. Lighter than clover, she'd said. Easier to handle.

I looked out through a crack in the barn wall. There were no lights anywhere except in the sky. I stationed myself at a gap in the planking on the north side, so I could observe the intersection where Stacy said she and Elroy had seen Larson killed.

I stood there a long time, staring into the darkening landscape. Behind me creatures in the barn stirred and fussed. Out there all was silent. I sank slowly to my knees and then squatted down.

My watch glowed nine-thirty. Half an hour to go. A car or small truck with no lights showing rolled to a quiet stop out at the intersection. Too early, unless the opposition was checking things out ahead of time. After a brief pause, it drove slowly out of earshot. Several minutes later I heard gravel crunching. Somewhere in the darkness an engine died. The engine had been so quiet I hadn't really heard it until the sound stopped. '*Who comes so fast in silence of the night?*' I wondered.

I lowered my head into the hay and tucked myself around the radio. With my shirt over my head and the radio, I thumbed the transmit button and in as quiet a voice as I could manage I said distinctly, "This is car eleven. Dispatch, I'm ten-ten at Junction. Car eleven is ten-ten at Junction. Out." I jammed the speaker of the radio against my ear to muffle the sound.

For a moment there was silence. Had I been heard? Was the radio working? Then somebody called Pete by name to ask if he was going be there a while. That was the only response. I hoped Arnason had heard the radio call. Slowly I rose to my knees, still peering out at the intersection I could no longer see. My fingers itched for a weapon, preferably one with bullets. My sense of being alone disappeared. Moments later came the soft, cautious, sound of somebody walking across the floor of the barn below me. I shut off the radio and jammed it in my pants pocket and looked at my watch once more. It read nine-forty. With great care I rose to my feet and crept toward the ladder. I could make out a faint glow from the hole in the floor where the ladder was. Whoever was down there had lit a lantern of some kind. I took a slow step toward the ladder.

There was a loud crack and the floor disappeared beneath my feet.

I landed sprawled on the straw of the ground floor of the barn while pieces of rotting planks, loose hay, and a small section of a beam fell around me. Momentarily stunned, my unfocused eyes picked out two things. A gas lantern had been hung from a peg at one side of the barn. Its hard light made sharp shadows in the corners of the room. That was one thing.

The other was Georgina Maxwell, who stood staring down at me. She held a small pistol pointed directly at my chest.

31

"Can you stand up?"

"I think so." The thick coating of straw and hay had cushioned my short fall. Looking up at Gorgina, I gingerly wiggled my legs and arms. I figured there'd be some serious aches later on, but everything worked at the moment. "What are you doing here?"

"Surprised are we? I guess you didn't figure me out after all, did you?" She spoke in a flat monotone. The gun in her hand didn't waver.

"You don't have to keep pointing that thing at me." I pulled my feet under my bruised rear end and slowly stood up. Georgina stepped back a pace to stay well out of reach. I brushed bits of hay off my head.

"Don't I? Now tell me what's going on."

"I didn't figure you were involved in kidnapping Lori." I peered around at the floor. Where was the radio? It had apparently fallen out of my pocket when I crashed through the floor. If she saw it, she'd realize something was up.

"Kidnapped? Lori? Of course not. What in hell is going on here?"

I looked at her in the harsh light of the lantern and considered what to tell her. Why was she here? Was she a silent partner? We stared at each other.

"C'mon, Marston. You must know something, or we wouldn't be here in this damn barn."

"I think your blackmail scheme has finally gotten out of hand, Georgina." Her eyes widened, just a little, but her gaze never wavered.

"I've got nothing to do with any blackmail. Show me some proof of that."

"You're the one who found the files Ron Larson hid here five years ago. I think you've been blackmailing certain people in town for quite a while with the documents you found."

"You figured that out, did you?" she demanded softly. "Damn!" She snorted. "You'll never prove it, even if the records turn up. I've been very careful. Assuming I've been doing what you say, who's going to complain?" She paused and apparently decided whatever she said there was little I could do without hard evidence. "I suspected those bozos for a long time. You might not know it, but I've been dealing with those guys most of my life. It wasn't exactly a secret around town that Borken and Houck had some deals together. And that maybe some of those deals weren't exactly on the up and up. I started thinking about how Martin might be involved about the same time Dick Borken and I started up."

I had a sudden recollection of Georgina Maxwell, shirt undone, straw in her hair, emerging from a stall in Kronk's horse barn. It must have been Borken she was with Saturday morning.

Georgina watched me closely. "Oh, I see. You didn't know about that, either. You aren't such a hot shot investigator, are you?"

"I'm a student counselor, not an investigator," I said flatly. I watched Georgina and listened for approaching vehicles.

"I began to wonder why Larson had been out here in the first place. It's not exactly the direct road to the dump." She coughed once from the dust in the air. "Eventually I decided to check out this barn.

"By the time I discovered the files, it was cold and there was snow so I was leaving tracks. After I found Ron's files, I decided to take a chance and leave them until the next spring, until the snow melted. And after it snowed again and covered up my tracks around this place, I figured the secret was safe."

"Unless somebody else figured it out or just chanced on the files."

She shrugged. "So I took a little risk. I wasn't sure what I had anyway. The next spring I came back and made a thorough examination. I went through the boxes and took a few records."

"Why didn't you get rid of the rest?"

She shrugged. "I wasn't sure about a lot of it. Didn't see how I could use the information. Then I would've had the same problem Ron had. How to keep all that stuff hidden. So I just left the other boxes here. I figured if anybody found them that'd be okay. There was nothing in 'em to tie anything to me. I made sure of that. 'Course I wasn't part of their land scams anyway."

"What about Borken?" I asked, watching her warily.

"What about him?"

"How involved in your blackmail is he?"

"Not at all, except he's hooked up with Johnny Houck and Tomlinson. So he's paying me something on the side, right along with those others." She smiled slightly. "He doesn't know it, of course. Doesn't know I found this barn and Ron's stash of records."

"I still don't understand why you're here now."

She shrugged, but her gun hand was unwavering. "I overheard Houck and Eddie Tomlinson talking at the law offices about this little meeting. They've gotten careless over the years. I decided to get here earlier and hide in the loft. Figured it might have something to do with those files. I was gonna hide and listen in."

There was a sudden creaking of rusty hinges and another door in the opposite wall swung open. Georgina spun toward the noise and then stopped dead still. Her hand with the little pistol was half-way between me and the door.

The first thing through the door was the business end of a double-barreled shotgun. I recognized the man holding the shotgun when he stepped into the light. It was Darrell Olson, the brute mechanic from Tedvedt's where the Miata was being repaired. The twin holes of the barrels looked enormous.

Olson stepped carefully inside, swinging the weapon slightly to cover both Georgina and me. I could see Olson's finger, inside the trigger guard, caressing the triggers. I wondered what kind of shells he'd loaded, but it didn't matter. At this distance, a single load of bird shot would do for both of us. Georgina stood there, half turned, facing toward the door. The pistol in her hand was now resting against her leg in the fold of her skirt. I wondered if the mechanic had seen it. She took a careful step backward, closer to the lantern.

"Stand still lady," he said. "Both of you." I wasn't moving. There was no cover, nowhere to run. What was worse was the man didn't sound the least bit nervous. He handled the weapon with a definite familiarity.

He stepped slowly to one side and Dick Borken and Ed Tomlinson walked into the light.

"What the hell?" Borken said, startled. "Georgina? What are you doing here?"

She raised her chin. "That's my question. What does Lori have to do with this?" She slid her right foot, the one toward me, back a little, keeping the gun hidden.

"Georgina?" Borken said again. He started toward her.

"Careful!" barked the man with the shotgun. Borken stopped and the man drifted another step to his left so he still had a clear shot at Georgina and me.

"We're here to talk, Marston." Tomlinson's voice was calm, assured sounding. "To deal. But this complicates things a little." He didn't look at her, but I could tell Georgina's presence was a surprise to him.

"Where's Lori?" My voice sounded gravelly. "Is she all right?"

"She's here. And she hasn't been harmed. Yet. Where are the files?"

"First I want to see her." I forced my voice to be matter-of-fact and as hard as I could make it. Commanding. Projected from my diaphragm, the way I'd learned to do back in the dim days when I was a neophyte actor in college.

"She's right here, Marston," came a new voice from the dark. Three more figures emerged into the light. Banker Houck had Lori by one wrist. Behind Lori, one arm clenched across her upper chest from his position, was a man I had never seen before. Lori's eyes were wide, her hair mussed and there was a dark bruise on her left cheekbone. Her bare arms were stark in the hissing lantern light. She parted her lips, but didn't say anything. She and I stared at each other. She acted calm, but I could tell she was frightened. So was I.

Houck held up one hand, palm out. "She's a bit of a wildcat, our Lori. Anse here had to smack her once when he picked her up at the bank, but she'll recover. If we can do business."

I didn't know who Anse was, but if things worked out, he and I were going to meet again.

"Here's how it goes," I said. "The deal is, you let Lori walk out of here right now, then I'll tell you where the files are."

Houck considered this. He glanced at Tomlinson. Lori watched me.

I took a breath to steady my thudding pulse and said, "Look, I'm not sure what's going on in this town. But what I think is a bank employee named Ron Larson stole some files, probably from the bank vault. Later those files surfaced and are apparently being used to blackmail some of you. Now obviously, I don't know any of this, and I haven't had time to go through the files. I've just put a few of the pieces together."

"You say you can't prove anything?"

"Right. I'm telling you I'll give you the files I stumbled across when you let us walk out of here. We'll go back to Minneapolis and you can go back to whatever it is you are doing." It sounded lame to me, but maybe they'd buy it. People who have to resort to killing to cover up their mistakes usually aren't the brightest people in the world. The problem was they'd already killed at least one person. It's been said that it gets easier with repetition.

"How do you want to work it?"

"Lori leaves first. After she's gone I'll tell you where the files are. Then you let me go. Lori's my protection that you'll keep your word."

"You look at those files?" Houck shifted from one foot to the other.

"No." I shook my head. Here was the weakest point. "Only some of the labels. Haven't had the time."

Houck appeared to be considering my offer. Then he looked at the shotgun bearer. Something passed between them that I couldn't interpret and I sure as hell didn't like.

"If you kill the three of us you'll never find those files," I said. I was struggling to maintain my calm. The radio was gone and I had no way to signal the sheriff waiting out there in the dark somewhere. I wanted to leap at Houck or the gunman and strangle the life out of them. "Once you have the files, no one will be able to prove anything."

I was getting a dark feeling that things were slipping out of control. The way Houck avoided looking at Dick Borken made me suspect they might kill Borken too.

Georgina's unexpected presence had destabilized the whole scenario. I looked again at Lori who kept switching her gaze from Georgina to me and back.

"We had a nice little deal going," Houck complained. "I tipped Borken and he made loans to the farmers after I turned 'em down. Then he foreclosed and sold the loan collateral. Sometimes we leased land back to a farmer. We all shared the profits. Nice tidy little income supplements." He looked at Georgina. "Had to replace the skim from the gambling after Georgina shut us down, you see."

"Nuts," Georgina muttered. "You've been running that scam a lot longer than that."

He was talking too much, telling us things they would never want repeated outside the old barn, records or not. Desperately I began to calculate how to reach the man holding Lori. I couldn't count on Arnason to save us now.

Houck went on. "Ron found out somehow and collected the records we kept to be sure we didn't screw up the bank's books and tip the examiners." Houck shrugged and spread his hands.

He was too relaxed by half.

"But somebody else found the records and started blackmailing us. Not very much, not too often. Who was it?" He looked slowly around. "For a while I thought it might be one of my partners." He shrugged again. "Sorry, I can't help what I was thinking. I guess that's why you're here." His gaze fastened on Georgina. Her face was a frozen mask. "Got a little greedy, did you? The club and the motel weren't enough? Or did your lover, Dick there, put you up to it?"

"Wait a minute, John," roared Borken, twisting toward Houck. "It wasn't my—" Suddenly everything fell apart. Borken's sudden move pulled everyone's attention to him. Georgina wheeled, crouched, and with two quick shots blasted apart the lantern, plunging the barn into stygian darkness. Somebody shouted an inarticulate warning.

The shotgun roared as I dropped to the floor. The muzzle flash was intense white. I heard thumping, a high scream and a grunt of pain. The other barrel discharged in a fiery shower of sparks. Outside a bullhorn crackled, a car horn blasted and lights came on, sending hard shafts of bright light stabbing through crevices in the walls. Dust from powdered straw and muzzle smoke billowed up in the beams. Shouts rose inside and outside the barn. I crawled across the floor toward where I'd last seen Lori. Two more shotgun blasts, those from outside, roared in my ears. There was the sharp crack of a heavy pistol.

Instantly there came a shriek of pain from near the door where I'd last seen Lori and a sigh of pain from close by. Where in God's name was she? More shouts. Hinges protested and the fragile walls trembled as bodies slammed about. I glimpsed figures struggling in and out of the beams of light, bodies falling through holes ripped in the siding. Vehicles roared closer. Sirens howled and mixed with the shouts.

My outstretched hand encountered a shoulder, then slid down along a limp arm. I felt the texture of a long-sleeved shirt and smelled blood. Georgina, it had to be Georgina. Her hands were empty. I didn't waste time searching for her pistol. In a low crouch I ran across the barn at an angle and along the wall toward where Lori had been standing. I stumbled over someone sprawled on the floor, discovered it wasn't Lori and kept going.

Things were getting calmer as deputies swarmed around, took control, smashed down the last resistance.

"Jack? Jack? Where are you?" Lori's cry came from close by, but outside the barn. A wave of relief washed over me. My knees trembled and I leaned against the barn wall, felt the timber tremble. Thank God! She was all right.

A shape rose before me. A man got to his knees and then to his feet. Beams from big flashlights were swinging around the barn and one flashed across his face. I recognized the man who had been holding Lori. Anse, his name was.

Without conscious thought, I reared up and lunged at the other man. He fell back and his elbow caught me high on the forehead. I swung one mad, roundhouse punch that caught Anse square in the belly, doubling him over. A satisfying jolt ran though my arm. The man fell away into the darkness. I went after him. More shouts, then forty arms and bodies collapsed over me and smothered my attempts to reach him.

"Hey, easy. Take it easy, Marston," a voice huffed in my ear. "We're the good guys." It was Brad Arnason, wrapping his arms around my body and wrestling me to the floor. He probably saved me from hurting myself.

More lights were brought and Lori rushed into my arms. We clung together, realizing we were safe and almost unhurt.

* * *

Sheriff Arnason walked slowly across the barn toward us. He'd just covered Georgina Maxwell's body with a tarp from one of the squad cars. "It must have been Darrell Olson who shot her. We found his pistol on the floor near where you said he was standing. With one spent shell." Arnason's lips lifted briefly. "The only other handgun in here was hers. Two shots fired."

"Yeah," I said. "She saved my life. Our lives. Shot out the lantern."

"I figure his shot was just happenstance. He was on his knees after Lori kicked him in the–"

"In the balls," Lori finished grimly. "Bastard kept putting his dirty hands on me."

"Softened him up, did you?" I squeezed her hand and she squeezed back. She was still trembling, or it might have been me.

"Anson is still recovering from that fist he took to the belly," commented Brad.

"How'd you happen to be so close when things fell apart?" I asked him.

"I told you earlier I didn't like the odds. After Houck and the others arrived, I moved my men up close right away. I wanted to be able to intervene fast if anything went wrong. I figured that even if we didn't get them all, we had a responsibility to try to protect you two. Hell, it's so dark we weren't even sure who was in here with you. Nobody saw Georgina arrive. I haven't seen her car." He looked around at the activity of his deputies. "We borrowed a few people from over the border."

"Borken and Houck and the others are on the way to jail. Borken's already talking non-stop. Deputy's got a little tape machine running on the seat beside him." He smiled mirthlessly. "Isn't legal, but we'll get the story, I figure. I've had a quick look at some of the files. Thing is, none of that stuff in those boxes you found appears to be worth much. 'Course it'll take some time for a thorough look."

"I expect you'll find other more meaningful records from those boxes somewhere at Georgina's," I said. "She must have been sending those files, a few at a time, to Houck and Martin. She probably made copies."

"You can never trust a thief," murmured Lori sadly. "But it's too high a price to pay. Way too high."

"Marston, I'll have one of the deputies drive you two to your motel. We'll have to sort all this out tomorrow."

I gave Arnason his keys and told him where to find his car. Lori and I sat in the back of the squad and held each other all the way back to Riverview.

32

I don't know what woke me. Maybe it was Lori sitting up in bed. When I raised my sleep-blurred eyes, I could see her dark form against the faint gray of the sky. The bedside clock glowed at me. Three-thirty it blinked.

I put out a hand to touch her silken hip. "Honey?"

She shifted slightly, away from my touch. Hunched over a little, then stretched out again. "Shh. I'm all right. Go to sleep."

Unwillingly, I did.

* * *

"Ow! Ohh, God!" I struggled to sit up in bed. "I seemed to have tortured some muscles my body forgot it had."

Lori, already up and showered, stood toweling her hair. Ugly bruises were developing on both her arms and the yellowish swelling on her cheekbone hadn't diminished at all, that I could see.

She glanced my way and said, "C'mon, tiger. Let's get going. I'd like to finish giving statements to Brad as soon as we can and get on the road. Even if we have to come back later for trials or something."

"Ah, the recovery ability of youth," Lori is a couple years younger than me. "'Tis a wonder to behold," I declaimed in my best theatrical tones. I hobbled into the shower where hot water soothed the abused parts of my body. When I returned to the bedroom, I was starting to feel closer to my real age. Lori was dressed and stood staring out the window. Her stillness unsettled me. "Hey," I said, crossing to her. I put my hands on her shoulders and placed a gentle kiss on the back of her neck. "You okay? Last night…"

Deep sigh. One hand raised to touch mine. "Yes, sort of. Mostly. Every so often it all rushes back. Yesterday, last night. A delayed reaction."

I pressed her shoulders. I could only begin to imagine what it must have been like. "Do you want to talk about it?"

Lori hadn't said much about her abduction and I hadn't pushed her. I knew she'd tell me when she was ready.

"I recognize the symptoms. I've read about them in my psych books and I've seen them in patients. I've studied this. I'll deal with it. It's not paralyzing the way it is with some. If I have lingering problems I'll have some consultations." She paused.

"But Jack, it was awful, even though they never hurt me physically. Things happened so fast. I had to wait while they admitted Ada at the hospital. I called Houck to tell him I was coming to talk to him about my dad's estate. After I saw the doctor, I hitched a ride to the bank. The receptionist told me Houck said to come back to his office. When I went through the door into a hall leading to his office, Darrell Olson was standing there. I remember thinking he was one of the guys we saw in the field the other night. Suddenly he had a knife pressing my cheek. He held it just under my eye." She shivered and I put my arms around her waist.

"He hauled me down the corridor and out a side door into a car. He kept telling me to keep my eyes closed and when he threw me in the back seat, he slipped a gunny sack over my head. It was dusty and dirty, but loose enough so I could breathe all right. He shoved me down on the floor in the back seat and put his feet on me. Then he tied my hands behind me. Somebody else drove. Anson, I suppose.

"They drove for a long time, sometimes on paved road and sometimes on gravel or dirt." She stopped, cleared her throat. She turned and draped her arms around my shoulders. We stood there close together, silent for a moment.

"We don't have to do this right now."

"No, it's all right. I want to tell you everything I remember."

"Up to you, babe." She sighed and gave me a gentle squeeze, a soft kiss on the side of my head.

"Finally they stopped somewhere out in the country and dragged me into a shack. I tried to get my hands free, but I couldn't, so I just sat there. I did figure a way to rub the sack on my head high enough so I could see more, but I didn't want it to fall off. I really tried to avoid seeing who the other man was.

"So there I was, for hours, until those two came back and hauled me out to Coleson's." She looked out the window again. "You know the rest."

"Do you think you are okay?"

She nodded. "I'm anxious. That's why I woke up. I think it's a natural reaction. Telling you helps, but I'm okay. Really."

I nodded. Lori stirred. "Now I'm hungry. Must be a good sign." She put a hand on my bare chest and gently pushed herself out of my arms.

I finished dressing and we went down to the restaurant. I discovered I was ravenous.

"Jack, are you sure? I mean, eggs, bacon, *and* pancakes is a lot for you."

"Hungry, very hungry, starving even," I mumbled, draining a large glass of orange juice. "Saving damsels in distress is hungry work. Anyway, these last several days of big rural meals must have enlarged my appetite, if not my belly."

It was obvious that word of last night's shootout and arrests of several prominent townsfolk out at Coleson's barn had raced through town. We were recipients of numerous glances, some just curious, a few carrying touches of anger. No one came to our table to talk to us, for which I was thankful.

After a second cup of coffee we decided to drive out to Worckowski's.

"We could just pack up and leave," I offered. "Just give our statements to Brad and drive home. The car must be ready by now, even if the guys at the garage are in the slammer."

"I know I said that. But now I don't want to leave until this is really settled," Lori said. "Here, turn right here."

"I hope we aren't tempting fate with another trip out here."

We returned our rental and sure enough, the Miata was waiting in the sunny garage lot. Lori had an extra ignition key so we didn't have to track down somebody to open the garage. The drive to Worckowski's allowed us to insure there were no lingering problems with the automobile.

"Only the warm prairie sun out there, this time." Lori slid over and rested her head lightly on my shoulder. I dropped my right hand from the steering wheel and gently squeezed her thigh.

"There's the driveway. We won't stay long." Her voice was a low murmur in my ear.

I swung in next to the spot where we'd parked the last time we'd been here. It seemed weeks ago, so much had happened in the interim. The screen door banged and a tall lean figure stepped out. He was cradling a rifle in the crook of his elbow.

"Lori? Anything wrong?"

"No, we came out to see how Ada and Brian are getting along. Where's your dog?"

"Hector? He's inside, with Ada. He never barks at strangers unless it's dark."

Worckowski came down into the yard. He stopped a few feet away and said in a careful, calm voice, "She's inside lying down. You can go say hello, but she's not up for much visitin', I guess. Brian's in his room. Says he still has a bad headache."

I could hear the controlled emotion in his voice. Lori went forward and brushed by him, touching his arm lightly.

"I'll just go in and say hello. Be out in a minute."

Terry turned toward the barn and I went with him a few slow steps until we came up against a board fence attached to the barn. He slid the long gun down until it disappeared beside his leg. Let out a prolonged gusty sigh. I wondered why he was carrying the weapon.

"I dunno, Jack. I never saw it coming. Ada. Didn't realize the pressure she musta felt. Never believed what was happening with Brian, either. She told me things she'd heard. Pleaded with me to talk to Bri and the other boys, but I just brushed it off. Didn't want to hear, I guess. Didn't want to believe Brian was acting like such a fool. Too busy, I said. Damn. You know, Ada hasn't said two words to me since I got to town and picked her and Brian up at the hospital. She just sorta stares at the wall. Before this, Ada and me, we've always been able to talk things out. Not like some."

"I expect that's one reason Lori thinks so highly of you," I said. "Terry, I see you're carrying a gun. It seems a little odd." I stopped and looked at him.

"Yeah, Well." He looked out under the bill of his cap. "The murders and all. Ada's afraid. I don't know what's happening any more in the county. Hell. Why would somebody kill Elroy? And Edith. Marston, do you think somebody has it in for our class?" He shook his head in disbelief. "It's just crazy."

"Maybe those two had something in common."

"But what? I just can't think of anything they ever did that somebody would want to murder them."

We were quiet then, standing together in the warm day, leaning against the fence. Words seemed difficult. We stood there without speaking for many minutes, but I had no sense of time passing. Later I was surprised to discover how long it had been.

The screen door creaked and slammed softly, and we turned toward the sound. Lori stood on the stoop, hand shielding her eyes against the sun.

Terry and I went toward her.

"I think it's going to be all right," she said quietly. "Ada's in better spirits now. Still angry though, Terry…at Brian, and at you. She wants to talk to you."

I could almost feel the tension start to drain out of the man along with another gusty sigh.

"Thank God. Her silence, that's the worst," he muttered and started up the steps. He stopped and looked back at us. "Thanks, you guys. Lori." Worckowski turned and went inside to be with his wife.

We went to the Miata. "No miracles," Lori said. "Ada was ready to go find Terry. I just got to be the messenger. Right place at the right time."

"Lori. Jack. Wait." It was Terry.

We turned and he called us back.

"Ada's going to put coffee on. She'd like you to stay a while. Me too. Can you?" Terry said.

Lori and I looked at each other. "You sure, Terry?" she asked.

He shrugged and turned back to wave us into the kitchen. Inside, Ada turned from the stove and smiled shyly at us. We took seats at the bare kitchen table and I said, "How is Brian?"

"No real damage," said Terry. "The doctor checked him out. No concussion, or only a slight one."

"I couldn't just let you leave, after what you did," said Ada. "I really made a fool of myself in town. I guess it was Terry's reunion on top of everything else set me off. I don't know." She shook her head.

"I remember your daddy had a terrible temper," mused Lori softly. "He broke a finger hitting the barn door one winter when it froze shut." We were silent for a moment. Ada nodded.

The aroma of brewing coffee was strong. It smelled good.

"What'll happen to Houck and the others?" Ada asked then.

"Indictments. Trials," I said. "Houck will lose the bank and Tomlinson will be disbarred. Borken will likely have to sell the store to pay his attorney. Murder trials can be expensive. It'll take a while to sort it all out."

"Are they all going to be charged with murdering Ron Larson?" Ada asked.

"I expect that'll depend on the county attorney and the way the case develops," I replied. "Or a confession by one of them."

Inevitably our conversation turned to the murders of Kronk and Guteman. "I keep wondering what they had in common," I said.

"Yeah, I wondered the same thing," said Terry. "And I keep coming up empty."

"Well," said Ada suddenly. "Would it help to look back at the annuals?"

Without waiting for an answer, she got up and went to another room. When she returned she was carrying five Riverview High School annuals, for the years from 1984 through 1989.

"These are the years you all were in high school," she said.

"Did you go to Riverview?" I asked Ada, picking up the 1985 book.

"Yes. I graduated in nineteen-ninety-two. Here." She leaned

over and flipped open a book to her ninth-grade group picture. Even though we were looking for clues to gruesome murders, the mood lightened noticeably among the three of them as picture after picture brought back good memories of events in their shared past. Mostly I just listened and watched.

"Look at that drift. The snow that year was so deep we couldn't see the fence posts around the yard."

And again. "Look, Jack. I wish you could see this picture in color. When the flax bloomed, the whole world turned blue. You should have seen the fields. I can remember the blue flowers stretching for field after field, almost to the horizon. Pretty."

"Why was there so much flax grown back then?"

Lori smiled. "Oh, that was the last of it. Years before, an agronomist from the University in St. Paul traveled all over this part of the state. He showed farmers how flax was a good cash crop. His influence was really strong in the forties and fifties. A few still had big acreages of flax when I was growing up, but it gradually went away."

"What was it for?"

"Flax?" Terry said. "Linseed oil, used in oil-based paints. The straw makes linen and the government used flax straw in the paper money it manufactured at the time."

"No kidding. Why'd farmers stop growing it?"

"Gosh, Jack, I really don't know. Maybe the prices they got went down and another crop took its place. My dad never grew much flax at all," Terry said.

Finally, we reached the picture in the nineteen eighty-one annual of Lori and Terry's ninth-grade class, the class picture with Tony Litvek.

"I remember his sister," Ada said. "She was taller than the rest of us, but really thin."

"That's right," said Terry. "They were twins, weren't they? Somebody said she got real sick and missed a lot of school before they moved to Riverview. She was two grades behind her brother."

"Dolores was her name," murmured Lori looking down at the page.

"I heard the family moved to Chicago that summer," said Terry. Ada nodded.

We went on through the rest of the book, but the lighter mood had evaporated. Ada looked up as she closed the book. "More coffee?"

Lori shook her head. "We better get going. We've still got to stop at the sheriff's office before we go back to the Twin Cities."

We said our goodbyes and drove back to town. There were three squad cars and several civilian cars in the lot behind the County Seat when we drove in. Brad Arnason, with a big grin on his face, came out to greet us.

"Let's go back to the conference room. We'll be more comfortable there." He was right. The three of us spent an hour in the room, sipping more coffee and running through our versions of the events of the weekend. The tape recorder spools turned silently, recording our recital of facts, suppositions and ideas.

"I'll have transcripts typed up and sent to you. No need to wait for them since they aren't formal statements," said Brad as we walked back through the offices to the front door. "Have a safe trip back." Lori and Brad embraced and he offered me his big hard hand. "Take care," he said. "We'll be in touch when it's necessary."

Back at the motel we were in the midst of packing when the phone rang.

33

Lori crossed to the table and picked up the telephone. "Yes?" Then, silence.

I watched her, tossed my dirty socks into the suitcase. All dirty. I realized I was out of clean underwear as well. Lori straightened up, looked my way, and a frown appeared. I hoped it wasn't aimed at me. In spite of the emotional rollercoaster we'd both been on these past few days, I was feeling pretty good, looking forward to the drive home and the opportunity to have a long, private talk.

"Ada," Lori said after a prolonged silence of just listening, "did he say anything specific? I know, but it's only been a couple of hours. Yes. All right. I'll call you." She hung up the telephone.

"Hey, hon, what's that all about?" I flipped down the cover of my two-suiter, watching her as I did so.

"That was Ada. She said Terry got a call right after we left and he ran out of their house without saying where he was going."

"Is that unusual?"

"Apparently. She hasn't heard from him since. Brian went to town to pick up his sister so Ada has no car at the farm. It's been a couple of hours now and no word from either Brian or Terry. Ada's called some neighbors and a couple of friends in town. Nobody's seen him. She's worried."

"Do you want to go look for him?"

"Would you mind?"

"Of course not. But first, let's call the sheriff."

Arnason wasn't in, but I told the duty clerk of our concern and she said she'd alert the duty staff and radio Brad or tell him when he returned to the office. I picked up the keys to the Miata and we drove first to Martin's Implements.

Nothing. Then we drove through Riverview in a random pattern, watching for Terry's truck.

Still nothing.

"Look. We have to cover more ground, talk to more people," I said. "Let's park on Main and each work one side of the street. Talk to people, see if anybody's seen him."

I parked at the north end of Main Street, half a block down from Martin's Implements. I surveyed the town.

Lori said, "I'll cross and work the west side." She started around the car and then I stopped her.

"Couple of things, babe," I cautioned. "Stay in sight. If you decide to go into a store, give me a high sign and don't disappear for more than five minutes. I'll stop and watch the door."

"Jack? What are you thinking? What can happen in River...Oh. You don't think...."

I shook my head. "I don't think anything right now. But I lost you once in this place and right now we have no idea what's up with Terry and Brian. So do me a favor. Five minutes and I'll be in there like a mad bull. And loud. Same routine if I disappear. Scream for help when you come."

Melodramatic? Over-reactive? Right then, I didn't think so. This town was getting to me. I could feel my elevated heart rate in my chest. When I thought about it, I was a little amazed that Lori had just plunged right in to the search, after her recent harrowing experiences. We went down Main Street and poked heads into open shops, called to people turning down side streets. No one had seen Terry or his truck. Once I forgot and started down a side street toward a tiny saddle shop. A piercing whistle stopped me. I'd forgotten she could do that. I waved at Lori and turned back.

Ralph's Cafe was closed and dark. I saw Lori go up the steps to the law office doors and shake them. Locked. A car screeched around the corner ahead and accelerated toward me. I recognized Brian at the wheel.

I stepped off the curb, waving. "Brian!" I hollered. He hit the brakes harder than necessary. The pretty girl next to him stuck her head out the window and grinned at me.

"Mr. Marston? What is it?"

"Louise?" She nodded.

"Have either of you seen your dad in town?" Negative head shakes. "His truck?" Same response. I could see a bandage on Brian's face, a reminder of his recent encounter with his mother's anger.

"Is something wrong?" Louise Worckowski started to get out of the car. There was a polite honk from a car waiting behind them. We were blocking traffic. I signaled the driver to go around us.

"No, nothing that I know of. But your mother wants you to go home right away. Okay?"

They both nodded and I stepped back from the side of the vehicle. I looked up to see Lori watching from across the street. I pointed us on.

In the next block, an old man was sitting in the narrow shade cast by the awning of Parsons hardware store. He had his chair tipped back and he was staring across the street. I almost wished we could change places. What I'd really have rather been doing right then was driving Lori and me back to Minneapolis.

"Afternoon," I said.

The man tilted his head slightly so he could see me. He didn't have to tilt very far. He was grizzled, unshaven. Tendrils of white hair escaped from under the greasy Pioneer seed corn cap he wore. It wasn't one of the newer ones with the plastic adjustment in the back. The man and his cap had seen a lot of years. Hard years under the hard prairie sun.

"Howdy," he said in a gravel voice.

"I'm Jack Marston."

"Hank Anderson. Haven't seen you around before."

He didn't extend his hand and from the one with badly deformed knuckles and fingers curled around an old briar in his lap, I could guess why not.

"No. I'm a stranger here myself. Came to town for the class re-union. You been here a while today?" I was starting to adopt some local speech mannerisms, I thought.

"Yep." Hank tilted his head back so he could stare across the street. "That your gal? Lori Jacobs? I 'member her dad. Good neighbor."

"That's right. I came to town as her guest. For the reunion. Now we're looking for a friend. Terry Worckowski. Wondered if you've seen him in town this afternoon."

"Yep."

"You have? When was that?" Something in my body language must have alerted Lori. When I looked up to locate her, she was already halfway across the street, striding toward us. I stepped back a step so Hank Anderson didn't have to crane his neck so far to look me in the face.

"Saw 'im in that Chevy truck of his. Drove south out of town. Don't know why. Him and his old man allus drove Chevys. Most everyone else hereabouts drives Fords."

"Mr. Anderson? Hank? It's Lori. Lori Jacobs." She knelt beside the old man. "How are you?"

I touched her shoulder and pointed back toward where the Miata was parked. She nodded. When I rolled up in the street next to the hardware store, Steve Parsons was standing beside her and they were both talking to old Hank Anderson. I was anxious to get going, but Lori called me over. I didn't bother to park.

"Steve," I said, coming up beside them. We shook.

"Tell Jack what you just told me."

"Hank's right," said Steve. "I was out here with him when we saw Terry driving south." He nodded at the street in the direction they had gone.

"'At's right." Hank said. "Somebody with him."

Steve nodded. "A woman."

"Who was it?" asked Lori.

"I can't say. I only saw the top of her head. She had dark hair, though."

"How do you know it was a woman?" I said. The strip of shade from the awning had narrowed and I felt the sun's heat on my neck.

Steve paused and thought. "You know, I can't really say. I guess it was just my impression."

I took Lori's arm and drew her toward the Miata. "Thanks, Steve, Hank. I guess we'll get along now," she said.

I thought about Steve's impression as we walked quickly to the Miata. I stopped beside the driver's door and looked south, along Main Street.

"What's out there?" I asked.

Lori squinted up at me. "Miles and miles of fields. Farms. Coleson's. Our old farm."

"And Wilson's Creek, right?" I said.

34

We got in the car and I drove south down the highway toward the edge of town for a couple of silent minutes while Lori just stared at me. "Wilson's Creek? What does that creek have to do with anything?"

"I don't know, Lori, maybe nothing at all. Maybe everything." I accelerated around a dusty old truck chugging along and we reached the southern border of Riverview. "Maybe we better tell Brad where we're headed." I pulled into the service station across from the 40-Mile Club and asked the attendant to call the sheriff.

"Just tell him that we're headed for Wilson's Creek."

"You sure Sheriff Arnason needs to know that?" the guy asked.

I started to make a smart comeback and then stopped. Reasonable question. I wasn't giving his the benefit of the background we had. "Yes," I said. "He will want to know. And please do it right away. It's pretty important." Then we roared back out on the highway.

"The next right will take us out toward Wilson's Creek, Jack. It's a little shorter than going out to our old farm first. Why do you think Terry's gone out there?"

"Look, I know this is painful. I realize now that what happened at the creek all those years ago still troubles you, maybe more than even you realize. I wish to God I'd never badgered you into coming out here for this damn reunion. But here we are and I think Terry may be in danger. I've been thinking about Guteman and Edith Kronk. I've been listening and listening and there is just one thing I've learned that appears to connect those two murders with Terry."

Lori furrowed her brow for a moment and then exclaimed, "Oh, God, Jack. The day Tony Litvek died. And me. I was one of the others who was right there. At the creek." I heard the sorrow in her voice. "Are you thinking that somebody here blames us? Somebody wants us dead because of what happened to Tony?"

"I don't know. Seems far-fetched, doesn't it?"

"But who? The family moved away after Tony died. I heard his sister was inconsolable. I told you how she cried at the funeral, remember? There's no one here from his family anymore. It doesn't seem possible."

"I know. It doesn't seem rational, either. But what if somebody in the class, or one of the other classes at your school has been harboring a grudge all these years? Somebody who was a close friend of Tony? Or of the family?"

The dusty green fields slid past while Lori thought about that. She shook her head. "I can't think of anyone. They weren't even in town very long. His sister was in seventh grade that year. Two years behind because she was sick."

"There is something else. I didn't mention it at the time, but when we stopped at Wilson's Creek on Friday afternoon, it looked to me like someone had been visiting the place. Had been there several times."

"What? Why didn't you tell me?"

"You were upset. We were…apart, not communicating much. I guess I just didn't want to intrude on your memories right then. You seemed sad and a little distant. Later, with everything that went on, it slipped my mind."

"Why do you think someone else had been there?"

"Tracks. Flowers. It looked like there had been several small bundles of flowers tied to that old piece of metal sticking up in the creek bed. Did you see it?"

She shook her head. "That old plowshare. It's been there for eons. No. I was mostly looking at the culvert where Tony hit his head. Remembering that awful day."

"There was a fresh bundle of flowers tied to the shank of that plowshare and remains of dried-up flowers scattered on the ground around it." I felt the Miata drift slightly on the gravel and slowed down. "It looked to me like someone had been replacing dead flowers periodically for a long time."

Lori stared at me. "As if it were a grave."

I nodded. "Or a memorial of some kind."

"Like the crosses and flowers we sometimes see along a highway where somebody died in a car crash." Lori pointed. "There's the road over Wilson's Creek. Turn left. We're almost there. If you're right about Tony's accident being the link, Terry could be in danger."

"So could you."

"But at the end, Terry wasn't teasing Tony. Neither was I. I mean, he was there, of course but he wasn't responsible for Tony's death. None of us was. It was an accident. But I still feel...felt...guilty."

"If I'm right about the motive, guilt or innocence may not matter."

"That's right. Only presence. But who is it?" Lori pounded her fist on her knee. "I can't imagine who it could be." She looked up. "Stop the car. If you're right and they came here to Wilson's Creek, they're just over that next rise."

I killed the engine and coasted the Miata to a stop on the edge of the road. We got out. A gentle breeze from the south blew into our faces. I put out my hand and Lori took it. Hand in hand we walked quietly up the road the last few yards to the top of the rise until we could see down into the gulley where Wilson's Creek ran under the road through a big steel culvert.

Terry Worckowski's truck was parked at the side of the road just before the culvert. The passenger door hung open. It was hot and very quiet, except for the murmur of the light breeze. Lori and I walked down the road until we stood half-hidden behind the bed of Terry's truck. We looked down into the creek bottom at the two figures there.

Terry sat on the ground, his back to us, on the crumbling lip of the creek. There hadn't been much rain this summer and unlike the spring day Tony Litvek had been swept into the culvert, today the creek was nearly dry. Terry's feet were in the damp black prairie mud.

His limp hands rested on the ground beside him.

A few paces behind him, holding a large pistol in both hands, stood a tall, lean figure in a loose white shirt and dark pants.

"Look," I murmured. The two figures were a few yards upstream from the plowshare, midway between the culvert and the makeshift memorial. A fresh bundle of flowers was tied to the top of the shank.

"They're right at the place where Tony fell in the water," Lori said softly. "Who's that with the gun?"

I felt her slip her fingers out of mine and start around the back of Terry's truck. "Lori, wait!"

"I'm going down there. I have to." I reached for her, but I was too slow. She went across the gravel and the weeds and scrambled down the steep bank. My breath caught. Halfway to the bottom she dislodged several small rocks that rattled down the slope. The figure with the pistol jerked around and stared at Lori.

It was Dolores Holbrook. She of luscious pastries and reunion dinners. Barbecues. Owner of Ralph's Cafe. Bringer of an espresso machine to the prairie. Sister of a dead boy. I knew it as I looked at her over the rear gate of the truck. I didn't know how, I just knew.

"Well, Lori Jacobs. How nice of you to join our little outing." The wind carried her over-loud voice, but I couldn't hear Lori's response. Terry turned his head and got to his feet. "Now I don't have to go looking for you."

I watched from the security of the truck. Watched my love go steadily closer to mortal danger. Dolores Holbrook waggled the pistol and pointed Lori closer to Terry. Lori apparently tried to go to Holbrook a couple of times, but Dolores motioned her to stay where she was. I sweated. They were talking. Arguing, it appeared. Finally I couldn't stand it any longer. Stood up. My head pounded.

The sound of the pistol shot was awfully loud. Lori flinched as a gout of mud from the slug jumped up near her feet. The mud splattered the legs of her blue jeans.

My mouth went dry. "Wait!" I shouted desperately. "Please!"

I went over the edge of the road and slid down the bank, nearly falling in my haste. My pulse roared in my ears, and I felt heavy thudding in my chest. Sudden sweat ran into my eyes.

"Oh yes," Larson said. "I wondered where you were. Marston, right?" Her eyes flashed sparks at me. "Get over here with these killers where I can see you."

"Look," I said, puffing. Found it hard to catch my breath. "Look. It doesn't have to be like this. We can help you."

"Sure you can, you and Miss Priss, here. You're just like the rest of the people in this town. Better than us, looking down your noses at us. My mother told me."

"I don't understand," Lori said softly.

The woman sneered. "Of course you don't."

"Do you want to talk about it?"

"Talk about it? Talk about it? Talk about what? I've got nothing to say to you." Her speech was sharp, abrupt. She was spitting. I could almost see sparks from her flashing eyes.

"Aren't you Dolores Litvek?" asked Lori softly.

"No, I'm Saint Teresa."

"I just wanted to be sure."

"Yes, I am Dolores Litvek. Anton was my brother. Remember him? Remember Anton? I came back to this stinking place and nobody remembered me. There wasn't even anything in the school annual about my brother's death. Was there?" Her question was an anguished scream.

"It was a long time ago, Dolores, but I remember Tony. I liked him."

"Anton! His name was Anton," she snarled. "Liked him? You were here, weren't you," she demanded. "The day Elroy Guteman pushed my brother into the creek? You were all here! You all helped murder Anton!" Tears started down her cheeks. Dolores swiped at them with the back of her hand.

"Who told you that? It wasn't that way at all. It was an accident. Won't you put the gun down so we can talk?"

"Talk. Talk. Everybody wants to talk. Talk won't help. My mother talked to me. Doctors talked to me in Chicago. Endlessly. Every time I got caught. My mother forced me to go sit there, answer their stupid questions. Then it was my husband. It's for your own good, Dolores he kept saying." She smiled, a twisted grimace of a smile. "You people."

She spat. "Anton was my brother. He took care of me. He protected me. He even tried to get our folks to hold him back in school so we'd always be in the same class. But I couldn't protect him." Her voice graveled and she sobbed once in deep anguish.

"We came here to this God-forsaken place and you people killed him. So now I'm killing you. That's right. I killed Elroy that night outside the club and threw him on that hay rake. You should have seen Edith's look when I told her about it, just before I stuck her to the stable wall. It was so easy.

"We never fit in here. I hate this place. All this empty space. When you killed him, I swore to Anton I'd come back some day and fix you."

"Dolores, please. Let me tell you what really happened. Too many people have been hurt." Lori tried a short step forward and the woman flinched, thrust the pistol forward again.

"Stop!" Litvek was wet-eyed and winding herself up. Getting tighter and tighter. I cast my eyes about, looking for something, anything to use as a weapon. There was nothing. I looked at Litvek's hands. At the weapon she held. It was a revolver. Six shots. One gone if she'd brought it fully loaded.

She rambled. Seemed to calm down a little. I measured the space with my eyes. It was too far. Unless she was incompetent with that pistol she'd get all three of us before I'd taken more than two steps. She wound herself up again. A dozen slights. More. Her mother, it seemed, had come reluctantly to Riverview with the family. A lot of her anger and resentment had been transferred to the daughter. Later in Chicago, Dolores married. Her husband, somebody named Trevor Holbrook, wasn't able to cope with her. They'd divorced. Again, Riverview's fault.

Suddenly she raised the pistol higher. "Say goodbye now," she screamed and squeezed the trigger.

I jumped sideways, flung myself at Lori, and we went down in the mud. I rolled toward Litvek in the sticky gumbo. I flailed a hand at where I thought Litvek's foot was. Missed. There were more gunshots, then silence. I looked up from the mud to see Brad Arnason with a rifle in his hand running down the slope of the pasture. Just behind him was a deputy, gun drawn. Dolores Holbrook, nee Dolores Litvek, lay on her side, dead from two bullets in her torso.

Terry moaned and rolled up to his knees, holding his arm. There was blood on his sleeve where the bullet from Dolores' pistol had gone through his bicep.

Arnason and his deputy arrived. Brad stared down at the woman's crumpled form. His hands were shaking. "I never shot anybody before," he muttered. The deputy helped Terry stand.

We stood silently, not moving or talking, in a semi-circle looking down on the body of Anton Litvek's sister, there on the bank of Wilson's Creek. The breeze murmured in my ears and the sun fled west toward the horizon.

OTHER BOOKS

by Carl Brookins

Sailing Adventures

The Inside Passage
Old Silver
A Superior Mystery
Devils Island
Red Sky

Sean Sean Private Investigator novels

The Case of the Greedy Lawyers
The Case of the Deceiving Don
The Case of the Great Train Robbery
The Case of the Purloined Painting
The Case of the Yellow Diamond

Jack Marston Academic novels

Bloody Halls
Reunion